BLOOD OF GOLD

DUNCAN MCGEARY

BLOOD OF GOLD

DUNCAN MCGEA

www.dragonmoonpress.com

ISBN 978-1988256-96-2

CHAPTER 1

"When's he coming back?" Laura asked for what seemed the tenth time. Her voice was flat, without inflection. To Simone, it was obvious she'd given up on everything else and lived only for the moment when *he* came around: fearing it, wanting it, all mixed up in her messed-up mind.

"I don't think he's coming back at all," Simone answered. She tried to say it kindly, but to her own ears, her voice sounded as flat as Laura's. She tried to put some life into her next words. "I think we need to try to get out of here."

"How?" Patty asked. "You been hiding some bolt cutters?" Just like her, to be so blunt. Since she was the oldest of them, Patty liked to think she was the most realistic of them, which might have been true. "Realistic" also meant she cooperated with the Monster more often than the other two prisoners. In fact, she had been the one who had enticed Simone into his car in the first place, the day everything had changed. Simone had been out with friends, going to the one movie theater in Crescent City, but she had missed her ride home. So she'd started walking home. She was feeling down, because she was pretty sure her friends had ditched her. It was cold, and when the car had pulled up beside her, heat radiating out of the open window, she had stopped and listened.

Patty had poked her head out the window, an older girl than Simone by a few years, but looking as innocent as child— which was what she was, since her maturity level had stopped at the age of thirteen, when she had been kidnapped.

"Hey, want a ride?" she'd asked.

So Simone had slipped into the backseat of that car, despite the looming presence of the huge man behind the steering wheel. The man had flashed a goofy smile—and that, along with Patty's disarming one, had convinced her it was safe.

For months, Simone had hated Patty for being the Judas goat, but as the months turned into years, she'd begun to understand what had motivated her fellow captive, even if she hadn't totally forgiven her.

"We just need time to get out, just a little time," Simone said now. It had always seemed to her that given enough of an interval between his visits, they could escape. But the Monster had always been unpredictable, and when Simone had thought about the timing of those visits, it had become clear to her that she would have been caught every time she'd had the impulse to flee. He seemed to have a sixth sense about when to show up.

And then there was…that girl…whose name Simone had never learned. The silent one with the big eyes, who had slipped her chains and run away…

Simone remembered the scream. They'd listened to the girl banging against the locked doors upstairs. Then came the scream, a cry that froze Patty and Simone in place and made their hearts skip a beat. Agony and despair and fear, all in one long wail that was cut off in mid-shriek. Patty and Simone had stared at each other under the thin light of the single light bulb, white-faced and wide-eyed.

They'd never seen her again. Not long afterward, he'd taken Laura.

They were each thirteen years old when they were kidnapped, and they'd been taken three years apart. The unnamed girl had been first, then Patty, then Simone, and finally, Laura. There had been others, though. There were five other names scratched on the wall. He had tried to obscure them, but Laura had had years to try to decipher them. Michelle, for certain. A Linda, it looked like. For the other three, she had just letters: Rh… Rhonda? by…Abby? Libby? Sh…Shirley? Sherry?

It had been more than six years since Laura had been taken—Simone wasn't certain exactly how long, since it hadn't occurred to her to keep track at first. But she could see it in his eyes: the Monster was getting bored with them, especially Patty, whom he barely touched anymore. Soon, he was going to want someone younger.

Simone had decided she was going to try to escape, no matter the consequences. It didn't matter what happened to her, but she had to keep him from finding another innocent victim.

The Monster had unexpected episodes of empathy when he relapsed to being human for short, inexplicable moments. When she'd showed him her raw, chaffed wrists, he'd allowed her to cushion the metal bindings with the cuffs of her shirt.

Something about the way he'd acted then, the last time he'd been there, had decided Simone on a course of action she had been contemplating for months. She'd stuffed as much of the sleeves of her shirt under the handcuff as she could without it being noticeable. He'd tightened the handcuffs tightly, but when Simone pulled out the padding, there was wiggle room. But still—she had not yet tried to extract her hands. It would be an irrevocable move, she suspected, if she succeeded. It would be difficult, if not impossible, to put her swollen hands back into the cuffs.

She'd been planning her escape for years. She'd taken notice of the metal bar that lay, covered in trash, in the corner of the basement, and of the rock that had fallen from the bare walls. She had counted the number of steps out of the basement and the distance to the front and back doors. She knew which drawer in the kitchen held the knives, and about the huge wrench under the sink.

She visualized her movements and imagined what would happen. Once or twice a year, he would lead one of them up the stairs and down the hallway, feed them a real meal at the kitchen table and let them go out into the backyard. At first, Simone had been pathetically grateful. Then she'd come to regard it as a form of torture, a tease, a glimpse of what real life might feel like.

It had steeled her resolve to use the information she gleaned from these brief trips to escape. But now that the moment had come, she felt paralyzed by indecision. It wasn't fear, exactly. It was more that she was uncertain how the world would react to her—and how she would react to the world.

The Monster been gone for over a week, which was days longer than any other time she could remember. He usually checked on them almost every day, or at least every two days. His hunger for their bodies was so insatiable that if too much time passed, he was rough with them. They had learned to hope for shorter intervals between his visits, because he was less driven and less brutal. That was the horror of it, that they cooperated with him, almost begged him for it.

But something had changed. Simone felt stronger than she had since she'd first been taken.

Why? she wondered. *What's happened to us?*

A few weeks before, he'd come down the stairs and there had been something different in his stride, something in his face. He always had a haunted look, as if demons were riding his back. But now his eyes were gleaming with confidence.

He reached for Laura first, as was his wont. But instead of stripping her, he bent her over and started nuzzling her neck. It had appeared almost gentle, except for the look of horror that had come over the girl's face.

"What…" she murmured, she who rarely spoke at all. "What are you doing?"

Simone had heard the sound of sucking. *Is he biting her?* she wondered. *Has he broken her skin? Is that blood flowing down her neck?*

He dropped Laura to the floor, limp and lifeless. Laura's eyes were growing dull even as Simone watched. Then he was on Simone.

She felt a sharp pain in her neck, and then a slow agony spreading down her body. Then she felt weak and sleepy, as if her life was being drained away.

When Simone awoke, she was in a puddle of blood on the bare concrete floor. Laura was still lying where the Monster had dropped her, but she was breathing now. Patty was sprawled on the broken-down couch in her usual spot, but she was unmoving. As Simone tried to rise to her knees, she heard Patty gasp and sit up.

"What was *that?*" Patty exclaimed. "What did he do?"

Laura was stirring. She groaned and rolled over, and then—surprisingly, for she had given up moving from her little bundle of blankets in the corner years ago—she got to her feet and walked as far as the chains would allow. She looked confused, and her eyes searched Simone's for answers. "I feel different," she muttered.

Simone understood what she was saying. She, too, felt transformed, as if she had more energy and strength. She looked at the corner of the run-down basement where the trash had been thrown. She could see a rat in the midst of the garbage, and felt a sudden urge to try to catch it and…

She shook her head. That made no sense. They'd been fed only the day before; she wasn't so hungry that she needed to do something like *that*. She glanced over at the rubbish pile—bag after bag that had once held Burger King and McDonald's value meals; empty boxes of cereal and granola; the remains of loaves of bread that had already been days old when they'd been purchased; whatever the Monster could pick up cheap and in bulk.

The pile of garbage had always been in the dark, so Simone had been able to safely ignore it. She'd become impervious to the smell, too. But now she could see it clearly, could see the maggots swarming over the remnants of hamburgers, the black insects eating the slimy lettuce. The odor made her gag, and yet also made her hungry.

After he'd done...whatever he'd done to them, he hadn't come back for three days, and the girls were getting tense, afraid of what he'd do to them when he returned. When he'd finally shown up, he hadn't even come downstairs. Instead, he'd thrown the corpse of a dog down into the cellar. It had landed equidistant from the three of them, at the far length of their chains. They'd stared at each other for a moment, then Patty and Simone had both scampered toward the dead meat. But Simone had gotten there just moments sooner.

She'd grabbed the dog and pulled it out of reach of the others. Before she knew it, she was tearing into the animal's flesh. She'd looked up, her face wet with blood, and seen the snarls on Patty and Laura's faces. Their jaws seemed to have elongated, with long fangs jutting downward over their lips, and they had a reddish glow in their eyes.

Simone had stopped in mid-feeding. She'd still been hungry, but at the last moment, she remembered that the others hadn't eaten either. She tore in half what was left of the carcass and tossed the parts to her fellow prisoners. Patty was savage in devouring her portion; Laura seemed aware that there was something odd in their behavior and looked out over the fur toward Simone with a question in her eyes: *What's happening?*

That had been four days ago, and they had used up what water was left in the basement. He usually left three buckets of water at the base of the stairs, one for each of them. Only Simone had shown enough restraint to have any left—a day's worth, at best.

The three girls had always referred to their captor as the Monster, but they'd always known he was a man—albeit an evil man. Now Simone realized he really *was* a Monster, and so were they.

"Why hasn't he come back?" Laura demanded.

Patty and Simone looked at each other. Both of them had heard the gunshots and explosions outside, but Laura either hadn't heard it or wasn't believing it. Something had changed, not only in the nature of their captor, but in their own bodies, and something was happening to the world outside as well.

"We should wait," Patty said. "He wouldn't want us to leave."

Simone scoffed. It wasn't the chains and locks that had kept them captive for so long. She felt strangely fearless, as if, for the first time, she could defend herself. Let the Monster return—she'd rip his throat out.

The basement was huge, as if it was below an apartment building or an office complex instead of a small two-bedroom house. It was this unusual feature that had probably attracted the Monster. He didn't live in the house. The windows were boarded up, the lawn was dead and the single functional light was a bare bulb that burned day and night over the steps to the basement. The basement walls were bare rock, crumbling, and the floor was cracked concrete. It was one large, open space, and the three corners farthest away from the light were eternally dark. There was a toilet under the stairs that each of them could barely reach. Small slotted windows near the ceiling had been covered up by cardboard, but they could see the passing of day and night.

After nearly six years, Simone still didn't know anything about the Monster—his name, where he lived, what he did for a living. Only that he wanted sex and wanted it rough, and didn't ever look them in the eyes or talk to them.

Simone wondered what would have happened if she had been alone. Though it wasn't something she would wish on her worst enemy, it was a blessing to have two other girls with her. Patty was difficult and Laura was simple, but Simone had learned to love them both—perhaps more than she ever had her own brothers and sisters, whom she barely remembered. The girls knew every single fact of each other's brief thirteen years of experience outside: every story, every feeling, everything they could describe. They'd spend day after day trying to bring the outside world alive, but only Simone had managed to hang onto hope.

Laura had begun as a frightened little girl who could still occasionally giggle at jokes and talk endearingly about her plans to become a veterinarian. As the years passed, she'd begun to fall silent, to become nonresponsive. Meanwhile, Patty had become more vocal, more strident, especially as the Monster began to lose interest in her. The more he ignored her, the more she tried to get his attention, nearly stripping whenever he came down the stairs, talking to him in a morbidly erotic way that made Simone blush.

Simone endured what the Monster did to her, pretending to be someone else, somewhere far away. She didn't fight him; she didn't encourage him. She certainly wasn't disappointed when he began to turn more of his attention toward Laura, though she felt for the younger girl, and sometimes—when Laura was being particularly nonresponsive—she tried to seduce the

Monster in much the same way that Patty tried.

"He's not coming back," Simone said.

She started to pull at her handcuffs, trying to squeeze the fingers of one hand into as narrow a space as possible. She reached her knuckles and couldn't get any further. She pulled harder, felt the bones almost crack under the pressure, felt her skin splitting and blood running down her forearm. But no matter how hard she tried, even with her newfound strength, she couldn't get her hand loose.

Simone cried out in despair. She fell back on her rear and put her arm over her eyes, feeling the blood seep onto her neck.

"Told you," Patty said. "We have to wait."

"We can't wait!" Simone shouted, sitting back up. In frustration, she grabbed the chains and yanked with all her pent-up fury. She'd done it a thousand times before and had always met the solid resistance of rock and steel. Now she felt something shift in her hands and heard a grinding sound. She looked over and saw that the hook was coming loose from the wall.

One last wrench and it detached and fell to the floor with a loud clang.

All three girls froze, as if waiting for the Monster to hear and come down the stairs and punish them.

Then Simone was gathering up the chains and wrapping them around her shoulders and arms. They were heavy, but she could move. She started up the stairs.

"Wait!" she heard Patty cry out.

"What?"

"Where are you going?"

"I'm going to get us free, Patty. Free from the Monster."

CHAPTER 2

Hoss and his followers were trapped in the Armory. The skylights washed most of the floor with daylight, while the breaches in the walls from the Wildering attacks exposed most of the rest of the warehouse to the sun. Only one corner was still dark, and Hoss and his twenty or so supporters were clustered close together there.

Facing them, as impossible as it seemed, were the vampires with blood the color of gold. The sunlight washed over them, exposing their pale white skin...but doing nothing more damaging to them. The legendary Terrill stood at the center of this group, with his human love, Sylvie, next to him. She had never left his side during the fight, though she could not bring herself to kill. She'd scrounged for ammunition and for weapons, and it seemed like every time Terrill had needed to be resupplied, she was there.

Clarkson, the blonde-haired member of the Council of Vampires, stood beside them.

Hoss still couldn't believe that Terrill was real.

Here stood the author of the Rules of Vampire, which had given Hoss the meaning of his existence. As a human, he'd been adrift, seeing things that those around him couldn't see, knowing the answers to problems but unable to get anyone to see the sense of his suggestions.

Then he'd been Turned. At first, that had been equally confusing. But then he'd found the Rules of Vampire, and everything had made sense:

Rule 1. Never trust a human.

Rule 2. Never leave the remains of a kill, or if you must, disguise the cause of death.

Rule 3. Never feed where you live.

Rule 4. Never create a pattern. Kill at random.

Rule 5. Never kill for the thrill. Feed only when necessary to eat.

Rule 6. Never steal in the short term; create wealth for the long term.

Hoss had become a believer in the Rules—and had made certain that the poor lost souls that found and surrounded him also believed. Because of this, they had survived the holocaust brought on by the Wilderings. At least, until now.

Surrounding the vampires, both blue and gold bloods, were the human vampire hunters, led by the two FBI agents, Callendar and Jeffers.

"They came to help us," Terrill was arguing. "Without them, none of us would have survived."

"All right," Jeffers said. "For that, I thank them. But for their future human victims, I damn them." He turned to his partner. "We have them in our power, Callendar. Let's finish it."

"These are not Wilderings," Terrill said. "These vampires follow the Rules of Vampire. They will not kill unnecessarily."

Jeffers laughed. "How reassuring. I'm sure that their victims will be glad to know they were 'necessary.'" He turned back to his fellow agent. "Come on, Callendar. We don't have any choice. This is our job; this is what we were trained to do. But even more importantly, it's what needs to be done."

Callendar hadn't spoken since the argument began. He had his head down, deep in thought. As the senior agent on the scene, it would be his decision: life or death for Hoss and his followers. Hoss wasn't sure, but he thought he knew the solution to their problem. But it would be better if it came from the humans instead of him.

Smoke curled over Crescent City. The wind was coming off the foothills and blowing the darkened clouds out over the ocean. Everywhere a Wildering had been caught by the sudden emergence of the sun from the clouds, there was a blackened patch of soot, a shadow of a once-existing being. Some of the foliage and human structures in proximity to the Wilderings' doom had caught fire as well, and parts of downtown were now blackened rubble.

The FBI agents and their police backup had just finished the unpleasant job of dispatching those victims of the Wilderings who had not yet Turned. This had entailed chopping off their heads, so the humans were covered with a mix of the red blood of those not yet Turned and the blue blood of vampires.

Now the cops wanted to finish the job. They had bona fide vampires in their power, trapped by the sun and by their weapons. But some of the cops looked uneasy, for they knew that without the help of this band of vampires, in all likelihood, they would have perished under the onslaught of the Wilderings.

As it was, only the unexpected emergence of the sun after days of fog and clouds had saved them from the Wildering onslaught. Half the population of Crescent City had been Turned into vampires, creatures consumed by hunger for human flesh. None of these newly Turned vampires had been instructed by their Makers in how to behave, so they had become a horde of Wilderings, consuming everyone in their path.

In the distance, the survivors could hear sirens approaching. News vans had found their way to the fairgrounds and were parking outside the Armory, waiting to see who—or what—would emerge. *It is going to be hard to sweep this disaster under the rug,* Hoss thought. *Vampires are secret no longer.*

Hoss and his followers were of the old school of vampirism, trained and restrained to kill only when necessary—and above all, to follow the Rules of Vampire, which Terrill had formulated long ago. But they were no less dangerous for it. Hoss was young and newly Turned, but he'd always been smarter than everyone around him, young or old. He'd figured out early on that the only way to survive was to do as the Rules suggested.

The only thing that confused him was that he'd just broken every Rule, one by one, and yet it had seemed like the right thing to do.

"This is bullshit," Jeffers exclaimed and raised his crossbow, pointing it at Hoss. "Let's end this."

In a blur, Terrill was at his side, snatching the weapon away before Jeffers could pull the trigger. "You'll have to kill me first."

Jeffers looked stunned, but not cowed. "Impressive. You really are a new breed of vampire. But there are only a couple of you gold bloods," he said loudly, so that the other cops could hear. "You may kill me, and you may take out a lot of us, but eventually we'll take you down."

"Actually," a voice said from the door of the Armory, "there are four of us." Officer Robert Jurgenson walked in, accompanied by a stunningly beautiful woman.

"Jamie!" Sylvie shouted, and sprinted toward her sister. "You're alive!"

The two girls hugged, the younger sister tall, dark and human, the older shorter, red-haired and apparently now one of the golden vampires. "Thanks to Robert," she said.

Their appearance seemed to finally decide Callendar. The newly Turned policeman was his former brother-in-law, and it was obvious that he didn't relish a fight to the death with this new breed of vampires, whose capabilities weren't fully understood.

"Enough," he said loudly. "This is what has to happen. I can't in good conscience let a pack of vampires go free."

At these words, both sides visibly tensed.

"So I will require a promise from them."

Hoss nodded. He'd thought this would be the compromise from the beginning and had been formulating his response.

Callendar continued. "You must promise not kill humans again. All of you...or you must leave this country forever. If you can't agree to these terms, we will have to finish this now."

"I accept," Hoss said. He turned to his followers and spread his arms. One by one, they all agreed to the terms.

"You believe them?" Jeffers asked, disbelieving. "These are vampires, Callendar! Lying, murderous, night-stalking vampires!"

"I will take their word," Callendar said. Then he raised his hand to forestall the protests. "But if you break your word to me, young man, I will hunt you and all your followers down, I promise you."

Again, Hoss nodded. He was already planning his trip to England. It was time he joined the real Council of Vampires.

Terrill finally relaxed. He'd done his duty to Hoss. It was clear that the young vampire and his followers were not yet ready to be tested by the golden blood. Now he could turn his attention to the woman for whom he'd long been searching.

Jamie looked worn, yet even more beautiful than he remembered—leaner, her face chiseled, missing all the baby fat that had obscured her high cheekbones. Her freckles, which had made her seemed innocent and unspoiled, now seemed to highlight the experience written on her face. She was leaning against the cop, Robert, and it was obvious they were a couple.

Jamie was Terrill's unexpected progeny. After decades of not feeding on humans, he'd had a moment of weakness, and the young woman had been his victim. In remorse, he'd tracked down the girl's family, and had unexpectedly fallen in love with her younger sister, Sylvie.

He'd sworn never to kill again, and despite great provocation and danger, he'd stuck to his vow. When he'd been trapped and forced into the daylight, it had turned out that all his suffering—the provocation and temptation that only centuries of resolve had helped him overcome—had Turned him human again. He was the first and only vampire to Turn back, since the beginning of time.

His own Maker, Michael, had long planned for a new kind of vampire to emerge, but Terrill becoming human had been unexpected. When Michael had Turned him back into vampire again, so he could fight in the coming battle, Terrill had become something new to this world: a vampire with gold blood, who could walk in daylight, who was stronger and faster than any blue-blooded vampire.

There was one important catch: only vampires who refused to kill humans could be transformed. Any other vampire would be destroyed by the infusion of gold blood. So far, few vampires had been willing to take the test.

"Jamie," Sylvie was saying. "Why did you run away?"

"I wanted to protect you," Jamie said. "I didn't trust myself."

Sylvie smiled sadly, tears welling in her eyes. "You don't protect someone by breaking their heart."

Jamie grasped her sister and buried her head in Sylvie's shoulder. Terrill heard a muffled sob. "I understand that now. I won't leave you again."

Around them, the police were cleaning up. Several of them stood near the cloistered vampires in the dark corner, as if still uncertain they wanted to let them go. Nightfall was hours away. The tension probably wouldn't dissipate until Hoss and his crew were gone, but Terrill felt the situation was stabilized.

"Now what?" he heard Clarkson say. He turned to the former Council of Vampires member. She had been an unexpected ally, and another in the line of vampires that Michael had tried to create. She had accepted the golden blood without harm.

Terrill shook his head. It still wasn't clear what he—and those who had tasted the golden blood—had become, or what the ramifications were.

"Damned if I know," he said.

Across town, the answers to Terrill's questions about his future were, at that moment, being formulated.

Marc had returned to the thrift store. It had been looted even before the Wildering surge had occurred. Ordinarily, Marc would have been dispirited. After all, he'd spend most of his adult life trying to help the homeless and the dispossessed, and it was disappointing that they were probably the ones who had raided the unguarded store.

But Marc barely noticed the disarray. He went to his office in the back and swept his arm across the desk, clearing it. His laptop was gone, but it didn't matter. What he wanted to write—what he was impelled by a higher force to write—seemed as though it should properly be written by hand. Because it came from God, not man.

He had watched helplessly while Fitzsimmons, the leader of the Council of Vampires, had killed Michael. The white-haired vampire—the oldest of his kind—had not resisted his death. Instead, he had turned to Marc and said, simply, "Remember this, son. Tell the story."

Marc found a fresh pen and began to write.

"The Ancient One, Michael, gave his life that we might live."

He stopped and stared into the distance. *How do I know all this?* he wondered. *Where is it coming from?*

It was as if he'd always known, and that he had been Turned so that he might understand and record the vast changes that were taking place in the world. Knowledge had come to him that there was no way he could have possessed, as if it had been passed down through the blood of Michael himself.

He knew that his true test was still in the future. Someday, he himself would have to take the sacrament of the Holy Golden Blood, as all vampires would. Then he would find out if he was truly worthy of the understanding that had been granted him.

He began to write once more.

"From the Blue Blood of the last true vampire, Michael, came the Golden Blood of Terrill, that the vampire race might be redeemed from evil and join God's creatures in the light of his wisdom.

"The vampire race need no longer hide in darkness, for they have been given the choice: join in the love of God, become Golden, and renounce your evil ways. If you refuse Michael's sacrifice, if you do not partake of the Blood of the Chosen, you will be damned forever and ever, no longer vampire, but a lower order of beast, one of the ravening horde, the Wilderings, who have no soul, no salvation.

"Come to the light, and ask humbly that Terrill give of himself, that you might be forever redeemed. Turn away from the darkness and your thirst for blood and become one with God.

"If you do not, if you refuse this offering, you will be hunted down and destroyed, and your soul will melt into the ground and become of the earth and be forever lost. Your kind are doomed to eternal darkness and emptiness. You shall be exterminated and you shall exist no longer.

"But join us, and you shall have everlasting life, in harmony with mankind and with God, and with all the peace of the world. Become Golden and walk in the Heaven on Earth that shall be eternally your right of Making. Turn, as you were Turned, and become Holy. Join Michael and his Maker, God above."

Marc wrote feverishly into the night, and in the morning, as a ray of sunlight landed on his exposed hand and burned him, he looked down and realized he had filled up all the loose paper in his desk and several notebooks as well.

He slept. When darkness fell and his vampire senses woke him, he returned to his desk and wrote through the night again. And again, into the next night.

Finally, it was complete. He hadn't written it—God had. It had flowed through him, already formed and complete. The word of God. He was the conduit, the holy vessel.

Marc wandered out into the dark, found an ATM and removed all the money in his meager savings account. The next morning was dark and cloudy, and he dared to venture to the local Best Buy, where he purchased the cheapest laptop he could find.

A few nights of typing and the manuscript was complete. It existed only on his laptop until one morning he uploaded the entire thing onto the Internet, with the simple title *The Testament of Michael.*

CHAPTER 3

The trapdoor at the top of the basement stairs was locked, but Simone pushed hard against it and felt the lock give way. It wasn't so much that the lock felt flimsy as that she felt very strong.

"Hello?" she called out softly. "Master? Are you here?"

It was silent. Her heart lifted and she climbed out onto the first floor. The house was completely boarded up, but Simone could see daylight leaking through the cracks between the plywood panels. It was so dark, she shouldn't have been able to see much, but it was as clear as day to her. It was as if everything was bathed in some strange form of illumination—every nook and cranny, everywhere it was dark, stood out sharply, but when her eyes passed over areas where there was normal light, her vision shimmered uncertainly.

Simone went to the kitchen, grabbed the big wrench from beneath the sink and sat on the floor, where she pounded at the links of chain nearest her wrists until one of them split enough for her to pry the chain off. Then she got to her feet and went to the drawer where she knew there was a big steak knife. She took it out and, holding it, felt safer. She had decided she wouldn't let the Monster take her alive again. She'd die first.

And yet…she was famished. She opened the refrigerator, and a foul odor flowed out over her. Apparently it wasn't plugged in, because everything inside had rotted. She started to slam the door, but held back at the last moment. There was a rotting Saran-wrapped steak sitting on the top shelf that still had a little red blood on it.

Before she knew it, she had removed the meat and was gnawing into it. Her brain wanted to reject it, but she was already swallowing, and her body was accepting it. In fact, it tasted better than anything she had ever eaten.

I may regret this, Simone thought as she ate the whole thing. *I'll probably get sick.*

But it didn't feel that way. Eating the tainted flesh felt entirely right.

Shaking her head in puzzlement, Simone moved to the back door. It was not only locked, but also blocked by heavy furniture that would take time to move. She trotted back down the hallway toward the front door, her bare feet slapping on the wooden floor. For the first time, she became aware that she was wearing only a flimsy nightgown.

She turned into the first bedroom and went to the closet, where he kept the coats they were allowed to wear when they went outside. She put on a long coat and ran her fingers through her tangled hair, and then proceeded to the bathroom to check out how she looked in the small mirror there. She dared to flick on the light.

What she saw—or rather, what she *didn't* see—didn't make sense. *Is the mirror gone?* she wondered at first. But no, there it was, reflecting the view all the way back into the dim hallway. In the mirror, the bathroom looked as it had always looked—but there was no one in it. She was standing right there, in front of the mirror, but there was no image of her.

Simone closed her eyes and swayed on her feet, feeling the blood drain from her face. She fell forward and caught herself on the edge of the sink. As her hands hit the porcelain, the knife in her grasp slipped and nicked her right forefinger.

She saw the blood oozing, though she felt little pain. The

blood was blue. Somehow, in the shadows of the bathroom and the dim light, the color was off. She shook her head at the sight and opened the cabinet to look for a bandage. The cabinet was empty except for a rusted razor and a squeezed tube of toothpaste.

It was the sight of these simple toiletry items that finally brought tears to Simone's eyes. It was such a small thing… but she hadn't brushed her teeth except with her own fingers for years, or put on deodorant, or shampooed her hair. Once a month, he allowed the girls a quick shower—for his sake, she thought, more than theirs. She suspected that they were so inured to the smells that they didn't notice them anymore.

She looked down at her finger and saw that the strange blue blood had stopped flowing. When she ran water from the faucet over her finger, she couldn't even see the cut.

How strange. Simone reached for the tube of toothpaste, lifted it to her lips and managed to get a small bit of it on her tongue. It tasted sharp and sweet.

I don't have time for this, she thought. The Monster could return at any moment while she mourned for a toothbrush. *Get out! Get out now!*

She hurried to the front door and examined it. There was no doorknob.

She almost despaired, but then she caught sight of scratch marks on the small, square piece of metal that would have held the doorknob. She might not have noticed if her dark-vision wasn't so clear. There were was a pair of pliers on the windowsill next to the door, just under the curtains, and it was obvious to her that that was how he opened the door.

She reached for the pliers, and her fingers brushed aside the curtain and extended into the daylight.

Her hand started to hurt; then, before her disbelieving eyes, flames started to curl up from her blackening fingers. She pulled her hand back, the pliers landing with a thump on the floor.

Simone held her breath and lifted her fingers before her face. Even as she watched, the blackened skin was repairing itself. There was no time to think about it. She picked up the pliers again and fumbled to open the door. She gripped the handles strongly and turned the little square extension. The handles almost bent, she was clamping down so hard, and it occurred to her that only a few weeks ago, before this transformation—whatever it was—she probably wouldn't have been strong enough to accomplish this.

The door opened and sunlight flooded in. Simone jumped back just in time. As she wondered what to do, the sunlight blinked out. She dared to peek around the door and saw that heavy black clouds were rolling in. She could stand the dimmer light, though it hurt her eyes and made her skin ache.

Simone saw a windowless panel truck parked on the street outside. *Parker Plumbing*, it said on the side.

She ran back down the hallway to get her fellow prisoners.

Laura and Patty watched her silently as she came down the stairs. She went over to the metal bar she knew was hidden under the trash heap, trying not to look at the maggots that heaved over the pile. She took the bar over to Patty and pried apart the links of her chain.

"We shouldn't do this," Patty said uneasily.

It was equally simple to get Laura free. And Laura was just as uncertain about her freedom. "What if he comes back?" she whimpered.

Now that it was done, Simone was surprised how easy it had been to get loose. In her heart, she had always known it wasn't the chains and locks that kept them imprisoned, but their own minds. She wasn't certain she would ever have summoned the courage to escape if the strange transformation hadn't overcome her. For the first time since the early days of captivity, she felt strong and certain, and willing to fight for her freedom.

It wasn't easy to convince either of her fellow captives to leave. Finally, she grabbed Laura by the arm and said forcefully, "You're coming with me."

Laura gave in and followed her meekly up the stairs. When they reached the top, they both stopped and looked down at Patty, who was staring up at them, her stubborn expression turning to one of indecision.

"Do you want to get out of here or not?" Simone asked her.

Patty seemed confused for a moment. Then she muttered, "Of course I want to get out of here." She followed them up the stairs.

Simone held the other girls back when she saw daylight coming through the open door again. When the light dimmed, she urged them forward.

"There's a truck across the street!" she said. "Get in the back."

She watched them run across the road and saw Patty reach for the handle on the truck's rear door. They both slipped inside and closed the door behind them.

Simone stood there. *Why am I hesitating?* she wondered. *I don't have anyone to give me orders. I only have myself.*

Then the clouds parted, and she couldn't leave the house. She stood back from the door and waited for another wave of shadows.

What would life be like outside? How would they be treated? What kind of world were they entering? In the distance, Simone could see smoke, and there was a steady cacophony of sirens of different tones and textures—police and fire and other emergency vehicles, all with their own unique sonic signatures.

She didn't know anything more than a frightened thirteen-year-old girl, she suddenly realized. Six years had passed outside, and she didn't know anything about it. Even the cars parked on the street looked strange. Who was the president? What kinds of inventions and devices had been created while she was gone?

She almost felt like turning around, going downstairs and putting the chains back on again. At least she knew that world.

A heavy black cloud passed overhead and she sprinted for the van, even as she saw a man emerging from the house on the opposite side of the street. She slipped into the darkened van before he could turn around and see her.

Only a few moments later, the young man got into the driver's seat with a sigh. He didn't look old enough to own his own business—in fact, he looked like he was barely out of high school. Slender, but athletic looking, with crew cut hair. "Idiots," he muttered. "All they had to do was turn on the water."

He shook his head and put the keys in the ignition.

Simone moved swiftly from behind his seat, grabbing the top of his head. Her fingers were exposed to the sunlight for a second. The pain flared until she wrenched his head back out of the light and placed the steak knife against his neck. She almost surprised herself with how fast she moved.

"Don't move, don't shout, just do as I tell you," Simone said.

The man started to turn his head to look at her. The pressure of his movement made his skin grow taut under her blade, and at the last moment, he had second thoughts. His eyes flicked up to the rearview mirror. There was nothing there. He looked puzzled for a moment, then closed his eyes and groaned. "I knew it was too early to go to work. But everyone was so insistent. Offering double and triple the usual rates."

"Drive us out of here," Simone said.

"Listen," he said urgently. "I'm taking you where you want

to go because I want to. Of my own free will. Just because you need to get there, OK? No need to get weird about it."

"Drive," Simone repeated.

"Sure," he said, trying to sound cheerful about it. "Where to?"

"Anywhere!" she shouted. "Away from here!" Without meaning to, she pressed the knife a little too hard and penetrated the skin. A trickle of red blood ran down the man's neck. Simone felt herself salivating and averted her eyes.

"All right, all right!" He fumbled with the gearshift, stalled in first gear and then tried again. He pulled out into the light traffic.

"What happened out here?" Simone asked, staring at the wreckage around them. Every block seemed to have a burned house, or a car wreck, or some other kind of destruction. There were police and National Guard troops everywhere. She looked out the passenger-side window and saw, in the shadows between two large houses, what appeared to be a couple of cops kneeling over a dead body. One of the cops swung an axe, and it looked as if the head fell away from the body. She shuddered. It had been a small girl, from what she could see.

"You don't know?" the man said. "Oh, you said, 'out here.' Been shut in, have you?"

"Yeah…" Simone drawled. "You could say that."

"Everyone went crazy there for awhile. As soon as it started happening, I locked the doors to my house and took my family downstairs, and we just hid out. When all the gunfire stopped, I came out. Then the phone started ringing off the hook— everyone needs repair work done, all over the place, will pay me anything I want."

"So you don't know what caused all this?"

"They're saying vampires," the plumber said quietly. He tried again to look at Simone in the rearview mirror, and again, there was nothing there. This time he dared turn his head all the way, and she knew he could see how gaunt and pale they were.

Laura laughed shakily. "Vampires? Has everyone gone crazy?" She sounded so sincere that Simone could almost see the man relaxing.

"All I know is, I heard some very strange sounds outside my house," he said. "People screaming, people snarling like animals. When it all finally stopped and I went outside, there were burned-up bodies everywhere. Just cinders, as if they had burst into flame. I saw cops running around with crossbows. *Crossbows,* for Christ's sake! So yeah, I almost believe it. Vampires fit."

In her astonishment at his explanation, Simone almost relaxed her grip, and she saw his fingers edging toward the door latch. She pulled his head back and hissed. *Did I just hiss?* she wondered. *Is that what we are? Vampires?*

It made sense. The sudden strength and speed, the hunger for raw meat. The effects of sunlight. She could smell the droplet of blood underneath the point of her blade as strongly as she'd once smelled a complete banquet. She realized that she'd been suspecting it ever since the Monster had attacked them, even before they began their escape.

"What's your name?" she asked the plumber.

"Rod," he said. "Rodney Parker. I'm a good guy. I'm married; three young kids. It hasn't always been easy, you know? Crescent City is a poor town—so I understand when people are desperate. I'm totally on your side."

Patty spoke for the first time. "Sure you are." Her tone was so sarcastic that he gulped and shut up.

"Just do as we ask, Rod, and we'll let you go," Simone said. They had left the outskirts of town and were on a winding road that led into the foothills. There was the occasional redwood stump and a few stands of surviving trees amid mobile homes, trailers and a few small stick-built houses. She recognized the neighborhood.

"Turn here," she said.

Rod pulled off the main road onto a small lane that made a sharp u-curve and turned back in the direction they had just come from. They hit another dogleg to the right and drove onto a dirt road. Awbrey Lane, the road sign said. Simone had lived out here for a couple of years when she'd worked at the Wal-Mart that was situated just over the hill.

"There," she said, pointing to a small manufactured home in a dense grove of trees. She'd driven by the place a thousand times. The house was just as she remembered, completely dark on even the brightest days. She had often wondered how the owners could stand the gloom. But then, no one had ever seemed to be home.

As they pulled into the driveway, she saw the broken windows that weren't visible from the road and realized the building was abandoned. It was perfect.

Rod pulled up to the door and stopped.

"I mean it," he said desperately. "I won't tell anyone. As far as I'm concerned, you just hitchhiked out here. Please, let me go."

"Get out," Simone said.

He hesitated, and she could see that he was preparing to run.

"Don't," she said. "I'm faster than you, and stronger— believe it or not."

It was obvious that he believed her. Something about the certainty in her voice had convinced him. Plus, it was clear that he knew what she was.

They broke into the house, and she marched Rod to the hallway closet and told him to get inside. He meekly followed her orders.

As the door closed, it occurred to her that she'd come full circle. The morning had started with her as prisoner of a Monster and had ended with her taking a man prisoner. Did that mean she was a Monster?

She wasn't sure what that meant, but it seemed right.

CHAPTER 4

Every time Fitzsimmons awoke in the cold and darkness, he'd forget who he was. As he lay in the silence, he would forget *what* he was. He'd dream of the day ahead, a humdrum kind of day: shopping, working, dining, lazing about.

Then he'd try to move.

And he'd scream.

Sometimes Peterson or one of his servants was nearby and would come and lift Fitzsimmons out of his enclosure. Other times he'd lie there for days in his own filth, helpless and raging. If he could have killed himself in those early days, he would have.

Peterson found it useful to keep him alive. He would hold a phone up to his former boss's mouth, placing a piece of paper with the lines he wanted Fitzsimmons read in front of him. Fitz was forced to try to sound normal. His genial old self. The other Council members thought he was traveling and had left Peterson in charge in his stead.

After the disaster in Crescent City, they'd flown into London during the daytime, when no vampires were around to observe them. Peterson had stuffed Fitzsimmons's truncated body into a suitcase and wheeled it past the tight security that surrounded the headquarters of the Council of Vampires. No one but Peterson and a couple of his closest progeny knew Fitz was here.

If Fitzsimmons didn't do as Peterson asked, he'd be tortured again and again, to the point of death.

And the next day—the next night, to be exact—he'd awake and start screaming again.

At first he wondered if his arms and legs would come back. He was vampire, after all, and all injuries eventually healed. But Peterson kept him starved, with just enough animal blood in his system to keep him alive and no more.

Once they brought him a child, bound in ropes, as helpless as he was. He drank the young girl's blood and spent the next hours, and then days, waiting for transformation. His wounds ceased to leak blue blood, but other than that, nothing changed.

He didn't take up that much space anymore, so he didn't need to be in a big room. The one he was in was a closet, really, with a bare bulb hanging overhead so that he could see to read what Peterson put before him. Sometimes when his captors left, they forgot to turn the light off, and Fitzsimmons wasn't sure which was worse: the darkness, or the light that showed the barrenness of what was left of his life. He memorized the cracks in the ceiling, made creatures out of them to keep him company.

In the end, he was left alone with his hate. It festered and oozed inside him until he was nothing but a raw and open sore. The vampire—the Wildering—who had done this to him was dead, but those who sought to take advantage of his weakness were very much alive. He planned his revenge, certain that the night would come when he'd arise.

Once a week, a servant came into the tiny room and scooped out the waste. At first, Fitzsimmons endured the humiliation without a word. One day, uncharacteristically, he mentioned how hard it must be for the vampire to have to clean up his mess.

The vampire, who looked like a young woman, smiled.

Fitzsimmons's mind started churning. He knew that his anger and resentment was off-putting, but his moment of empathy had resulted in a moment of relaxed vigilance. On the servant's next visit, he smiled at her and asked her name.

"Chloe," she said.

"I'm sorry you have to do such a dirty task, Chloe."

She shrugged and bent down to wipe something from his face.

From that day on, he talked to Chloe as if she were a friend or a family member—a niece, perhaps; perhaps even one of his progeny. Their little talks grew longer, a little more familiar, with each visit. It seemed to Fitz that she started coming to him every few days instead of once a week. He was winning her over, he was sure of it.

"If only I could get out of here," he ventured one day. "I bet if I had enough blood, my limbs would regrow. You wouldn't have to do this anymore."

She frowned slightly, as if she was considering it.

I've planted the seed, he thought. *Now I must nurture it.*

The next visit, they talked about where they had grown up as humans. He told her the story of his Making and then waited for her to reciprocate. She mentioned she was French and had been Made in the mid-twentieth century, which made her old enough to know the ways of vampires, but still relatively young. She would say nothing more about her Making.

They talked about their human childhoods, which, as was typical for vampires, had been miserable and hopeless. It was the downtrodden who most often found themselves the victims of vampires.

They even shared a laugh or two as the weeks went on. Finally, they were talking like old friends from the moment she walked into the room.

It is time, Fitzsimmons decided one day. She might turn him down, but he didn't think she would report him.

"You wouldn't have to do this job if I could just regain my mobility," he said. "Bring me some blood, Chloe. Perhaps an animal, or a small child. I don't really believe it will take that much. Then you won't have to do this demeaning job any longer."

"I don't find it demeaning," she said.

"No? But surely you don't like doing it."

"I don't mind."

"But how did you get assigned to it?" he pressed, certain that there was a story behind it.

"Oh, I didn't get assigned. I volunteered."

"Volunteered?"

She laughed at the look on his face. "You are so obvious, Fitzsimmons. I just wondered how long it would take for you to actually ask."

"What do you mean?" He started feeling dread as he saw her sneer at him.

"My Maker was Southern.,." she said. "You killed him, remember? You betrayed him."

"He was a traitor," Fitzsimmons muttered.

Chloe laughed. "Oh, come now, Fitz. We both know that isn't true. He was in your way, that's all. You had him eliminated."

"Then why are you here?" he asked, and he hated the tone of dismay in his voice. He'd been getting his hopes up, he realized. He'd really begun to think she was going to help him. Now, it was worse than before.

"Well, I didn't want you rotting away too soon. I want you to be like this for a long time. For eternity, if I can manage it. I'll teach my progeny to come in and do this nasty job after me, and their progeny after them, if need be."

Fitzsimmons was silent. He closed his eyes as she kept talking.

"But I need not come quite so often," Chloe said. "I've had enough of your manipulative bullshit. I think maybe once a month is sufficient for keeping your waste from eating away what's left of you."

"No…please…"

"*Please?*" She sounded as if she couldn't believe he'd said it. "The great Fitzsimmons, pleading for mercy? How pathetic."

Her voice was coming from directly above him. He opened his eyes just as she leaned down and spit into his face.

Fitzsimmons felt a vast hate explode in his chest, and it seemed to him that he almost levitated out of the box. It was as if he was a cobra, simply waiting for the moment when the prey got close enough. He had his fangs sunk into her neck and was sucking her blood before she could even cry out.

Chloe struggled to push him away. He kept biting and sucking, but finally she pushed his limbless body off. Blue blood sprayed the room, arcing out over him, and he found himself trying to catch it in his open mouth. Then she was falling backward. Her head hit the wall and she slammed to the ground.

No! Fitz cried out inside. He could feel the energy from her blood coursing through his body, but he couldn't do anything about it. He was as helpless as ever.

Chloe was gurgling on the floor, out of sight. Her torn-out throat was a severe wound, but she'd recover eventually, especially when they came looking for her and fed her fresh meat.

The frustration was enough to make Fitzsimmons scream, but he only let himself moan, a high-pitched keening. He tried to rock the little coffin he was in back and forth, and was amazed when he felt it move an inch to one side.

Then he was thrashing with all the newfound energy he had, and when that was gone, he started using what was left of his reserves, and then it was sheer willpower rocking the tiny coffin, back and forth, back and forth. He was crying blue blood in frustration, unable to keep himself from shouting in anger.

And then—just as he felt the last of his energy disappearing—Fitzsimmons felt himself falling. He'd tipped the coffin off the table. As he hit the floor, he fell out of the coffin and rolled across the floor.

He landed on his stomach, and, raising his head, he found he could slither forward, inch by inch. Only a few feet away, he could see Chloe on her back, her head turned his way but her eyes unfocused.

Then her eyes cleared, and they filled with hate as she saw him. She started to rise to her knees.

Thinking about it later, he wasn't sure how he managed it, but somehow, he slithered across the floor and sank his teeth into her left ankle. He felt the bones split and the foot fall away. As she screamed, he turned and sank his fangs into her right ankle, and bit that foot off, too.

Even without feet, Chloe tried to stand, but she immediately fell again, her head hitting the edge of the table as she went down. She lay moaning, half dazed. Fitzsimmons started to slink his way toward her throat, the new blood and meat giving him renewed energy. He reached her throat as she regained consciousness. Her eyes flared with hatred and pain, and then, as he latched onto her open wound, he saw fear in them.

He bit down, again and again, finally reaching her spine, which he snapped.

She stopped moving.

He lay silent, luxuriating in the feeling of both his body and his hate being fed.

Then he ate the rest of her.

Fitzsimmons could feel new arms beginning to sprout, but it was happening slowly. His legs were coming back even more slowly. He had consumed all of Chloe, and had even broken her bones and sucked her marrow. Now he was contemplating trying to eat her bones, though he wasn't sure how much good that would do.

It had been two days since he'd killed her. He wasn't sure how much longer he had before they came to check on her.

After three days, he had four stumps, with which he could maneuver himself around the room. He reached the door, and to his surprise, found it was locked. *Why would they lock it?* he wondered. But Peterson had always been a careful bastard.

He positioned himself near the door and waited.

That afternoon, he heard the lock begin to turn. One of Peterson's bodyguards came in. He was looking at some paperwork he had in one hand and holding a tape recorder in the other. He was relaxed, and obviously unaware that Chloe was missing.

Before the bodyguard had gone two steps, Fitzsimmons had his fangs sunk into the man's shins and was tearing at the tendons. The guard stumbled and fell.

If anything, he was easier to kill than Chloe had been. He lay screaming, his hands clutching his legs, as Fitzsimmons scrambled like a crab toward his throat. At the last moment, the guard threw up his hands, but it was too late. Fitzsimmons had him by the throat and was tearing away, gulping up the meat of his neck and face. The frenzied screaming turned into gurgle, lost volume, and then stopped altogether.

It took another day to completely consume the guard. Since this latest victim had obviously been sent on a task, Fitzsimmons doubted he had much time left. His arms and legs continued to grow, but far too slowly.

He decided to commence his escape even though he wasn't yet fully reformed. He had short, stubby hands with tiny fingers and the beginnings of thumbs, so he was able to grasp the guard's keys in one hand and hold the trigger of the gun with the other. He probably wasn't going to be able to use either, but if he could just somehow manage to find one more victim, he was certain that his healing would be complete.

Just one more meal.

Fitzsimmons reached the end of the hallway. The door there was unlocked, too. He opened it a couple of inches and looked out.

Then he tried to slam the door closed, but it sprang open, pushing him back into the hallway. He landed on his back, and struggled to turn onto his side and get back onto his stumps.

"Impressive," he heard Peterson's voice say. "We've had cameras and microphones on you the entire time, but I needed to see it with my own eyes."

Fitz's nemesis stood a safe distance away, with two of his guards between them. The other vampire, who had the appearance of an old man, was smiling down on him.

"I wanted to see how far you'd get," Peterson said, "though it's a shame about Chloe. I warned her to be careful. You've always been a tricky son of a bitch."

He motioned for the guards to hold Fitzsimmons down. Only then did he approach. "Well, now we know. Vampires can grow back limbs. I always wondered. However…" He removed the sword from his cane. "I don't think we can allow that."

As Peterson stood over Fitzsimmons, a look of satisfaction came over his face. He slashed down, chopping off his former boss's left arm, then his right.

Fitzsimmons was too numb, too stunned, to cry out. He felt a sharp pain as his vestigial legs were chopped away. Then he passed out.

He woke in the dark, back in his little coffin.

He screamed, unable to stop himself though he knew that his thrashing and his cries were being observed and recorded. He no longer wanted to die. He wanted to live. Such hate as he felt was like a magic potion, strong enough to manifest itself into reality. He was certain that his time would come.

CHAPTER 5

Kelton didn't remember being Turned. He'd awoken to the sound of explosions. Turning on the radio, all he got was garbled messages about groups of people attacking other people for no reason.

They wanted everyone to evacuate to the National Guard Armory building at the county fairgrounds.

It hadn't taken him long to realize that this was the best chance he'd ever have to spree kill. From everything he'd read, he fit the definition of a serial killer—but he'd always had the desire to kill a lot of people in a short time, too. Trouble was, spree killers were always caught, most often going out in a gun battle or turning their weapons on themselves. Kelton didn't have suicidal tendencies. No, he just wanted to know what it would feel like to kill a bunch of people.

He drove to the wealthier side of town, which he usually stayed away from. Much easier to prey on the downtrodden— fewer alarms, fewer police patrols. But he'd always harbored resentment against rich people, and this was his chance to act on it.

Fires had broken out all over the city, but the fire trucks were in this part of town, taking care of the rich. Kelton caught a fireman between houses and approached him with a big smile, sticking the long blade of his knife up into the man's chest before he could call out, careful not to get blood on his big waterproof fireman's coat. Kelton put on the coat and the helmet and started going house to house.

With all the activity in town, people were being more wary than usual, but were also knocked out of their routines and easily seduced by the promise of safety. His uniform and his vaguely official demeanor reassured them. He'd ring the doorbell and stand there with his goofy grin, and they'd open the door for him.

He had approached this final home like any other. It was a small house near the ocean. It was in the open on a bright, sunny day, and yet it seemed to be in shadow. It both drew him in and repelled him at the same time. He almost turned around and tried the next house.

Are you a coward? The thought came into his mind as if from some outside source. Kelton had never run from anything, and this mental taunt made him keep going.

He talked his way into the house; the little old lady didn't even question him. He picked her up as she keened a weird little scream and threw her on the floor of the living room. He knelt over her, deciding he'd make short work of it—kill her and be gone.

Then the room seemed to turn completely around. Someone else was there. He rose and started running for the door.

STOP! The command was shouted directly into his mind. *TURN AROUND!*

His sense of direction was disrupted, and when he looked toward where he thought the front door was, he found himself looking in the wrong direction. Everything seemed different: the size of the room, the color of the paint, the age of the woman lying on the floor staring up at him with round eyes, as if she, too, had sensed something strange had happened and wasn't sure if she was more frightened of the change or of him.

Kelton couldn't breathe, but it seemed as though he didn't need to breathe, or move, or think. A coldness flowed over him, and he felt his life drain away—everything he had ever liked, every good thing that had ever happened seemed to spiral down a dark hole in his soul. What remained was the hate and the resentment, which had always been the biggest part of him, but was now magnified a thousandfold.

That's how he was Turned.

When he awoke, he was filled with a hunger and thirst such as he'd never known. The old woman was gone. Now, as if laid out especially for him, was a young woman, naked and bound. He felt the usual desires, but also something new. His need for sex was overwhelmed by his thirst, and as he fell on the woman, he found himself sinking fangs into her neck and sucking her dry. Only afterwards did he remember he was horny as well. And, to top it off, he was hungry. New and old desires melded together.

It didn't seem strange to him that he was eating another human being. He only wondered why he hadn't tried it before.

On the second night, he skipped all the preliminary steps and simply burst through the doorways as if they were made of paper. He was strong, stronger than anyone or anything. He'd always restrained his urges, knowing that he couldn't indulge them for very long before he was noticed. Even moving around the country, he couldn't fully give in to his desires.

But this was different. This was the end of the world. Kelton didn't stop with the first house—outside was chaos and death, and he knew that what he was doing was indistinguishable from what everyone else was doing. He was just doing more of it.

At the third house he entered, a shotgun blast hit him, and it hurt, but when he chased down the shooter and tore him apart, consuming every bit of flesh on his body, the pellet wounds were already healed.

After a couple days of this, Kelton remembered the girls. Had he left them enough water?

Even as he thought this, he wondered if he needed them anymore. It was time to move on, and this was his chance to get rid of them and destroy the evidence.

The three girls were gone. The door to the house was wide open, and he could see the pliers lying on the floor of the hallway. *Should've killed that Simone girl while I had the chance,* Kelton mused. She'd been trouble from the moment he'd brought her to the basement. If only she hadn't been so beautiful. Tall and dark, she'd shed all her baby fat and was starting to look like a model. He'd kept her around for a little spice. Patty had begun looking like a middle-aged woman, all pinch-faced and squirrely, all mousy limp brown hair and pastiness. Laura was nice, in a dumb-blonde, pimply-faced, busty sort of way, but she had given in to him so easily that she wasn't any fun anymore.

What can they do to me? he wondered. Not much. They were vampire now, just like him, and they'd be unlikely to just show up on the steps of the police station. Still… better get rid of the evidence. He took the gas can out of the back of his pickup, went downstairs and sloshed the liquid over the piles of garbage.

The chains had been pulled out of the wall and the links pried open. He shook his head. He should have realized that if his strength had been increased by the transformation, then no doubt theirs had been, too. *Dumb.*

In his defense, he'd been busy. The complete chaos outside had been a once-in-a-lifetime chance to glut himself on blood and death. He'd fed on the first two victims, and then he'd just killed for the fun of it. Vampire or human, he didn't care. He just felt sexually charged by the violence.

Kelton felt himself getting aroused at the thought of the coming conflagration of the house, and before he lit the match, he satisfied himself, spraying his seed into the middle of the living room. Then he tossed the match at the gas can and walked out of the house as it burst into flame and practically exploded behind him.

Setting fire to the house was what he'd planned to do anyway, after he killed the girls and doused them with gasoline. But now, with all the fires around town, there wouldn't be any questions from the authorities. He'd get a nice, tidy two hundred thousand bucks of insurance, with little chance they'd accuse him of arson. And there wouldn't be any bodies to raise the alarm.

Not that random bodies would have much impact these days. In fact, there would have been no impact—it was his perfect opportunity. Still, he kind of got a kick out of the idea that his sex slaves were still alive and on the run. It wouldn't have occurred to him to let them go, nor could he have resisted the temptation of one final, brutal rape before killing them. But now that they were gone, he found he was all right with it. He'd had a surfeit of death in the last few days. He wouldn't have thought that was possible, and he doubted he'd ever have another chance to satiate himself. So the thought of three girls still existing in the world was somehow very pleasing.

Maybe he'd have time to look them up later.

As soon as he figured out just what the hell he was and what the hell it meant.

The sun was starting to poke out from the clouds, and Kelton was exposed. He glanced back at the house, but he could already see the flames flickering in the windows.

"Hey, neighbor," he heard someone say. Two doors down, Harvey Stockman was coming down his steps. His mouth dropped open as he saw smoke come billowing out of Kelton's home. "Oh, my gosh. I'm sorry about your house!"

"Burst gas line," Kelton said. "I was planning to tear it down anyway. This just saves me the trouble."

He walked over to his neighbor, with whom he'd conversed

maybe three times in the last dozen years. Kelton felt twice the size of the little man; he was taller by a foot and a half, and broader in the shoulders and thighs. Maybe Stockman had him beat in the belly department, though. Kelton had always been strong, but now he felt like he could have taken his chubby neighbor and ripped him in half.

"Happening all over town," Stockman said. "I was having plumbing problems, myself. You haven't seen a plumbing truck around anywhere, have you? The guy went out for a part and said he'd be right back."

"What was the name?"

"Parker Plumbing."

So that's how the girls got away, Kelton thought. *Good to know. Meanwhile, I need to get out of the sun.*

"Hey, can I use your phone?" he asked. "I should at least be on record for calling this in. Though I doubt anyone will show up."

"Phone wasn't working, last time I checked," Stockman said doubtfully.

"Let's check again." Kelton grabbed him by the arm and guided him down the sidewalk quicker than the little man could keep up without breaking into a trot. They went inside just as sunlight washed over the front lawn. Kelton felt the back of his neck start to flare, and then they were inside the dark, cool house.

Stockman's equally chubby wife and his two chubby kids were in the kitchen, and their eyes grew big when they saw Kelton looming in the doorway. Kelton put on his best smile. Years ago, by accident, he'd stumbled upon a big artificial grin that seemed to work with people, though he didn't know why, and he could turn it on any time. As long as people didn't look him in the eye and see the perfect blank coldness there, he was pretty convincing. He was always careful to be looking at something else when he turned on the charm.

The house was the perfect place to hide out until nightfall. And it came with the added bonus of some chubby snacks.

The Stockman house had a full pantry. Kelton had never seen a fridge and pantry so full of sauces. He poured some hot mustard over Stockman's leg and tried that, then threw the bone over his shoulder, where it landed with a clank against the other bones. Nothing tasted better than raw meat, but he felt an obligation to try all the seasonings—he didn't want them to go to waste.

The table seemed to turn on its side, and he gripped the edge to steady himself. He recognized the feeling as the same one he'd had in the old lady's house, when he'd been Turned. He closed his eyes and then opened them again, hoping the dizziness would go away.

It seemed cold in the house. No, hot. No, both. It was a temperature that was comfortable, that's all Kelton knew.

Then he realized that something was behind him.

He turned around, knife in hand, ready to rush whoever it was who had come into the room.

There was a strange blackness filling the corner of the room.

The intruder was in the shadows—which should have meant that Kelton could see him clearly, since his night vision was now better than his day vision. But the shadows cut off the corner of the room as if it wasn't there; as if *nothing* was there. Kelton could hear the man, but couldn't see him.

"Who are you?" he demanded.

Your Maker. Again, the words came into his mind, the inner voice flat, not so high that it could be called high, not so low that it could be called low. It couldn't be called anything—it just existed in the middle of sound, consisting of tones that had never been heard before. Kelton didn't think anything could scare him, especially in his new form, but this made him shiver and his heart skip a beat.

"Why are you here?"

I am your Maker, the voice from the void said again. *I have chosen you.* The voice didn't travel by airwaves, but entered Kelton's bones and churned his marrow.

Kelton believed him—it—whatever the creature was. Should he thank him?

"What…what do you want?"

I want to help you to fulfill your desires. I want you to never stop. Nothing can stop you.

"The sun…"

After tonight, the sun will no longer bother you. My Darkness cannot feel the light.

The shadows moved toward him, and Kelton caught a glimpse of something whipping out, reaching for him. Something heavy landed on him, something heavier than the world, and yet he stood unbowed. He felt a sharp pain in his throat, but this time the creature didn't drain him; instead, it seemed to be pumping something into him, some of the cold and the darkness—and it felt familiar, like all the hate he'd ever felt, distilled and flowing eternally through his veins. Over and under the sensation, he heard the creature speaking into his mind.

I have chosen you, as I have chosen your forebears, for long millennia. For I have chosen only the vampires with the strongest desire to kill and to consume. I have selected only those who understand that they are not humans Turned into vampire, but something completely different. Superior in every way to their fleshly origins. You are the culmination of a long line of Darkness.

The shadow man was gone when Kelton woke up, but the cold and dark remained inside of him, as if he was now part of the shadow.

CHAPTER 6

The Testament of Michael just appeared one day, seemingly everywhere at once. It spread through every social network and was mentioned on the major networks' evening news broadcasts. It was talked about in the newspaper gossip columns and magazines. It may have been reported mostly with a wink and a smirk, but there were plenty of believers.

The devastation of Crescent City was originally attributed to an unknown pathogen, and the ensuing rioting to mass hysteria. But enough visual verification existed from video and cellphone recordings that infiltrated the Internet that the government was having a hard time explaining it all away. Then there was the eyewitness testimony—some of which was actually credible. The amount of evidence seemed too overwhelming for all of it to have been manufactured.

Someone had found a cellphone on the street. The video footage on it showed a man running toward the camera faster than seemed humanly possible. As his face became clearer, you could see the fangs already covered in blood, the look of hunger in the creature's eyes. There was just something so believable about it that a screen grab from the footage—the last frame before it went dark—had become the signature image of the event. Sure, it could've been faked, but most people instinctively understood that this had been what some poor soul had seen in his or her last moments.

It was so evident that something unusual had happened that conspiracy theorists were taking the opposite tack than usual—that is, that so much evidence of vampires existing meant it must be faked—which, ironically, gave the stories more credibility than ever. Surveys showed that in addition to the usual twenty percent of the populace who will believe anything, another twenty percent thought vampires "likely," and more than half thought them "possible."

Books about vampires shot to the top of the best-seller lists, and shows about vampires filled movie theaters and started a heavier-than-usual rotation on TV.

Coming on the heels of the news stories, *The Testament of Michael* had arrived as a validation of the reality of vampires.

"Listen to this." Sylvie was reading aloud from her laptop. They were back home in Bend. Jamie, Sylvie and Terrill were sitting at the kitchen table, and early-morning sunlight was streaming through the windows. Terrill had almost winced when Sylvie had pulled back the curtains to flood the room with light. It was hard to get used to the fact that he—and the other vampires with blood of gold—could survive in the full light of day.

"'From Michael came Terrill, who defied Satan and refused to feed on the souls of the innocent. Terrill, who went to his doom without complaint, who became Human because of his love of Mankind. Terrill, who sacrificed himself yet again that he might fight the new threat of the Wilderings.

"'He was the first of the Blood of Gold. From him came a new race of beings—neither human nor vampire, but the best of both...'"

"Jesus," Terrill breathed.

"No, not Jesus. I think he's calling you Terrill," Jamie said, laughing. There was a look in her eyes as she looked at him, though, as if she was half serious.

"And you're telling me the author—this Marc—is someone you know?" Terrill asked.

"If it is who I think it is, he's a young man who helped me. A nice young man. I called him 'Marc with a c.'"

"But how does Marc know all this stuff?" Terrill exclaimed. "Where's he getting it?"

"God told him, obviously," Jamie snorted.

"Who's next? Matthew, Luke and John?"

"Hell if I know," Jamie admitted. "To tell you the truth, he's pretty convincing. I feel like I should fall to my knees before you, Master."

"Oh, shut up," Terrill muttered.

In all his long existence, he had never been as happy and content as he'd been since he and Sylvie had returned home from the disaster in Crescent City.

Humans seemed to believe that everyone had a soul mate in life, if they could but find them. But Terrill had lived many lifetimes, and he had never felt like this.

Sylvie was young, so incredibly young, but she seemed wiser than him. Her emotional response to the events around her was always kind and thoughtful and seemingly right. It was a knack he'd never learned.

Now, as he watched her read the newspaper aloud, she seemed so alive, but so vulnerable. Several times during the Battle of Crescent City, he'd seen a Wildering target her, as if knowing how important and how vulnerable she was. He hadn't told her how many times she had almost been killed. It worried him. She was a human, frail and weak. And she was the lover of the vampire who was perhaps the most hunted of all vampires—and now, apparently, the founder of a new type of vampire.

She'd be safer if she was Turned. Terrill had no doubt that Sylvie was ready for the golden blood, but he also sensed that she would reject the offer. She was too alive as a human, and it was by observing her grace and beauty that he continued to appreciate the differences between humans and vampires.

Jamie and Robert had rented the house next door, and Clarkson had found an apartment down the street. They were lying low. So far, the only people who knew who they were and where they were hiding were managing to keep their mouths shut.

Terrill wasn't worried about Father Harry, or his good friends Grime and Perry and Billy, but the word was out in the homeless community they were part of, and it was only a matter of time before someone decided there might be money in the story. Terrill wasn't even sure he would blame whoever sold them out.

"We have to go into hiding," he said.

"I thought that's what we were doing," Sylvie said.

"We're hiding in plain sight. That won't be adequate for much longer. We have to go somewhere no one knows us."

"Jamie and I have some land," Sylvie ventured. "Up in the Strawberry Mountains, near John Day. Dad used to go hunting up there. I think I can find the keys to the trailer…but I don't know if I can remember how to get there. Jamie?"

Jamie had come over for breakfast—a side of raw bacon. Robert was sleeping in, still recovering from his ordeal. She nodded. "I think I can find my way there. If not, I know the people at the base of the mountain. They can give us directions."

"Then let's pack up and go," Terrill said, standing up as if ready to leave that minute.

"Do you think it's a good idea to be out of communication range?" Sylvie said, not stirring from the table. "If anyplace is outside a coverage area these days, it's the Strawberry Mountains."

Terrill sat down again. He hadn't thought of that.

Sylvie was already getting busy on her laptop. "Apparently, there is a Wi-Fi cloud over Eastern Oregon that is owned by some millionaire," she said after a few minutes of searching. "There wasn't enough money for the big companies to invest in it, so he put his own five million dollars into the project and—get this—he offers it free to anyone in the area. I think we'll be all right."

"Jamie? Get Robert ready. I'll go track down Clarkson," Terrill said. "I think until all this blows over, we'd best stay out of sight. With any luck, this *Testament of Michael* will fade away and everyone will forget all about vampires."

Jamie nodded, but Terrill could see she didn't believe that would happen. To be honest, neither did he. *The Testament of Michael* had a strange pull on him, as if it was being directed at him, as if it was trying to tell him what to do.

As if Michael was speaking to him personally from beyond the grave.

Sylvie had woken up that morning with a fever. She was hacking and coughing and blowing her nose every few minutes. Terrill realized that he hadn't been around anyone with one of humanity's little diseases for a very long time. It was annoying.

"You know, if I just Turned you, you'd never get sick again," he told her. "Then I would haven't to follow you around throwing away Kleenexes."

She looked at him with a frown, then saw that he was teasing. "So all I have to do to avoid a cold is become undead? Pretty high price to pay, wouldn't you say? Thanks, but no thanks."

Terrill laughed. He watched her walk over to him, her body so fluid, so full of grace. When she plopped herself down in his lap, his heart seemed to melt into the rest of his body.

She sneezed in his ear.

"I'm serious," he said, frowning. "You are so vulnerable to

everything. Bugs, accidents, anything at all. If you Turned, you'd be safe from these things."

"No, thank you."

"Why not?"

Her face was against his shoulder, but he could tell she was seriously considering the question. "Because…it isn't natural."

"It is completely natural. According to Michael, it is just evolution."

"No, it is not the natural order of things. I don't think it is something that someone chooses. It happens to you, but you don't go seeking it. You remain what you are until you aren't. I know that doesn't make much sense, but that's how I feel, Terrill. I'm human and should remain so."

"But you love me, right?" he said, genuinely puzzled. "If you think I'm OK, then why wouldn't you be OK?"

"I love you *in spite* of you being vampire," she said quietly. "I don't love you *because* you are vampire."

"What about Jamie? You could be like her. She's renounced all killing, and she seems fine with it."

"I'm not ready," Sylvie said.

Terrill left it at that. He'd always worry about her, and the fact that she was, like all humans, vulnerable to a thousand little things. At least she hadn't completely shut the door on the idea. She just wasn't ready.

They spent the rest of the day packing, and it was dark by the time they were done. They decided to wait for morning, then leave.

Not long after sunset, there was a knock at the door. Jamie went to answer it.

A strange vampire stood there, his eyes glowing with religious fervor. He was skinny, dressed in rags and smelled of the charnel house.

"'The Blood of Gold shall transform you, absolve you, make you one with God,'" the vampire said without preamble. "'Partake of Terrill's blood and thou shalt be redeemed, reborn in God's grace.'"

"Terrill? It's for you," Jamie said.

Terrill sat frozen at his desk, uncertain what to do. Sylvie got up, went to the door and led the vampire into the house. "What's your name?" she asked kindly.

"Parks," he mumbled. "Jon Parks."

"Are you hungry?"

"NO!" he shouted. "I will not drink the blood of the innocent!"

"How about some raw pork?" Jamie said. "I'm sure this pig was guilty of something."

Terrill laughed. He couldn't help it. The whole thing was ludicrous. This poor creature was under some delusion that Terrill was holy, somehow. That he would wash him clean of his sins.

Terrill looked down at his arm. His skin had taken on a kind of bronzed tone, as if permanently tanned. It was the gold blood. There was no denying the gold blood.

"You've got to do it," Sylvie said, as if she could read his mind.

After Jon had fed, they led him to the living room and had him sit down in the middle of the carpet. Terrill wondered what he should do next. Sylvie went to the kitchen and brought back a knife.

"A few drops should do it," she said.

Terrill stood over the skinny vampire, who was trembling, blinking rapidly in excitement. His fangs had grown, and he was nearly vibrating with anticipation.

Reluctantly, Terrill cut into his forearm, and a line of gold blood grew until it began to drip. He held his dripping arm over Jon's open mouth and found himself saying, "This is my blood. Accept it and be one with me."

The others were looking at him with wide eyes. He ignored them, for at that moment, he truly did feel something awe-inspiring. *I can save the vampires*, he thought. *I really can.*

The vampire Jon Parks suddenly stiffened and lay down on his back. Then he began to shake.

Uh oh, Terrill thought. *Not again.*

"Tell me you haven't fed off a human recently," Terrill said, feeling cold.

"I wanted…I wanted…" Jon muttered, looking sad. Then he looked up at Terrill. "I'm weak."

Terrill stepped back, expecting him to explode, as Stuart, the leader of the Wilderings, had when he'd ingested Terrill's blood. Instead, the skinny vampire's flesh slid off his bones and instantly decayed into a putrid puddle. His back arched and his bones disconnected from each other, his skull rolling off to one side.

They all stood in a circle over the putrefying remains, too shocked to move.

Finally, Jamie spoke. "Next time, could we do this outside? I don't think we'll ever get those stains out of the carpet."

No one laughed. Sylvie nodded, as if this was a serious comment. "We'll have to come up with some procedures, that's for sure. Maybe some test. Some way to weed out the less than sincere."

Terrill was stunned, not just by the preceding events, but by Sylvie's words. It struck him that this was going to be a constant occurrence, that as *The Testament of Michael* reached more and more vampires, some were going to seek him out, both worthy and unworthy.

"We're not waiting until morning," he said. "We're leaving tonight."

The others didn't argue. Their two vans were already loaded and gassed up. As soon as they cleaned up the mess, they locked up the house and left, telling no one where they were going.

An hour later, a SWAT team stormed the house. After a short time, the team leader emerged and approached the FBI agent in charge.

"It's clear," he reported. "Looks like they packed up. Other than a god-awful smell, there's nothing here."

Callendar nodded. He sensed that they had just missed the vampires. Secretly, he was relieved. This raid hadn't been his idea.

After Crescent City, he'd been put on leave. Orders had come in for him to be FBI liaison to the Canadian government across the border from the oil fracking fields of North Dakota. He'd just laughed on reading that—North Dakota! They couldn't have found a more isolated spot for him to be exiled.

He didn't care anymore. He only had two years left until he'd put in his thirty years, and he didn't care where he spent them.

Then, unexpectedly, he'd been called to Washington, to find himself, along with his partner, Jeffers, in the office of the director of the FBI. Jeffers hadn't been in charge at Crescent City, and Callendar had been glad that he'd avoided most of the blame. They'd given each other a big hug, something they had never done before in front of other people.

Director Landry didn't greet them, didn't even look up from his desk. Instead, he started reading something off his computer.

"'Fear not the hunter, for if thou art innocent of spilling the red blood, thou shalt be absolved of all crime. Drink thou of the Blood of Gold and thou shalt live in peace alongside mankind until the end of thy days.'"

Landry looked up, frowning. "What do you know about this?"

"I have read The *Testament of Michael*," Callendar said. "That's all I know."

"But what is this 'blood of gold?'"

"Did you read our report?" Callendar asked, and the director nodded. "Then you know that Terrill and his followers walked in sunlight. Nor did I see them kill any human. I think I believe what the book is saying, sir."

"'Fear not the hunter,'" Landry intoned. "I'm not sure we want that to be the message people hear. It's been decided to take this Terrill and as many of his followers as we can find and bring them under our...protection. We want them alive, if possible."

"If possible?" Jeffers asked.

"I mean that," Landry nodded. "That isn't some code to take them down. We need to find out what this Terrill is about. We need a sample of that blood of gold. So do everything you can to keep at least one of these new-type vampires alive—if possible, Terrill himself. Understood?"

"Yes, sir," Callendar and Jeffers said.

"We have word that they're holed up in Bend, Oregon. You're flying out tonight along with our crack SWAT unit. Bring them back, agents. Bring back the blood of gold."

Now, as Callendar stood in the darkness outside the small house where Sylvie lived, he was half relieved. He didn't think it was up to the FBI to decide what happened to Terrill and his followers.

No, that was up to God...and the Shadow that opposed him.

CHAPTER 7

"I want to go home," Laura said. Behind her back, Patty rolled her eyes with an exaggerated shake of her head.

"We're your family now," Simone said. "We're your sisters." And, as with any sisters, there was tension and rivalry. Laura apparently didn't remember that she'd spent several years in foster care or camped out on couches at friends' houses. No one had even reported her missing.

"I want to go *home*," Laura repeated.

Simone realized with a shudder that she was talking about the prison they'd just escaped from. "We can't do that," she said gently.

Laura stamped her foot and left the living room. The abandoned house nestled in the thick grove of trees had been empty for a long time. There was a thick layer of dust on everything. Patty had found a battered broom in one of the closets and set about busily sweeping. There was a single bed in one of the bedrooms, and Patty had immediately declared dibs. Simone had stared at the soiled mattress dubiously and agreed. Laura didn't seem to care.

They found a few rickety chairs and tables spread through the three-bedroom house and gathered them all into the living room. But no matter how Simone tried to decorate the room with flowers and prints out of moldy books, it still felt like a prison.

The first night, Simone had gone out foraging, finding a few pieces of furniture and bedding in storage sheds that she doubted the neighbors would miss. They had released their captive, Rod, from the closet that night, with the warning that he would be tracked down and hurt if he tried to escape.

Surprisingly, he offered to help them. "I could hook up the electricity to the neighbors'—they won't notice until they get next month's bill, if then. With electricity, I can hook you up to the well and you'll have running water."

Patty cheered up at the offer. "I'll guard him," she said. "But I'm warning you, Rod, I'll rip your head off if you try anything. I'm feeling pretty hungry."

By the next morning, they had a functioning household. Simone insisted they seal up all the windows so no light would escape. They didn't really need to have lights on, but it seemed to comfort them somehow, as if they were living a normal life again.

That satisfaction had lasted about two more days.

"Laura's right, you know," Patty said now. "We can't stay here."

"Why not? We've got everything we need," Simone argued.

"We don't have food," Patty said. "I keep looking at Rod like he's a pork chop or something. I don't know how much longer I can hold out."

"That will be true no matter where we go. At least here, we're safe. We'll find some animals somewhere, eat them."

Patty shook her head. "You always were a townie. You don't understand these country folk. They all know each other; they all know what's going on in the neighborhood. We won't be hidden for long—especially if we start stealing their precious livestock."

"We'll go farther afield," Simone insisted.

"You have a bigger problem on your hands," Patty said. "I'm not sure I care whether I feed on a human. I never did like people much, and I like them even less now. We're vampires, Simone. We aren't *them*."

It's wrong! Simone wanted to shout. But she, too, had been getting the urge to taste human blood. It only seemed wrong when she thought about it—but if she just followed her emotions, she found she really didn't care anymore, either.

No, she thought. *I won't do it.*

But she was going to have trouble restraining her "sisters"— and she would be loyal to them no matter what. Rod seemed like a nice enough guy, but what did she really owe him? He was human, and Simone woke up every night feeling less and less like a mortal. A coldness had settled over her, a calculating hunger she'd never felt before. Of the three of them, she was the only one who had had a solid home life, who had ever subscribed to the moral values imbued in them by school and family. Her two sisters had never had that luxury—for them, life had always been a dog-eat-dog existence. It wasn't much of a stretch to a vampire-eat-human existence.

It wasn't the fault of all humans that the Monster had imprisoned them. He'd been a Monster before he was Turned, but not everyone was like that. But Simone found that her anger didn't distinguish as much between "good guys" and "bad guys" anymore. Humans were a different species now. They were prey—food.

She shook her head. They hadn't crossed that forbidden boundary yet. Simone sensed that once they did, they were lost. They would be forever hungry and damned. So far Laura and even Patty, in spite of her bravado, were too frightened to wander far, too scared to hunt. But that wouldn't last much longer. The hunger was building.

She went into the kitchen, then down the hallway. Where was Laura? With a mounting panic, she checked the three bedrooms.

She was hurrying back to the living room to tell Patty when she heard voices coming from Rod's closet. She opened the door. Rod was sitting cross-legged in the corner. Curled up next to him was Laura, in the same posture that Simone remembered from night after night of lying on the cold cement floor of their prison: on her side, wrapped in as small a ball as she could make of herself.

Rod looked up. "She's all right. She just wants to escape for awhile." He seemed genuinely concerned about Laura's welfare.

Simone didn't answer him. She crouched over Laura and pressed her until she got to her knees. From there, she managed to get the girl to her feet. Rod started to follow them out. "Stay!" she ordered, then mumbled, "Thank you."

More than ever, she was determined to save this man. Rod had thought he was being kind. He hadn't seen what Simone had seen upon opening the door. Laura's head had been only inches away from the man's legs, and her fangs had been extended and glistening.

Simone had found Laura just in time.

Kelton walked out into sunlight, never doubting. He could feel the cold, damp soul of his Maker settling into his bones. He was like a passenger in his own body—nominally in charge of his movements, but knowing that someone else was really making the decisions.

The sunlight came down on him, but it seemed to stop a few inches away. It wasn't so much that he could now survive in daytime; instead, it was as if the sunlight never reached him, as if the darkness that filled him repelled all light, and he was a concentrated patch of night gliding through the hours.

He saw someone approaching. The man hesitated, looking as though he wanted to cross the street, but then got ahold of his courage, hunched his shoulders and walked quickly past.

Kelton put on his goofy smile, but instead of reassuring the stranger, it made the man grow pale, and he seemed to be holding back a shout.

Huh, I guess I've lost it, Kelton thought. *Well, I always did wonder why the stupid grin worked.*

Feller was lost. He was FBI—he'd always been FBI. Without his job, he was nothing, nobody. He was vampire, a scavenger feeding off society. He hated himself. Every morning, he fought the temptation to open the curtains and let the sunlight burn him out of existence.

This was the story he told himself, even as he knew he was lying. In truth, he loved himself, loved being a vampire, and could care less about being an FBI agent. He went hunting every night and felt no qualms about it.

He awoke with the fall of darkness, as he did every night, thanks to the internal clock that all vampires possessed. Instantly, he knew he was being hunted. They were trying to be quiet, in their clumsy human way. They were two floors down, working their way up the stairwell of the abandoned apartment building. Feller counted the footfalls. There were six of them, all young, judging by the vigorousness of their steps. All young men, and all armed, judging by the sound of confidence in their voices.

Feller thought about slipping away, then decided, *No, I'm hungry and I'm mad, and these young men need to be taught a final lesson.*

Feller wasn't exactly sure why he hadn't left town.

Everyone in Crescent City was on high alert. The entire surviving populace knew about vampires, and gangs of youth spent every night searching the shadowy corners for the creatures of darkness. The humans had the upper hand this time. They always had the upper hand when they were aware and vigilant, for they could move around by day and by night and always had the superior numbers. One on one, vampires were more dangerous, but, armed with the latest weapons, modern humans would win in the end.

That was why vampires had always lurked in the shadows and caught their unsuspecting prey by surprise. As a vampire hunter, Feller had always been against acknowledging the existence of vampires, because it would panic the public. Now he saw clearly that it had been simple turf-protecting on his part, self-serving, like most of his motives. He hadn't really cared about vampires—even the best vampire hunter usually confronted only a bare handful in a lifetime. No, the world of vampires had just been his turf to consolidate and expand.

One thing about being a vampire—you no longer harbored illusions. You saw life clearly, in all its brutal reality.

That's why he was surprised by his own hesitance to leave the area. The further he moved away from here, the more unsuspecting the humans would be. This was probably the most dangerous place on Earth for vampires, for not only was the citizenry up in arms, but possibly every professional vampire hunter in the world had descended on this one small coastal city in Northern California.

Perhaps it was the challenge. Killing the hunters—that took real skill.

As a former vampire hunter, Feller knew all the tricks. So far, he had managed to avoid any confrontations with humans who actually posed a danger. He was breaking his own rules tonight of never challenging more than three opponents at a time, but he was feeling good, feeling strong. All the burns had healed.

When Robert had opened the curtains in that death room, Feller had been caught flat-footed. He'd fled, but not before most of his skin had burned away. He'd hidden in the rafters of the old motel until darkness had fallen, and then fled into the chaos and destruction outside. Even the other vampires had avoided him, a skeleton with red meat on it, eyes bulging from a bare skull, the bare bones of his feet slapping against the pavement.

He'd found a human, sniffed the little old woman out from hundreds of yards away, torn open the door and fallen on her. She had died with a resigned moan. But she had only been enough to begin the healing. Many more humans had died before Feller was himself again.

As the gang of youths crept up the staircase to his floor, he decided to remain where he was, hidden in a closet. They would check, of course. He was counting on it.

He heard them giggling and shushing each other. It had probably been days since they'd actually seen a vampire. They weren't really expecting to find one. They were just reliving the glory of previous days.

When the kid opened the closet door, his eyes weren't even focused. They were already moving away, on to the next thing. Then his head snapped back in a double take. It was too late.

Feller fired his FBI-supplied Glock twice, the silencer barely making a sound. The young man fell limply to the floor, folding almost without a sound. One of his friends called out tentatively, "Sergi?"

Feller fired in the direction of the voice, then walked out of the closet into the middle of the room. Only one of the remaining youths had a gun, and Feller fired into his head.

Then it was down to three opponents, the number he preferred to deal with.

He was on the first kid before any of the three could move, using his claws to rip into his neck. He left his victim standing, blood spurting out into the room, not yet aware he was dead.

One of the surviving hunters attacked Feller with a big Bowie knife. He almost caught the vampire by surprise with an overhand blow, but then the kid slipped on the blood-soaked floor and slid into Feller's grasp. Reaching down, Feller took hold of his head and twisted it. The hunter's neck snapped, but Feller kept twisting until his head came off. He rolled it toward the last hunter.

The lone survivor was running, as the humans always did. Feller caught him at the top of the steps, bit into his neck and drank deep. This was the real prize: the warm red blood of a still-living human. When he was done, he'd go back and feast on the dead, but nothing could match the sheer exhilaration he felt at sucking the adrenalized blood of a terrorized teenager.

"Well done," he heard a voice say.

Feller dropped the dead man and reached for his gun.

"No need for that," the voice continued. Feller used his sharp night vision to scan the stairs, the hallways, the room behind him. There was nothing there—no, wait. There was a shadow. A darkness where there should have been clarity. Feller could see into the darkest shadows, but he couldn't penetrate this void.

A huge man walked out of the shadow. That is, he became visible—but the darkness still accompanied him. His voice was low and neutral, yet not quite masculine. It was a voice that seemed to be made of many voices.

"What do you want?" Feller asked. He raised his Glock and considered firing. It wouldn't kill the other vampire, but it might slow him down. Feller didn't care that this new opponent was one of his own kind. He felt nothing toward other vampires and suspected they felt nothing toward him.

The huge vampire gave him a big grin, or at least appeared to be trying to. It was a rictus, a death mask, and Feller—who thought he'd seen everything—felt a chill. "My name is Kelton. I have been granted powers that most vampires don't possess."

"Good for you," Feller said. "So what?"

"If you follow me, I will give you the power to walk in sunlight," Kelton said.

Feller lowered his gun. This was what made being a vampire dangerous—humans merely needed to uncover them, just draw back the curtains, overturn the rock, and they would win, with all the daylight hours at their command. At night, the fight was equal, but unless vampires had time to prepare for the morning, they were always going to be vulnerable. Even Feller, the former vampire hunter who knew all the tricks.

"You can do that?" he asked.

"Yes...but you must descend into a deeper darkness than ever you have known, from which there will be no return."

"Let's do it," Feller laughed. "I have no desire to return to what I was." He holstered his gun and opened his arms.

The other vampire scooped him up before he was quite prepared, and Feller felt his neck being sliced by huge fangs.

As a cold lassitude swept through his blood, he had a final thought: *I hope this wasn't some sort of trick.*

In his mind, he clearly heard the words, "You have been chosen."

CHAPTER 8

Rod sat in the dark and wondered if he should try to escape. The closet was big enough that he could lie down, but he wasn't sleepy. He felt an unexpected pity for these poor girls, especially once he figured out who they were. Everyone in Crescent City knew about two of the girls; how they had disappeared into thin air. Most thought them dead, or taken far away.

Rod wanted to help them.

Stockholm syndrome? he wondered. He didn't think so, but then, someone suffering from Stockholm syndrome probably wouldn't, right?

The door opened, but he couldn't see who was there. It was equally dark in the hallway. It always freaked him out a little, how the girls could move around in the dark as if all the lights were on. Now, they usually only turned on the lights when he was there.

Someone slipped into the closet beside him.

"Laura?" he whispered.

"No," he heard a husky voice say. "It's Simone. I want to ask you some questions."

He sat up, hitting his head on the shelf above him. He tried to keep the sudden lump out of his throat. "Sure."

Ever since that first day, Rod had tried not to stare at her, but it was difficult. Simone was the most beautiful girl he'd ever seen, dark-haired and slender, without any guile in her face. She was like a young girl in demeanor, but totally woman in form. He felt almost guilty being attracted to her, because she was like a young girl in demeanor—but she was totally woman in form. Her low voice was unbelievably sexy. Her no-nonsense manner was immensely appealing, especially now that he knew what she had experienced. It was her presence, more than anything else, that had kept him from trying to get away.

She started to ask him questions about what had happened in the world since she'd been locked up. The events of 9/11 had occurred after she'd been kidnapped, so the wars in Afghanistan and Iraq were news to her. She found the Arab Spring intriguing. The fact that America had a black president astounded her. Rod started to tell her about how far the Internet had come when he got a sudden inspiration.

"Here," he said. "Let me show you." He dug out his cellphone. The light from its screen lit up the inside of the closet. Simone's face was only inches from his, close enough for him to smell the soap she'd used to clean her hair. *Close enough to kiss,* he thought. There was a gleam in her eye as if she could read his intentions. Then they both moved back a little, as if mutually embarrassed.

"What is that?" Simone asked.

"It's my cellphone," he said. "I can get Internet service on it."

"A phone?" she said. She reached out and grabbed it. "So small!" she marveled, turning it over and over in her hands. Then she sat and stared at him, still holding his phone. "Why didn't you call for help?" she said finally.

Rod was embarrassed. Of course, he'd been thinking about it ever since he'd been locked in here, alone. The girls had seen the phone and examined it as if puzzled, but hadn't seemed to be aware of what it was or what it could do. Smartphones and Wi-Fi hadn't existed when they'd been kidnapped.

"I, ah…I'm not sure," he stammered. "I want to help you…"

"Help us?" She sounded suspicious. "Why would you do that?"

"You don't remember me, do you, Simone?"

She gave him a look, as if to say, *Obviously not.*

"I was in Mrs. Hogner's seventh-grade math class with you. I had a crush on you."

She examined him, then shook her head. "I'm sorry. I don't remember much about those days. School seems so...far away."

"I still think you're pretty cool," he said. *God, that sounded lame.*

She looked puzzled. "What about your wife and kids?"

"I lied."

"What?"

"I thought you'd be less likely to kill me if I told you I had a family. I didn't recognize you at first."

Hearing this, Simone looked so sad that he couldn't help himself: he reached out and put his palm on her cheek. She winced at first, then leaned into his caress. It wasn't so much him, he sensed, but simply that she craved human contact. Her eyes started to well up, and he dared to take her in his arms and hug her.

After she had cried herself out, she leaned away from him and ran her hands across her eyes, wiping away the tears. "Do you really want to help?" she asked. Her voice was all business again.

"Anything," Rod said. He meant it. All thoughts of escape had vanished.

"Go to the neighbors. Tell them you have bought this house. See if they will sell you any of their livestock—anything at all. My sisters—I mean, Laura and Patty—need some raw flesh to eat, or...or I'm not sure what will happen."

"OK," he said. "I have a little money in the car. I'll see what I can do."

Simone started to get up, then sat back down and took his hand. "If you can't help us, then you must leave. I can't be sure than we can control our hunger much longer. Promise me you won't come back unless you can bring meat."

He nodded. He noticed that she hadn't asked him not to call the authorities. She trusted him, it was clear. She gave him back his phone and led him out of the closet. It was dawn outside, and a small amount of light had infiltrated the hallway. As they stood outside the door before joining the others, they turned to each other and hugged. Rod resisted the urge to try to kiss her, though he'd never wanted something so much in his whole life. She kept her head down during the hug, as if afraid he'd try it. When they broke apart, she gave him a grateful smile.

He spent the next few hours going door to door with the neighbors until he found an old man who was willing to sell him one of his goats. It was a scrawny thing, on its last legs, but Rod bought it.

When he got it back to the house, he was alarmed at how the three girls tore into the unfortunate animal. He went back to his closet so he wouldn't have to watch. He took out his cellphone. That morning, he'd only had ten percent power left, but once Simone had given him the freedom to move around, he'd used his recharger in the van.

The previous evening, Rod had come across *The Testament of Michael*, which was all over the Internet. It had given him an idea.

He called up his blog, his Facebook page, Twitter and every other site he could think of, and he told the story of the three young girls, tortured and abused and in need of help. He knew he was broadcasting it to the world, to both the good guys and the bad guys, but he didn't think he had any choice. In fact, he thought he'd be lucky if anyone noticed.

"To Terrill…" it began.

"Master, why were we created?"

"Please, call me Terrill," he said. He looked down at his followers, who were arrayed around him. They were staring up at him with adoring eyes.

Ridiculous. What he really wanted to do was run far, far away.

"This isn't about us," Terrill said.

"Not about us?"

"We sprang from man," Terrill said. "We are manifestations of mankind's hopes and fears. What is evil but the darkness in the human heart? And no matter where a human goes, his heart goes with him."

He sat on the picnic table, surrounded by a couple of dozen vampires. Most had taken the Sacrament of the Blood of Gold, but a few were holding back, uncertain or undecided. So far, almost everyone had survived the test, for a vampire had to be committed to make the long journey through the High Desert of Eastern Oregon and up the narrow, winding roads into the Strawberry Mountains from John Day. By the time they finished that journey, there weren't too many doubters left.

Even when they thought they were ready, though, Sylvie and Jamie made them wait, made them listen to Terrill explain the consequences. Never again could they kill man or woman, they were told. Never again could they drink human blood. They could never go back.

Since the consequence of failure was immediate death, there were always a few doubters. Terrill almost preferred it that way. This was taking on all the trappings of a cult, and it made him uncomfortable. He probably ought to keep his mouth shut, he knew, but he couldn't help spouting off when he had an audience.

And there was Marc, at the end of the bench, writing down his every word. Marc refused to take credit for the authorship of *The Testament of Michael*. "I heard his voice," he said. "Every word was Michael's."

Terrill doubted it—Michael had never been big on religion. He certainly never talked in the religious terminology of the Testament. Terrill's Maker, the most ancient of vampires, had told him that the evolution of this new type of vampire had been planned and guided for millennia. *We're nothing but the end of a long line of breeding,* Terrill thought. *Like prize cows.*

That didn't sound very lofty, however, and the Testament certainly was drawing in those vampires who were tired of killing. That's what Michael wanted, wasn't it?

Terrill stopped talking, and when it became clear he wasn't going to continue, his disciples wandered off, discussing his words. Terrill almost laughed at the serious tones he overheard. What would happen if he just took off? Never came back?

The cult would go on, he realized. Maybe even more vibrantly than with him there.

He shuddered at the thought. He didn't much want to be a martyr, but the logic of a cult almost demanded a sacrifice.

Clarkson entered the clearing from the hillside above. They had Wi-Fi reception only at the top of the nearest hill, so there was always someone stationed there. The former Council member was a breath of fresh air for Terrill. She treated him as an equal. She apparently wasn't buying into the legend of Saint Terrill. He'd begun to tell her of his worries about this turning into a cult, but she'd cut him off, saying, "It's a cult when it's only a few people—it's a religion when it's a lot."

"I thought you ought to see this," Clarkson said now. She handed him a phone and he started reading.

It was a blog by someone who gave his first name as Rod. It was entitled "To Terrill."

"I have read *The Testament of Michael,* and I think you might be our only hope. I am helping three young women who escaped the clutches of a serial rapist and murderer. They are safe for the moment, but I don't know what else to do. I'm worried about them. They don't know I'm doing this—they are completely innocent of the ways of the Internet.

"Here's the thing. They are vampires—vampires with the minds of thirteen-year-old girls, which was their age when they were abducted. Yeah, yeah, most of you will stop reading at this point, but it's true. Crescent City had an outbreak of vampires. Maybe you read about it. So these innocent girls, who suffered years of imprisonment by an evil man, were turned into these creatures, and now they are suffering. None of this is their fault. They don't deserve it.

"So far, they have not killed anyone, but I can tell they won't be able to hold off much longer. I'm not worried about myself; I'm worried about their souls. They didn't ask for what happened to them.

"Terrill, help save these poor unfortunate girls."

Terrill handed the phone back to Clarkson. "OK. What can we do about it?"

"I want to go get them," she said. "Bring them back here."

"They don't sound ready for the blood of gold," Terrill said.

"We can at least protect them," Clarkson insisted, "until they are ready."

Terrill sat back down on the picnic table and thought. Was it really his responsibility? He felt for these girls, and for their human protector. But what could he do?

"How will you find them?" he asked finally.

"I already have," Clarkson said. "I contacted Callendar at the FBI, and he gave me the cell tower coverage. I should be able to find them from that."

After the unsuccessful raid on Sylvie's house in Bend, Callendar had passed word through back channels that the FBI was looking for them, and that he'd try to hold off the hunters for as long as possible. "I owe you that much," he had said.

Clarkson had been antsy ever since they had arrived in these isolated hills. She had taken it upon herself to monitor the outside world, but Terrill knew that what she really wanted was to be engaged with it.

"All right, but be careful," he said. "We're probably not the only ones who read this message."

Clarkson nodded. She'd grown out her blonde hair, which once had been nearly white and cut close to her head. Now her hair was long and a soft golden color. Where once she'd been pale and forbidding, now she looked like a tanned beach girl. Her severe manner hadn't changed much, though. She still seldom smiled—or frowned, for that matter.

"I want to go too."

Terrill turned in surprise to see that Marc was still sitting on the bench at his feet and was looking up at them. He had an open expression, big brown eyes, and was skin and bones. He only ate enough raw meat to stay alive. Terrill thought he'd stop eating meat altogether if he could. Now that would be a true miracle—a vegetarian vampire.

Don't you want to write down my every word? he wanted to ask.

"I'll leave my recorder here," Marc said, seeming to answer his unspoken question. "I'll get others to tape you."

"Why?"

"Your words must not be lost," Marc said.

"No, I meant why do you want to go?"

"I think I know who these girls are. There were a couple of kidnappings of young girls in Del Norte County who were never found. I think their names were Laura and Simone. If it's them, they've been missing for over ten years."

So? Terrill wanted to ask. *Why are you interested?*

Again, Marc seemed to answer his thoughts. "They are innocents. They must be saved. The blood of gold can save them."

Terrill looked over at Clarkson. She seemed to be pleading with him with her eyes to say no. She was going to be disappointed.

"All right," he said. "I'd feel better if you didn't go alone, Clarkson."

I wish I could go with you, he thought. *Anything to get out from under the burden of sainthood.*

CHAPTER 9

By the time Hoss flew to London, he'd lost most of his followers. As he'd been about to leave, a little girl had pulled on his coat. *Who the hell would Turn a six-year-old girl?* Hoss had wondered. *A rule breaker, that's who.*

"Yeah?" he'd asked.

"Who's going to enforce the Rules of Vampire if you leave?"

"What's your name?"

"Charlotte."

"Well, Charlotte…you're going to enforce the rules." *After all,* he had thought, *who's bossier than little girls?* "You hear that?" he'd shouted to the others in the motel office. "Charlotte's in charge!"

Then he had left. *To hell with them,* he'd thought. *They're on their own.*

Jodie had stuck with him, but then, she seemed completely enamored with him, demanding more of his time and energy than he could really afford. Then again, he was a teenage boy first discovering sex. It turned out he always had the time and energy for that.

His first converts, Pete and Jimmy, had also come along. But once the Battle of Crescent City was over, most of the others had wandered away from his protection, no longer feeling the need to follow the Rules of Vampire, which Hoss insisted on.

Hoss didn't hold out much hope for their survival. The humans were aware of them as never before, which meant the Rules were more necessary than ever before. But the Rules had to be voluntary if they were to mean anything at all. As far as Hoss was concerned, that had been the biggest mistake that Fitzsimmons and the Council of Vampires had made: they had turned the Rules into laws, punishable by death.

Hoss had flown London to meet with the Council to press his case: that by enforcing the Rules through punishment, they were weakening their impact, not to mention just asking for vampires to disobey them. The Rules were only effective if each vampire, as a way to stay safe, internalized them; or, for some vampires, made them an ethical choice.

To Hoss's great surprise, he was ushered into the Council chambers within a day of arriving in London. Jodie was left behind in their hotel room, to her great disappointment. Pete and Jimmy, on the other hand, seemed just as content to stay out of the politics. The two small-town boys were already feeling overwhelmed by the long trip and the big city.

The Council chambers looked like any corporate meeting room—indeed, they were located at the back of a bank. There was a concave table in the center of the room. Hoss could smell the blood on it, and his eyes followed its contours as they tapered to a point—a drainage point, he realized. He felt a cold chill.

There were ten members of the Council, representing England and the rest of Europe. He'd been told before entering that Clarkson, the blonde vampire he'd met in Crescent City, had been the American representative, but was now considered a traitor. Meanwhile, Fitzsimmons was still in America, he was told. So there were eight councilors in attendance. Along the walls, behind the councilors' chairs, stood their aides—those most likely to be next in line for a seat at the table.

At the age of thirteen and newly Turned, Hoss was by far the youngest vampire there. He suspected it was unprecedented for a vampire so young to be given an audience at a Council meeting. He was not the youngest-looking vampire—there was a councilor at the end of the table who didn't appear much older than ten, if you didn't look too closely into his ancient dark eyes. He was so small that he had to sit on a raised seat. *This is Hargraves*, Hoss thought. Peterson had given him a quick rundown on the councilors who were likely to attend.

"Fitzsimmons hasn't yet returned from America, and he asked me to chair this meeting," Peterson said by way of introduction. "But he and I agree that what happened in Crescent City was extraordinary, and that we should introduce to you a young vampire who was instrumental in helping resolve the situation there.

"Don't let his age fool you. This young vampire met us at the airport with a local Chapter of the Council of Vampires."

Hoss heard one of the older councilors snicker.

"Without his help, we would have been quickly overwhelmed," Peterson continued. "I know it sounds precocious, but I suspect this chap is a kind of genius. He had organized his followers into an effective force. He knows the Rules forwards and backwards, and what's more, he believes in them completely."

Again there were amused mutterings, and Hoss wondered what was going on. *This is the Council of Vampires—don't they all believe in the Rules? Isn't that why they are here?*

"Without Hoss, here, I doubt I could have returned to give you an account of the extraordinary events in Crescent City, which is contained in the reports on the table in front of you and which I assume you have all read. Therefore, when Hoss asked to speak to us, I felt that we owed him that much. I also thought it would be a good idea to hear some fresh ideas…Hoss?"

Before Hoss could rise, another of the councilors spoke up. She was an overweight woman of indeterminate age, who had a jolly appearance and a high voice. "Don't be fooled by Belinda," Peterson had warned him. "She'll kill you as soon as look at you."

"Before Mr...." Her cheerful expression turned puzzled. "Hoss, is it? Do you have a full name?"

Do I? Hoss wondered. Yes, he'd once had a name, but it was long gone; it had belonged to an innocent child. He didn't feel like remembering it, much less revealing it. "Just Hoss," he said.

"Very well, Hoss. Before Hoss presents his case, I'd like to ask him a few questions."

Hoss looked at Peterson, who shrugged as if he couldn't do anything to prevent it.

"Yes?"

"Is it true that you and your followers allied with the humans against the Wilderings?"

"We did."

"I see," Belinda said. She looked around the table with raised eyebrows. "So you're saying that you broke almost every Rule of Vampire?"

Seeing the grim looks of the other councilors, Hoss suddenly understood that he was in trouble. Once again, his gaze fell on the table, which seemed designed to channel blood to narrow point near the legs. It had been used recently and often, he realized. But instead of being frightened, he found himself angry.

"I did," he said defiantly. "If the Wilderings had won, then the existence of vampires would have been exposed, putting all of us in danger. I determined that it was best to help the human vampire hunters put down the plague, because they wanted to keep the secret as much as I did."

"Did it remain a secret?" Belinda asked.

"Officially," Hoss said.

"Nevertheless, it appears to be common knowledge. So your gamble didn't pay off, did it?"

"It's a better result than what would have happened if I hadn't intervened."

"Still, you decided on your own to break most of the Rules."

Hoss thought about objecting, but then simply nodded. He could see it wasn't going well. The other councilors hadn't changed expression as he explained himself; they hadn't relaxed, as they would have if they were accepting his words.

"I think the young man showed great resourcefulness," a deep voice said. It was coming from one of the men along the wall, and Hoss identified him as Roger Combs.

"There is one more individual I must tell you about," Peterson had said. "He isn't officially a councilor, but he controls at least three of the Council members. He is a short man, fastidious in dress, looking like a nineteenth-century clerk from a Dickens novel. Do not be fooled by his stature.'

Four of the eight councilors seated at the table froze at the new speaker's words. *Interesting,* Hoss thought. *This vampire controls at least half of the current Council. Can't everyone see that?*

"I think this young vampire deserves our applause," Combs said.

Everyone in the room started clapping, some more enthusiastically than others, but Hoss got the sense that what Combs wanted, Combs would get.

Belinda frowned and looked as if she wanted to object, but glanced around and realized she was outnumbered. She looked down at the table, blue blood suffusing her countenance.

"I understand you had something you wanted to tell us, Hoss," Combs continued. "Please proceed."

Hoss took a deep breath. He'd prepared a long and reasoned discourse, but decided at the last moment to keep it short and simple. "I've come to you today to plead for a relaxation of the punishments for breaking the Rules of Vampire. As conceived by Terrill, these rules were meant to be guidelines, to keep vampires safe. Nothing more. It is a perversion of the original meaning of the rules to make them mandatory."

"How else are we to get other vampires to obey?" asked Jerome Bacher, the German representative.

"Vampires will obey what vampires want to obey," Hoss said, and Combs chuckled at this. "While they may pretend to follow the letter of the law, unless they actually agree with it, they won't follow the spirit of the law. So making the punishment draconian for failure to comply not only doesn't work, it serves to undermine the very meaning of the rules."

"Isn't this true of all laws?" Jerome objected. "Are you suggesting that all laws be voluntary?"

"Again, we are vampire. We aren't human. We aren't meant to follow laws, though we might be open to suggestions, if they make sense."

Combs laughed again, and this time others joined him. "I've always said so. We vampires aren't meant to be tame."

Hargraves spoke up, his young voice sounding high in the small room. "Perhaps we should wait for Fitzsimmons to return from America before we make any decisions."

"Agreed," Peterson said, and two of the other councilors quickly approved. It was four to four, and everyone looked to Combs to see what he would decide.

"I agree," Combs said. The tension went out of the room, tension that Hoss hadn't even realized was there.

Always helps when you delay the hard decisions, Hoss thought. But he, too, found himself relaxing.

"Meanwhile, we appear to be missing an American member of our august group. I hereby nominate Hoss for that position," said Combs. "I believe we need some fresh ideas, from someone who isn't just aware of the new technologies, but has lived with them and knows how to use them."

There was a stunned silence in the room.

I'm thirteen years old! Hoss wanted to object.

"I second the motion," Peterson said unexpectedly. Hoss had a sinking feeling mixed with a sense of excitement. Both camps in the Council were on his side, and within a few moments, the vote was taken and he was approved.

Peterson pulled out the chair to his right. "Take a seat, young man. Welcome to the Council of Vampires."

After getting handshakes and pats on the back from seemingly everyone in the room, Hoss found himself alone. *Nice,* he thought. *They congratulate me, but none of them want to be around me for long.*

Somehow he wasn't surprised that the exception was Combs. The little man was waiting for him outside the chambers, hand extended and a big smile on his face. "Sorry to spring that on you," he said. "But we need an American member to get anything done."

"It's all right," Hoss said.

"Come with me. I have dinner waiting in my suite."

Hoss followed the older vampire, though he knew Jodie was probably waiting for him back in his hotel room, naked and already in bed. But he doubted that Combs would take no for answer.

In Combs's suite, there was a liveried servant and a two-person dining table with a white linen tablecloth and immaculate place settings. Combs offered Hoss some red wine. "It's been mixed with fresh blood, and I like the zing," he explained.

Hoss hesitated, then accepted. With his strict upbringing, he'd never had any alcohol in his young life. His mouth puckered up at the acidic taste, but he was determined to drink enough to see what all the fuss was about.

The conversation wandered, Combs asking him about school and friends, and then slowly but pointedly drifting into questions about the Wildering battle. Then came the question that Hoss thought was probably the entire reason he'd been invited there.

"Tell me about the vampires with blood of gold," Combs insisted. "Tell me about Terrill."

By then, Hoss was feeling fine. The soft white tablecloth, the congenial surroundings, the sophisticated host: all if it seemed like a great adventure. He took another gulp of the blood-laced wine, then said, "I don't know much. They seem stronger and faster than us. They can walk in daylight. Other than that, I don't really have much to tell you."

"But anyone can become a golden vampire?"

"No…my understanding is that they must renounce all feeding off of humans."

Combs laughed, and Hoss joined him. So this was what it was like to be an adult! How wonderful that he didn't have to wait any longer! And his host—this was a wise and great man!

"Well, that doesn't sound like much fun," Combs said.

"Anyway, I only saw them for a short time. You'll probably need to talk to Fitzsimmons when he comes back."

The room started to spin a little, and Hoss put down his wine glass with a clank against the porcelain plate. "Sorry," he muttered.

"Strong wine if you're not used to it. Listen, I have a spare bedroom if you need to stay."

Hoss considered it. His hotel was across town, and getting

there would require a taxi ride. But he had a sudden image of Jodie waiting for him, and he tried to get up. "I need to get back," he said, but then flopped back down into his chair.

"Stay! I insist," Combs said. "I've got a surprise for you." He raised his finger to the servant, and a few moments later, a couple of giggling girls were led into the room. They were human. Hoss could smell their blood from across the room, and he realized he hadn't really fed since he'd crossed the ocean.

The two girls were way too young to be dressed so skimpily. *But that's just the small-town boy in me*, came a thought. It was his thought—and yet it wasn't. It was if it came to him from somewhere outside himself.

Hoss felt a tug at his sleeve and rose to his feet. He approached the two girls, and one of them, the smaller one, took him by the arm and led him to a bedroom. Hoss tried to unbutton his shirt, but his fingers didn't seem to work very well, and she laughed and helped pull it over his head. Then his pants were down around his ankles and she was on her knees in front of him. He flopped back on the bed.

Jodie will be pissed, he thought. But his body was responding, and the girl was very skilled. When she was done, she crawled up beside him and nestled against him. The blood in her neck was only inches away.

She'd been so nice to him. He didn't want to kill her.

Feed! the voice in his mind insisted. *Take her!*

He sank his fangs into her neck and she started, then relaxed, almost as if she was expecting it, even accepting it. *Or*—he thought underneath his bloodlust—*as if she's being controlled.*

The thought of control seemed to sober him, and as he continued feeding, his brain started working again.

There is something wrong here, he thought. *Someone is trying to manipulate me.*

CHAPTER 10

Rod was free to come and go as he pleased, though Patty often squinted at him as if she still didn't quite trust him. She'd get his attention in some subtle way and then give him a look that said, *Don't be trying to get away, buddy.*

Meanwhile, Laura seemed to be barely aware he was there. She didn't acknowledge him, and whenever he came near, she would move away, always keeping a distance between them.

But he wasn't going anywhere. He didn't want to leave Simone's side at all. They were constantly together now. He left the house only for necessities and then hurried back, worried the girls would leave without him. Fortunately, though they fed in a manner that was frighteningly ferocious, they didn't have to feed that often, not as often as humans needed to eat.

Simone wouldn't look him in the eye after their almost-kiss, but she didn't shy away from him, either.

He was trying to imagine the horror she had been through. It was almost inconceivable that she'd ever feel safe again. He wouldn't blame her if she never allowed another man to touch her for the rest of her life. But he'd be patient; he'd wait for as long as she needed. It was enough just to be near her.

They were sitting at the rickety, makeshift table they had constructed out of bricks and an old door. Rod was showing Simone how to use a smartphone. The Wiki app seemed to especially grab her attention, and she spent hours using it to find out about the missing decade-plus of her life.

"It's all so familiar," she said. "And yet so strange…"

Patty marched into the room and stood over them silently until they both looked up. "Laura's gone."

"What do you mean, 'Laura's gone?'" Simone said.

"I mean she's freaking gone!" Patty said. "Vanished, vamoosed, skedaddled, out of here!"

"Where would she go?" But even as Simone asked it, a look of realization came over both of the girls' faces.

"She went back…" Simone breathed.

Patty nodded. "I should have known."

"Went back!" Rod exclaimed. "Why would she do that?"

"You wouldn't understand," Patty snapped.

"We have to go get her," Simone said. She got up from the table, handing Rod's cellphone back to him. "When did you see her last?"

Everyone was quiet as they realized that Laura had been like a ghost floating around the house over the last few days and that none of them could remember talking to her recently. No one remembered seeing her since waking up at dusk, and now the night was almost over.

"She can't have gone far," Simone said in a faint voice. "I'll go. It's my fault. I should have watched her closer."

"*Your* fault?" Patty snorted. "What are you, the boss?"

"I can help," Rod said. "Nobody will look twice at me. I can drive the van and the two of you can hide in the back."

Simone looked at him gratefully, and he blushed.

"We can't all go," Patty said. "Someone needs to stay here. Laura might return."

As they stood there in silence, it became increasingly obvious what the right solution was. Finally, Patty spoke up.

"Simone, you should stay here with Rod. There is no telling what I might do if you leave him here with me." She looked at Rod and licked her lips, and he could see she was only half joking.

"Can you drive?" Rod asked.

"I grew up on a farm," Patty said. "Of course I can drive."

"Stick shift?"

She gave him a withering look. He dug into his pockets and handed her the keys. "There should be enough gas, but if not, see if you can't trade some of the tools in back for cash or fuel. If you need to park during the day, they'll never question you if you park along the beach road."

She reached out and snatched the keys out of his hand. There were only a couple hours of darkness left.

Laura wandered off from their hiding place without meaning to and without a plan. She just wanted to get away. She was tired of being ignored by the others. Simone had Rod to talk to, and Patty—well, Patty always had Patty.

It wasn't until she was walking north along the highway that she realized she wasn't going back. No matter what, she was never going to be cooped up again, unless…unless it was because *he* wanted her.

Thanks to Rod's magical phone, Laura had realized that no one had even submitted a missing person's report on her. She'd been thrown away, just like that. At least *he* desired her; at least *he* talked to her. He could even be nice sometimes. Like that time he'd brought her ice cream. Or when he'd let her lie in the backyard, staring up at the stars. He didn't have to do that.

They had called him the Monster—and that was before he'd become a *real* Monster. But Laura hadn't really thought of him that way. To her, "Monster" had become almost a term of endearment. She'd whispered it in his ear once, and he'd reared back and looked at her strangely, but then had gone back to what he was doing. From then on, she kept the feelings to herself, but when she thought "Monster," it didn't have the same meaning as it did to the others.

The outside world was bewildering, not just because it was different, but because it was so much faster and brighter and scarier than she remembered. What had happened to her body was frightening. She had desires that weren't natural. Down in the basement, she'd been safe. She knew what to expect every day. Sure, she didn't like…what he wanted from her. But that only happened once in a while. She could just shut her mind off while he was doing those things to her.

The hardest part was leaving her two friends. Well, she wanted to call them friends, but were they really? Had they chosen each other? Would they have ever hung out together if they'd met outside? Patty might have gone out on the town with her a couple of times, but she doubted Simone would have exchanged two words with her.

Simone called her "sister," but Laura sensed that the other two had always kind of looked down on her. Because she was Monster's favorite, that's why. He'd always gone to her first. He liked her best. They were too old.

She heard the horn only after the truck had already gone by, so close she could feel the wind from its passing. It was one of those enormous pickups that they seemed to have nowadays— as long as a stretch limousine and just as spotless. Coming from the country, she didn't understand clean, unmarked pickup trucks. Pickups were supposed to be used, otherwise what good were they?

The huge truck swerved as it came to a stop. A middle-aged man, tall and rangy, with a bald head and a bushy mustache, got out. He stood there for a moment and then approached her. "You all right? You shouldn't be walking along in the dark like that."

He had his hand on a holster attached to his belt. He'd be wary of anyone out here alone, she thought, especially with all the chaos and danger of the last week. Still, he seemed genuinely concerned.

"Sorry," she mumbled. She tried to walk around him, but he grabbed her arm. It was all she could do not to turn and snarl at him.

"Why don't you let me give you a ride to town?" he said. His voice sounded kindly. But then again, when the Monster had sounded kindly, it was when he was most dangerous.

"No, thank you," she said politely.

"Listen, you can ride in the bed of the pickup if you're worried. I'll be driving. You'll be fine."

Laura peered down the road. It was pitch dark. The lights of the town seemed a long way off. "OK," she said.

"Good!" the man said, sounding almost surprised. "That's good!"

He walked back to the truck, put his hand on the door handle, then looked back at her.

Laura surprised herself by walking past the back of the pickup and going to the passenger side of the truck. She climbed up onto the seat, feeling like a little child, perched up so high.

The bald man got in quietly, slowly, as if trying not to alarm her.

He started the truck and the radio began blasting—some guy was shouting nonsense lyrics at her. Rap, she remembered, though she'd probably only listened to it a few times in her life. The bald man quickly turned down the radio, then searched the channels until he came across a station playing classic rock. With the sound of "Piano Man" playing, he pulled out onto the highway.

Patty was pleased for Simone that she had found Rodney, who was obviously hopelessly in love with her. Patty was also desperately jealous. She needed to get away. Their shy glances at each other were just too much. "Get a room!," she wanted to shout. If Laura's disappearance hadn't given her the excuse, she would have found some other reason to leave.

She expected to find Laura walking alongside the highway. Laura was pretty simple in her choices. She'd find a road and follow it. She probably wouldn't even think to hide when she saw headlights coming toward her.

Patty reached the outskirts of Crescent City without spotting her friend. Once in town, Laura could have taken any number of side streets, so after driving around fruitlessly for a while, Patty drove to their old prison, even though it was possible she'd get there before Laura.

It was as if the universe had a hole in it.

The house wasn't there. In its place was a still-smoking heap of rubble, a small part of the blackened frame still standing. When Patty got out of the car, a burnt-mildew smell assaulted her heightened senses. It seemed to her that she could smell every moment of her life buried under that rubble—all the crappy meals and soiled clothing, and…the Monster. She could smell him even through the smoke.

She could also smell the stench of death. It was coming from a house on the same side of the street, two doors down. She walked swiftly toward the partly open door, looking around to see if anyone was observing her.

She found the remains of four people inside, two adults and two children, from the looks of it, though it was hard to tell. Beneath the stench of rotting corpses, she smelled something else—subtle but unmistakable. The Monster. *Her* Monster. He'd done this. He'd been here.

She went into the first bedroom and looked out the window. From there, she could see most of the street. She sat down on the bed and waited.

The man driving the pickup smelled comforting. He smelled of cigarette smoke and whiskey, with an underlay of oil and fast food hamburgers. He smelled just like her father—and like Monster. But Laura could also smell his animal flesh, could hear his heart and sense the blood coursing through his veins. She drooled, and a string of saliva splatted onto her T-shirt. She shot a glance at the driver, but he was pretending not to have noticed.

The drool had dripped off of her elongated fangs, which she was having more and more trouble hiding. She turned her face to the window and tried to think harmless thoughts, but nothing came to her. She hadn't felt safe for so long, she simply couldn't remember the feeling.

"You OK?" the man asked.

"Yeah, fine," she murmured. It was hard to speak clearly when her fangs were extended.

She felt him examining her—could almost sense him looking at her thigh where her too-short skirt was riding up, and then looking at her breasts, which she knew were large for her small frame.

She started to tense, not sure what he was going to do, not sure what her reaction would be.

She felt his hand on her shoulder. He probably didn't mean anything by it; it may have only been a comforting gesture, but she reacted as if he was attacking her. She turned her head and bit into his wrist.

He cried out, and the pickup swerved onto the shoulder of the road. He overcorrected and suddenly they were shooting across the highway and into the trees on the other side. The truck started rolling, and Laura felt her head crack against the window and heard the glass break. The truck finally stopped, upside down. She came to her senses almost immediately.

She still had the bald man's wrist in her mouth, and it was half chewed through, as if she had never stopped eating even during the accident. She looked over at him and saw that his head had been sheared off by a tree branch that was embedded in the back of the headrest. Without thinking about it, she kept chewing, finishing off his fingers, then his hand and on up his arm to his neck. She didn't stop until the top half of him was gone, except for the bones.

Laura crawled out of the wreckage, then had a thought and went back and searched his wallet. It was filled with twenties—more money than she'd ever seen in her life. She took the whole wallet and started walking down the highway toward Crescent City. Dawn was glimmering on the horizon. She'd have to find shelter soon. She looked down at her coat. It was covered with blood. She took it off, used the inside to wipe her face and hands and tossed it to the side of the road. Her stomach was full, and she felt good for the first time in a long time.

Motels were among the first buildings on the outskirts of town. She went to the office of the first one she saw and rang the bell. An old lady emerged from out of the back, blinking as though she'd slept the night in the armchair in front of the blaring TV.

"Checking out?" she asked.

"I want a room," Laura said.

"You want a room *now*?" The woman seemed suspicious.

Laura handed over five twenties. "How many days can I get for this?"

The old woman pulled the front of her bathrobe together. She got a shrewd look on her face. "Give me another twenty bucks and you can have three nights."

Laura dug into the wallet, keeping it out of sight below the counter, and handed over another twenty. When the woman tried to give her paperwork and tell her the checkout time, Laura almost-shouted at her, "Just give me the keys, lady! I'll fill out all the paperwork and stuff later, all right?"

The woman took the keys from a drawer, looking startled. "It's at the end. Last unit. You could have told me you needed to use the bathroom."

Laura grabbed the keys and hurried down the broken concrete of the walkway. She quickly unlocked the door and slammed it just as the first rays of the sun came over the edge of the parking lot.

Then she lay back in the bed, feeling completely satiated for the first time since she'd been Turned.

Eating the man who'd picked her up had been easy. She probably would have killed him anyway, even if they hadn't had the accident. She hadn't felt a thing. Not a tinge of doubt.

I'm going to like being a vampire, she thought as she fell to sleep.

Deb Hutchins watched the girl slip into the room. Showing up at dawn and being in such a hurry for a room? Well, didn't that just seem a little suspicious? She was well aware of what had been going on in Crescent City, though her motel had been far enough away from the fighting to avoid damage, and she'd benefited from the lack of decent rooms left in town.

She didn't kid herself about the quality of her motel. When she was young, she'd thought running a motel was a no-brainer. Take people's money for simply making their beds and cleaning the bathrooms? Piece of cake!

Then things had started to break. She'd worked hard for years trying to keep up with the entropy, but the money had never been enough to do anything but fix things, never replace them. Her husband had run off with one of the maids, and she'd never trusted another person to clean since then. Now she was old and worn out, and tired of the crap people did in her establishment.

When that cop had come in, giving her his card and telling her there was money to be made for any report of a vampire, she had taken the card but never expected to use it. But now there was a hundred bucks in it for her. Not bad, especially since the girl had been stupid enough to pay in advance.

Now, where had she put that card?

She fussed around the messy desk, then looked around in frustration. Ah, there it was, tacked to the bulletin board.

She called the number on it. "Officer Butler?" she said, lowering her voice. She'd heard vampires had heightened senses. "This is Deb Hutchins at the Beachwood. I think I've got one!"

CHAPTER 11

Sergeant John Butler was cruising around Crescent City, looking for vampires. He'd been promoted to sergeant mostly because there weren't enough cops in town to promote before him. The department was desperate. He knew that and didn't resent it. He still liked patrolling around town in his cruiser, keeping on top of the action, though he should have been doing paperwork back at the office.

Butler had fought at the Armory alongside the FBI guys, Callendar and Jeffers, and most of the other cops from the area. He'd also fought alongside vampires, including his old boss, Robert Jurgenson. These unusual allies had fought off the Wildering horde and then disbanded, each aware that the next time they met, it would be as opponents.

Then *The Testament of Michael* had started to appear, in pamphlets all over town and all over the Internet and the news. No matter how much the authorities denied it, too many people had tweeted, posted on Facebook and taken pictures and video, and it seemed like everyone had started believing in the Golden Vampires, and suddenly it wasn't so clear-cut that vampires were always malevolent. Perhaps humans and vampires could live together, if the vampires could give up their evil ways.

Butler didn't know what to believe. He'd seen the faces of the monsters—the slavering bloodlust of the Wilderings. But he'd also seen his old boss protecting his woman, acting all noble. Robert—good old honest Robert Jurgenson. It was hard to imagine him as a vampire, but even harder to imagine him killing.

So Butler knew about good vampires and bad vampires.

But even more importantly, he knew about vampires with money and vampires without money. Vampires with money would pay to save themselves and their friends.

He had been visited in the middle of the night by a huge vampire who could have killed him in his sleep. The creature had stood in the shadows, and there'd been something different about him—he seemed more knowing, more sinister than most vampires.

"You hunt vampires," the voice from the darkness had said. "You kill them."

Butler hadn't been sure how to respond. "Ah…it's my job," he'd finally said. He had started to reach under the bed, where he kept his shotgun—not that he thought it would do much good.

"I won't interfere," the Darkness had said. "Do as you will. But I am looking for three vampires who have the appearance of girls, from the ages of eighteen to twenty-five years old."

"Yes?"

"I want you to contact me when you find any vampire who meets this description."

"Why?"

"I will pay you ten thousand dollars if you find the right girls, but only if they are alive. Call me at this number." A piece of paper had came floating out of the darkness. Butler didn't move toward it until the Shadow had disappeared.

That was different, he'd thought. *A vampire who will pay for information!*

So far, he'd called the number six times. Each time, his description of the girl had apparently ruled her out and the vampire had hung up on him. Butler had dispatched the vampire girls as usual.

So much for vampires with money. Meanwhile, vampires without money were worth a bounty.

Oh, they didn't call it a bounty. "A reward for information" was how it was phrased, but it didn't seem to matter to those paying whether the "information" was the whereabouts of a living vampire or the corpse of a dead vampire. Whenever possible, Butler preferred the latter, to the tune of five hundred bucks per headless corpse. He had every teenage hooligan in town out looking, mostly acting as scouts, though sometimes they actually brought him a body. He offered to pay them, or—if they were willing to take less—supply them with beer. They usually took a six-pack or two of beer.

A full two weeks after the battle, the pickings were getting slim. All the vampires had either been killed, left town or were deep in hiding. Things were getting back to normal. Butler admitted to himself that he was ready for some routine duty. It had been exciting while it lasted, but it had also been dangerous. Now that it was almost over, he was remembering how close to death he'd been more than once. Vampires were swift and hard to kill.

His cellphone rang, and for a moment he was confused at the ringtone, a *Twilight Zone*-sounding thing. Oh, yeah. It was the number he'd put on the card he'd handed out. It had been a full week since he'd last gotten a call.

"Yeah?" he answered.

It was the old bat who ran the rundown motel south of town: Beachwood, it was called, though it was miles from the beach.

"I've found one for you," the woman was saying, speaking so low Butler could barely hear her. "Hard to tell under all the grime, but she looks about sixteen years old."

"All right, Deb!" he said in a cheerful voice. "Don't go near her. I'll be right there."

He turned the patrol car around and accelerated down the highway. He felt an adrenaline rush and tried to calm himself. He looked in the rearview mirror to make sure he had all his equipment in the backseat. It wouldn't do to underestimate a vampire, especially one who had survived this long.

It looked as though the return to good old boring routine duty would have to wait for another day.

Patty woke up with her toe on fire. She opened her eyes to see her big toe burning like a candle. *Curious*, she thought. Then the pain struck her and she yelped and pulled her foot away from the light streaming through the window. She'd fallen back on the bed and dropped off to sleep. Fortunately, only her feet had been exposed to the morning light.

She hobbled to the kitchen, looked in the refrigerator and found some raw steak. The house reeked of rotten meat, but she wasn't desperate enough to eat two-day-old corpses. Even animal meat was better than that. She gobbled down the steak in a few gulps. Her toe started healing almost immediately.

Looking out the window over the sink, Patty spotted the three teenagers coming down the street from a long way off. They were peering into the windows of every house. Sometimes they went to the door and knocked. If someone answered, the kids acted sheepish, as if they were apologizing for getting the wrong house. As soon as they were out of sight of the residents, they dropped the humility act and were back to their cocky selves.

They're looking for something, Patty thought. *Most likely, they're looking for me—or someone like me.*

They were big guys, maybe high school football players, and they carried wooden bats. If you looked closely, you could see that the handles had been sharpened to points. From a distance, they looked innocent, like kids coming back from a ball game. But they were systematically searching the neighborhood.

They seemed interested in the burned-out house, going around and lifting lumber, shingles and masonry as if looking for something. A body, perhaps? They walked down the sidewalk toward the house Patty was hiding in, and she stood a little further back from the window. She saw them catch the scent of the dead bodies and stiffen, unconsciously lifting their wooden stakes and holding them at the ready.

It was late afternoon. Patty could barely see in the light, it was so bright. She looked around. There was nowhere obvious to hide. She ran down the hallway, looking to see if there was an attic. Instead, she found the outline of a trapdoor in the floor. It looked exactly like the trapdoor in the house she had spent the last decade under. Apparently it was a feature of the houses in this subdivision.

The trapdoor wasn't obvious. She'd probably only noticed it because she'd seen one before. There was a throw rug in the next room and she ran over and got it. Then she opened the trapdoor, backed down the steep steps to the basement and tried to maneuver the rug over the top of the trapdoor as she closed it.

Just in time. She heard a timid knock, followed by the doorbell, and a short time later, by someone pounding on the door. Then she heard the teens break the kitchen window and tumble into the house.

"Gross, man!" one of them shouted.

"Well, one of them's been here, that's for sure. We just need to find out if the ghoul's still here," said another.

"How much is Butler paying, again?" one of them whined. He sounded as if was ready to quit this particular adventure.

"Last I heard, we could get fifty bucks. Or even better, a couple of six-packs."

"That's a ripoff."

"Yeah, well. So take the fifty bucks and try to figure out how to get the booze yourself, wanker. I don't know about you guys, but I'm planning to get totally hammered tonight."

Patty heard them walk over the trapdoor, and it was obvious they were going to miss it. She had an urge to fling open the door and spring out at them. Suddenly she was more hungry and thirsty than she'd ever been in her life. They wouldn't be expecting her. She could kill them in seconds, she sensed. It would be so easy.

But…she still hadn't killed anyone. Strangely, it was the look of disappointment that she envisioned on Simone's face that stopped her. What the hell? She didn't even like the bitch… most of the time. But she loved her like a sister, just as she loved that empty-headed Laura.

"Shit," one of the teens said, sounding disappointed.

"There's always Kate."

"She's my sister, man! You expect me to turn in my own sister?"

"Well, you said you wanted to get hammered."

"It's my *sister*! Well, at least, my stepsister. But still, if I have to turn her in, I want at least half of the beer."

The trio of vampire hunters left the house, laughing. Patty was so angry she didn't even hesitate. She wasn't sure why she was angry, or why she cared about some girl she didn't even know, but she was as incensed as she'd ever been.

It was too much, the way men treated women. She'd had enough, damn it.

She threw open the door and ran to catch the boys, but they were already out on the sidewalk. She watched them go down the street. Just as they turned the corner, the sun seemed to blink out. Patty looked up to see dark rain clouds rolling toward her. They stretched as far as she could see, and there wisps of rain falling in the distance.

She ran out of the house and followed the boys.

CHAPTER 12

Kelton woke up inside a rattrap trailer. The space was barely big enough for him and his six followers. The owner had been their last victim, taken just before dawn. Kelton looked over the table and saw that Feller had snagged the other sleeping space, while the other vampires were sprawled about the linoleum floor, dried blood caked on their mouths and chins.

They were all converts to the Shadow and could walk in the daylight, but that didn't mean it was comfortable for them. Kelton, for one, much preferred to operate in the dark, where he was nearly invisible when he wanted to be as long as he stuck to the shadowy corners. It wasn't so much that he could walk in daylight, he decided. It was that the light couldn't penetrate the thick layer of gloom that surrounded him. It was if he had a protective force field

It made him a little conspicuous, frankly. The fact that he was a huge, shaggy-haired man made it worse. He looked like a mountain man and was surrounded by a dark cloud that people couldn't see, but could sense. And now he was accompanied by six other suspiciously hard-looking men. No wonder everyone stared. Not a great thing if you happened to be a serial killer.

He opened the trailer door. There was still enough daylight that it disturbed the sleepers. They turned away from the light, groaning. Kelton kicked angrily at the man lying closest to the door. He hated that he was being forced to associate with these losers. He'd always been a loner. He liked it that way.

But the Shadow Master insisted.

The bones of their last victim were spread out on the ground outside the door, where they had tossed them as they ate. It didn't matter; there wasn't anyone to witness the carnage this far from town. As the week progressed, they'd had to travel farther and farther from civilization to find food. The authorities were finally getting things under control. Most of the Wildering vampires had been destroyed. It was getting harder to find new disciples or to feed the ones he already had.

Not that Kelton would have ever found these followers on his own. Like the Turning of Feller from an everyday vampire into a Shadow Vampire, the Shadow Master had selected each of these hard men. The empty voice that emerged from the floating darkness had told Kelton where to find them. Though it was Kelton who had injected his blood into them, it was the Master who gave it power.

Kelton recognized two of the men as career criminals who had spent half their lives in prison. Another he'd seen on the news, getting arrested for DUI every other week. The other three converts had been surprises. Feller, of course, as an FBI agent, wouldn't have been someone Kelton suspected would have such a rotten core. The last two men were pillars of the community: Howie Smith, the head of a local bank, and Jeff Miller, a schoolteacher.

They'd found Smith feeding on his employees, the bank vault wide open, bodies all over the floor, alarms ringing but nobody responding. Before they'd left, they'd filled canvas bags with money.

Then they'd found Miller alone at the high school, eating some sophomores. All girls. All blondes. They were members of the junior varsity cheerleading squad, for which he was the coach.

Turned out, both of these outwardly stalwart citizens had been successfully preying on their subordinates for some time.

As Kelton injected his blood into Miller, he'd drawn back in surprise—the man reeked of evil. Just the taste of him made Kelton realize that the schoolteacher took a creepy sort of glee in killing innocents slowly and painfully. Kelton had always thought there was no man worse than himself, that he was the baddest of the bad. He was finding, to his consternation, that in comparison to some of these other vampires, he was merely bad.

As he drew back from the unnerving sensation of injecting Miller, some of his own blood spilled, and under the fluorescent lights of the high school classroom, he saw for the first time that his blood was black—not just a dark blue, as he'd assumed. It was dull black, not reflecting light in any way.

It was then that he'd started to have misgivings.

Now, as he stood in the doorway of the trailer, blinking unhappily at the last light of dusk, he felt the Master returning.

At first, Kelton had actually believed the Master was corporeal, that he existed on the same plane of reality—that he somehow appeared from a dark abyss to give instructions. Slowly, he'd come to realize that the Shadow wasn't really there, except as a projection in his mind. For a short time, he'd wondered if it was figment of his imagination, but the Master had laughed at him. He'd done something to Kelton that made him feel as though every cell of his body was being pinched, dissected and pinned to a burning wall of flame.

"I am real," the Master had said. "I'd advise you to never forget that. We will meet soon enough."

Kelton looked back into the trailer. At the far end, the Shadow began to appear. Or, more accurately, the reality of that space vanished and was replaced by a vacuum. It was cold—it made them all shiver. The converts who were still sleeping on the floor sat up and scooted away from the void.

Miller shouted, a harsh sound that sent a shiver down Kelton's spine, but the cry was swallowed up by the Shadow, which cut it off abruptly.

"Why are you sleeping?" the Master demanded. His voice echoed inside their heads, and Kelton could see the others jump in alarm.

"We have to rest, to feed," Kelton said.

"No, you do not. You need to find more followers. This is happening much too slowly."

"It was easier at first," Kelton said. "There was so much chaos that no one noticed. Now, we risk getting caught."

"I don't care if you get caught. There will always be other vampires to take your place."

Kelton tried not to think. He tried to clear his brain, because he could feel the resentment swelling just underneath the surface, and he didn't want the Shadow to sense it.

"Miller! Smith!" the Master shouted. Both vampires scrambled to their feet, standing at attention. "You must know of others like you. Vultures of a feather flock together. Go! Seek them out! Turn them to the Shadow!"

"Yes, Master," Miller said. Smith nodded as if the Shadow Master was there to see it.

"You have the ability to inject your blood into others," the Master continued. "Those who are suitable will immediately become my followers. Hurry—do it now. Don't stop, day or night. Find those who have evil in their hearts and their souls. The great battle approaches, when the Shadow will fight the Light. We don't have much time."

"You others..." The Darkness faltered for the first time. "Do your best," he said to the other three vampires, sounding exasperated. "Go seek out your fellow jailbirds. Turn them to the Shadow and I shall reward you. Fail me, and..."

The three ex-cons all screamed at the same moment, their eyes bugging out, their muscles rigid with pain. They collapsed to their knees. Then it was over. They staggered to their feet and rushed past Kelton and out the door. They ran down the driveway. At the highway, the three men looked at each other, then headed in different directions.

Miller and Smith followed. Miller was tall and gawky, with sideburns. He wore horn-rimmed glasses and had spiky hair. He didn't even look at Kelton. Smith went next, fat and sloppy, his bald head glistening. "Pardon me," he muttered as he brushed past Kelton. They walked down the driveway together. Kelton saw them shake hands and then walk off in opposite directions.

Kelton sighed. He didn't like this arrangement anywhere near as much as he'd thought he would. Being an immortal vampire, stronger and faster than any man, able to walk in daylight, with bags filled with money—it was a dream come true. Except it wasn't his dream anymore. He belonged to the Shadow.

He waited for instructions, trying to keep these thoughts to himself, uncertain what the Master could hear and what he couldn't hear.

"I hear everything," the voice said.

Kelton was amused to see Feller jump, as if he'd also been caught thinking the wrong thoughts.

"You two are still my best hope," the Master said. "Miller and Smith are too deep into their own darkness to be of much use to me. The others are wicked enough, but don't have the brains or the social skills. So I'm counting on you."

"What do you want us to do?" Kelton asked.

"I won't be able to direct you toward new followers, as I have in the past. The six we have found so far were easy for me to sense—they radiated their malevolence so strongly that I discovered them even at a distance. It won't be so easy from here on out. I will be busy doing other things, so you will have to find converts by yourselves. Use your instincts—I've given you powers you've barely begun to explore. Trust your senses…"

There was a pause. In the background, Kelton heard the Master shouting at someone. "Go away! I'm busy!"

He sounds less like a Master of Shadow, Kelton thought, *and more like an ordinary harried businessman.* He quickly squelched the thought.

"Do your best," the Master said, filling their minds again. "You won't be alone for long. I'm coming to join you."

Kelton sensed Feller freeze, and realized that he, too, was holding his breath. "Here?"

"Yes, soon. Don't slacken your efforts. I will know and I will punish you, do you understand? But do as I ask, and I will reward you."

Both Kelton and Feller nodded, and that seemed to be enough. The space where the void had been—or *hadn't* been—snapped back into view. They exchanged glances and shrugged.

"Any ideas?" Kelton asked.

"Hell, my ex-wife, if you're looking for evil. Unfortunately, she lives in L.A."

Kelton was stumped. It had always been him against the world. He knew he was different, that he would be judged evil by others, though he felt nothing of that himself. Everyone else, in comparison to him, was normal. Or so he'd thought. He never would have guessed that a local high school teacher was a more prolific serial killer than him. It never would have occurred to him that a bank manager had wracked up a significant death toll without ever being suspected.

So what the hell did he know?

Of course, from a human perspective, almost all vampires

were evil. But Kelton was beginning to see that there were as many different types of vampires as there were people. Sure, most vampires killed to feed, but that was their nature. Was that evil? Did killing for food make them evil? Or only if they took enjoyment from it? Or only if they killed unnecessarily? Or…what?

They loaded up Kelton's car and headed out. The Master had said, "Trust your instincts. Follow your senses."

What the hell does that mean? Keller wondered. *I'm not instinctively sensing a damn thing.*

"Wait," Feller said. "Turn off."

Kelton slowed and turned into a nearby driveway.

"Go back a couple turnoffs."

Kelton turned the car around, and seconds later, they pulled onto an overgrown road. He heard the heavy brush grind against his car and winced. He reminded himself that he had bags of money in the trunk and could buy dozens of cars.

They pulled up to a trailer that was even more dilapidated than they one they'd just left.

"I recognized the name on the mailbox," Feller said quietly. "Whenever an FBI agent is transferred to a new town, we're given a list of parolees—they can be useful informants. I always pay attention. I remember the name Halliday from the list. Child molester, no less."

"Shit…really?" Kelton said. "Child molester? Do we have to?"

"You heard the Master."

"Well, OK. But you get to bite him, understand? I ain't doing it."

"It's just blood," Feller said, then repeated as if trying to convince himself, "It's just blood…nothing more."

They saw one of the curtains move to the side a little. A voice from inside called, "I've got a shotgun!"

Kelton looked at Feller, who shrugged. "A felon in possession of a firearm? Yeah, that *never* happens."

They got out and walked toward the door. Kelton let Feller take the lead, expecting the door to fly open and a shotgun blast to go off. "How do you know he's a vampire?" he asked.

Feller looked at him curiously. "Can't you feel it?"

Kelton searched within himself, and…yes, there it was: a sensation of blood attracting blood. Another vampire was near.

Feller tried the door, but it was locked. They nodded to each other, and then both punched the door at the same moment. As humans, all they would have done was broken their hands. As vampires, they shattered the door.

"Go away!" Halliday screamed. "I haven't done anything!"

Kelton saw the man cowering in the far corner of the cluttered trailer. To his surprise, Halliday was average-looking—indeed, almost good-looking, in a sallow sort of way. Average height, a little heavy around the middle, limp brown hair. Not what he expected a child molester to look like.

"I've changed! I did my time at Pelican Bay! I spent three years in solitary! I'm taking my meds!" the man cried.

"We aren't here about that," Feller said, sounding like an FBI agent.

"What do you want?"

"You're a vampire."

"How do you know that?" Halliday was even more frightened now, looking ready to piss his pants. "It wasn't my choice—my former sister-in-law, she bit me! She always hated me."

"We know because we're vampires too."

"But that's impossible. I saw you! You were walking in the sunlight!"

"That's why we're here," Feller said. "We can give you the power to walk in daylight too."

"We here to make you an offer," Kelton said. "We can make you stronger, faster than other vampires. We can turn you into a different kind of vampire, one who doesn't have to cower in fear. In return, all you have to do is submit to the Master of Shadow."

"Who's that?"

"Never mind that. You're damned already; this just lets you enjoy it more."

The little trailer grew silent, except for the buzz of a huge black fly over the sink. *What a way to live,* Kelton thought. *This guy is just as much a prisoner now as when he was in prison.*

"No," Halliday said dejectedly. "I won't do it."

"I don't think you understand," Feller said. "You'll be able to blend in with the humans, but you'll be better than them. Nobody will ever be able to push you around again."

Other than the Master, Kelton thought.

But Halliday was still shaking his head. "I meant it when I said I've changed. I have no unnatural desires anymore. I've banished them from my soul. I want to be a good person—I eat only animals."

Kelton examined him, uncertain. The Master had made a big deal out of how his followers needed to voluntarily submit to him and give themselves to the Shadow. But what difference did it make?

"Hell with it," Feller said. "Hold him down, Kelton."

Kelton was on Halliday in a flash. The vampire wailed like a girl, but Kelton picked him up, threw him on the bed and held his thrashing legs. "All yours," he said.

Feller grabbed the man's arms and leaned over him. Halliday sighed and quit struggling. Kelton watched the black blood being injected into his neck. It didn't seem to be flowing in like it should have. It would stop a few inches in and then flow back out. Feller kept trying, until Halliday convulsed so violently that both he and Kelton were thrown backward.

Halliday had his hands around his neck, which was shrinking, narrowing as they watched. Halliday's face turned dark; his eyes bugged out. He stopped breathing. No sound could emerge from his throat, because there was no more throat. It narrowed to a small patch of skin and then disappeared. Halliday's head rolled down his chest and onto the floor.

"Well, that didn't work," Feller said.

"I think they're supposed to agree to join the Shadow," Kelton said. "They have to really mean it."

"So not only do they have to be evil," Feller said, exasperated, "*really* evil, but they have to agree to this? How the hell are we supposed to know if they'll do that? How can we find anyone?"

"Oh, I don't think that will be a problem anymore," Kelton said.

Feller turned around and stared at him. "What do you mean?"

"Did you hear what he said?" Kelton asked. "He just got released from Pelican Bay—the supermax, where they put the worst of the worst."

Feller started laughing. "It's only three miles from here! Of course! How obvious!"

"Only one problem," Kelton said. "We have to break in."

"You forget," Feller said. "I was FBI. I still have my ID. If we go during the daytime, they'll never suspect a thing."

Kelton joined in the laughter. The Master of Shadow would be pleased. He wanted an army, and there was a big, mean, evil recruitment center waiting just over the horizon.

CHAPTER 13

Laura snapped awake the second the sun dropped below the horizon. She'd noticed this tendency before—it was like an internal vampire alarm clock. She was ravenous. The driver of the pickup had only whetted her appetite. She wasn't going back to animal meat, not if she could help it.

The clothes she was wearing, which had been scavenged from the houses around their hideaway in the trees, had begun to stink, especially the bloodstains. The garments didn't quite fit—some were too small, some were too big. She'd tried washing them out in the shower, so they were tolerable, but they were all wrinkled.

She wanted to look pretty. She hadn't had anything new to wear since before she'd been kidnapped. The Monster had brought his prisoners some makeup and told them to make themselves look presentable, and Simone—who had had the most practice before she was captured—tried to show Patty and Laura how to apply it. But Laura had looked in the mirror in the bathroom once, and she wasn't fooled into believing she actually looked nice.

But that didn't mean she *couldn't* look nice. She had a curvy body—she knew this. The man she'd eaten had tried not to stare at her breasts, but she'd caught him looking. If she was going to trap men, she'd need to play up her looks. There was a mall that stayed open in the evenings on the south end of town, not too far to walk to. She pulled the money out of the bald man's wallet. There was over five hundred dollars there, along with credit cards.

Laura kept one of the credit cards and tossed the wallet away. She couldn't imagine anyone walking around with five hundred dollars in their pocket. In her normal life, she'd been given five dollars here, five dollars there: never much more cash than that. Her foster mom had written checks for larger amounts, some of which had bounced.

Laura closed the motel room door behind her and glanced at the office across the parking lot. She caught a glimpse of movement, the curtain closing, a shadow behind it. *I'm going to take care of that busybody,* she thought. *But not before I've got my three nights' worth.*

The parking lot was nearly empty. There was a car near the office and another about halfway down the row. Laura didn't want to feed too close to where she was staying. She started off down the highway.

She caught a ride after only a few hundred yards. *Another horny middle-aged man*, she thought. But she resisted attacking him, because she wanted to at least be presentable when she went to the mall. The man brushed against her boobs when he opened the door to let her out, but didn't do more than that.

Laura went into the first clothing store she saw, then paused just inside the door. It was really fancy, way more fancy than she was used to. She felt out of place, and almost turned around and left.

"Can I help you?"

It was a girl not much older than Laura. Her tone seemed to suggest that there wasn't anything she could really do to help Laura.

"Hi!" Laura said brightly. "I just got back from summer camp, and my clothes are a mess. Daddy told me to get some new ones." She pulled out the wad of bills and the credit card. "He said to use his card if I could, but if you can't take it, I'll just spend the cash."

The clerk's demeanor changed immediately, and she flashed Laura a smile. She was tall and skinny, almost gawky, but her clothes looked good on her, Laura noticed enviously, hanging off her bony frame just right.

"I'm sure the card will be just fine," the clerk said. "My name's Susan, by the way."

"I'm Laura." She stood there flatfooted. *Now what?*

"Will you let me help you?" Susan asked. "If you don't mind me saying, you've got a nice body, but not one that will be easy to dress. I'm really envious—I can't gain weight no matter how hard I try."

Laura almost ripped her head off right then and there, then realized that the girl was just trying to be complimentary. This was probably her first job, and she was just as awkward in some ways as Laura. "That'd be great. I'm really not sure of my sizes these days. Things have changed so much in the last year."

"Tell me about it!" Susan laughed. "I think I can guess your sizes pretty close. Like I said, you'll need smaller sizes, but ones that will accommodate your curves. Fortunately, I think I know exactly what you need."

Eight hundred dollars' worth of clothing later, Laura looked in the mirror and couldn't believe what she was seeing. As long as she didn't look at her face and hair, it was as if she was looking at a sophisticated, sexy woman.

She held her breath as the card was run through some kind of electronic device. But the card sailed through, and Laura signed the receipt with her own first name and the last name on the card, Kirkpatrick.

She was enjoying bantering with Susan and was somewhat surprised that she could feel so comfortable doing it. *Spending eight hundred bucks doesn't hurt,* she reminded herself. Susan was only being nice to her because she had to be.

"Thank you again," Laura said as she walked out. She was carrying two huge bags, and was wondering how she'd get back to the motel room with them. She spied a salon, went in and did the same "daddy's little girl" routine, and again it worked.

Now when she looked in the mirror, she looked great from top to bottom. Her hair was clean and cut, her facial blemishes covered up. It was like staring at someone she didn't know.

She needn't have worried about getting a ride back to the motel. She'd barely walked a block before a shy young man stopped and picked her up. He barely said a word the whole way, barely looked at her. She decided to let him live, though originally she'd had him marked as her next victim. Even though she was hungry, she loved her new clothes so much that she didn't want to mess them up.

"Uh, can I…uh…can I take you to a movie or something?" the young man stammered when he pulled up to the motel.

"You got something to write on?" Laura asked.

He handed her an oily gas station receipt. She wrote down a string of nonsense numbers on the back and handed it back with a smile. He nervously reached for it, and she let her fingers linger under his for a second.

He stalled his car on his way out of the parking lot. Laura could see him leaning over the steering wheel, red-faced. She smiled and went to her room. She didn't notice that a third car was now parked in front of the motel at the far end, and that someone was watching her from behind the wheel.

What a hottie, Butler thought. *Wowza.* It wasn't often you saw a girl dressed like that in Crescent City. Was she even a vampire? Hard to tell from a distance, so he'd just have to trust the motel manager's instincts. Certainly it was suspicious that she'd spent all day in her room, only venturing out at night to go shopping. That wasn't normal behavior.

He pulled out the piece of paper that the vampire had given him and called the number on it. "I think I may have one for you," he said when the line was picked up.

"Describe her."

"She's a gorgeous blonde, sexy, dressed to the nines."

"That's not one of them," the voice said, and hung up.

Screw it, Butler thought. *I don't care if the reward is ten thousand bucks if all that's going to happen is getting hung up on.* He sat there in a funk. It was probably time to admit that most of the vampires were dead. He'd polish off this one and then get back to routine police work. Then again, ten thousand dollars was a lot of money.

He picked up his phone and redialed.

"Don't hang up," he said. "It might help if you would describe the three girls you're looking for."

There was silence on the other end, then, begrudgingly, the vampire answered. "The oldest one, about twenty-six, is tall and skinny, kind of plain, with mousy brown hair. The second-oldest one, about twenty-two or so, is nice-looking, with black hair and an average stature. The third girl, about eighteen years old, is short and busty, blonde and pimply."

Butler recalled that Deb Hutchins had described the girl originally as covered in grime. For some reason, he was certain that the third girl was the one he'd just observed.

"I think the blonde one is here," he said. "She's all gussied up—new clothes, hairdo, makeup—but her physical features are right."

"Where are you?"

"It's the Beachwood Motel," he said. "It's at…"

"I'll be right there," the vampire interrupted, then hung up.

Less than ten minutes later, a Toyota with scratched green paint pulled up next to him. There were two vampires in it.

The huge vampire Butler remembered from before got out and eased himself into the backseat of the unmarked police car. He swept all the vampire hunter equipment aside with a strange look on his face. "What room number?"

"The last unit," Butler answered. He resisted reaching for his gun or turning around, sensing that he wouldn't be quick enough. The FBI had a term for vampires like this: Alphas. He'd let someone else deal with this vampire, perhaps when all three girls were found and paid for.

"Here's your money," the Alpha vampire said. "Keep your eyes open for the other two."

The money was in a paper bag. Butler didn't count it, as he sensed the vampire didn't care about money and was eager for results. "Don't you want to check her out first?"

"No—it's her. I can smell her." The huge vampire opened the car door and got out. "Get lost."

Butler didn't question the order. He started the car and drove away, trying not to seem in too much haste. He'd have to pay Deb Hutchins later. He hoped for her sake that she didn't get in the middle of whatever was about to happen.

Laura examined the array of short leather dresses, tight silk blouses and sheer lingerie that was spread out on the bed. *Maybe I should have gotten some clothes that were a little more functional,* she thought. She was still hungry, but she didn't want to get blood and gore on any of her new things. She'd allowed Susan to throw away her old clothes without thinking.

She heard a knock on the door. She didn't even look outside, pretty certain it was either the awkward teenager who had dropped her off or the motel manager who wanted to scam some more money off her.

She opened the door and stopped cold. Her hand flew to her mouth, and she knew her eyes had gone wide and round.

Her heart raced. There he stood. The Monster.

She wanted to run. She wanted to leap into his arms. Instead, she just stood there with a blank look on her face.

"Hi, Laura," he rumbled.

"Come on in," she said, walking away from the door. Nonchalantly, she started to put her new clothes on the hangers in the closet.

He turned around and spoke to someone outside. "Wait in the car, do you mind?" Then he went over and sat on the bed.

This obviously wasn't going the way he'd expected. Laura almost laughed at the astounded look in his face. He'd probably thought he'd have to overpower her, put his big, beefy hands over her mouth to stop her from screaming. Laura found she wasn't frightened of him. Now that he was here, she felt safe again.

"You look nice, babe," he said, watching her warily, as if he expected her to bolt. "I should've bought you nice things long ago."

"Yeah, you should have," she said, walking back and grabbing another blouse that was lying on the bed near his hand. She put a little extra flounce in her step.

"You don't have to worry about that ever again," he said. "I've got so much money, I can buy you anything you want." She walked past him again, and he grabbed her and swung her around onto his lap.

She let out a delighted squeal.

He nuzzled her neck. "Not that we have to pay for anything. We can take what we want. Nobody can stop us."

She pulled away from him and stood up, straightening her short skirt. "I hear vampires are getting wiped out."

"Old-fashioned vampires, maybe," the Monster said. "Me and my friends are something new, babe—we're invincible. I'm beginning to think you might want to join us."

"Why would I want to do that? You're mean. You treated me bad."

"I'm sorry about that," he muttered. "I guess I didn't know what a great girl you are."

There was one last piece of lingerie left on the bed, a pair of frilly black panties. As she reached for them, he grabbed them first and held them up to his nose. "I'd like to see you wear these," he grunted.

"Oh?" she answered. She snatched the panties from his hand. She started to undress, demurely turning her back on him. He stared at her smooth back and wide hips. She wiggled into the tiny garment and turned around.

She walked over to him and straddled him. He fell back onto the bed.

It was the first time Laura had ever voluntarily given herself to him. Kelton couldn't believe it. How had he missed that she'd become so beautiful and sexy? Sure, she was a little old for his taste, but underneath her grown-up body, she still acted like the little girl he remembered.

This hadn't turned out anything like he'd expected. The moment he'd seen her eyes, looking at him half in fear and half in desire, he knew he had her. He probably hadn't needed the chains for years. She was completely his, heart and soul. She hadn't known anything else. She'd been abandoned by her parents, barely tolerated by her foster parents, teased and bullied by her classmates; he was probably the only constant she'd ever known.

Laura mistook his lust for love.

Well? Am I mistaking compliance for love? he wondered. *Not that I care; it's just curious.*

She lay in his arms, running her hand through the thick thatch of black hair on his chest.

"Where are the others, babe?" he asked.

"I can show you," she murmured.

He rose and started getting dressed.

"So soon?" she pouted. "Aren't I enough?"

"We're family," Kelton said. "I don't want them to get away. Come on, squeeze your butt into that tight dress of yours and let's go."

She got up, frowning. It was an ugly look, and now that he was satiated, she didn't look quite so appealing. She looked much more like the pimply-faced fatty he remembered and whom he'd been ready to get rid of.

"All right," she said. "I'll show you where the others are. But first, you gotta let me do something."

"Anything," he said. "As long as it doesn't take long."

Deborah Hutchins was enraged when she saw the cop drive away. Where was her money? She should have known it was a scam.

She slammed the door to her office and flopped into her armchair. The usual *Law and Order/Bones/CSI* programs were running on their continual loop on the same channels. She found the old shows comforting, though she'd probably seen all of them—more than once.

The bell over the office door went off. She almost ignored it, then remembered that the cop hadn't paid her and that she was nearly broke after using the girl's advance payment to keep the electricity on.

She pushed herself out of the armchair and opened the door.

There was a huge man standing there, and she instinctively understood he was a vampire. Standing next to him, looking as small as a child, was one of those women who used too much makeup. She was big-busted. This was a woman who was sexy now, but would be fat later.

"I'd like my money back for the last two nights," the girl said.

Deb did a double take. Was this the same girl? How was it possible?

"I spent it already. No refunds." Deb pointed a bony finger over her shoulder in the general direction of a small sign on the bulletin board.

"But see, I need it," the girl said, smiling. "I need to eat."

"Can't help you," Deb said, sounding stubborn even to herself. *Just give her the money!* a small voice in the back of her mind screamed. *Give her anything she wants! Get her out of here!*

"Well, I really am hungry. Even your scrawny body looks good right about now…"

Deb had picked up her phone and was calling the cops when she felt someone land on her back. The girl had vaulted over the counter without even touching it. She was snarling like an animal, and there was a bestial look on her face. As Deb fell back against the closed door to her living room, she saw fangs begin to grow in the fat little girl's face.

"No, please," she said. "I don't have anything."

She felt a sharp pain in her neck and something fluid ran down her chest, warm and soft. *I don't have anything,* she repeated to herself. *I don't have anything. I don't have any-*

Kelton took Laura back to Halliday's trailer, where Feller was waiting impatiently.

"What the fuck did you bring her for?" Feller asked when she stepped out of the car, her dress riding all the way up to her crotch. *Charming,* he thought sourly.

"She's a Shadow Vampire," Kelton said. "I'm sure of it."

Feller eyed Laura doubtfully, then shrugged. *No telling what is in the heart of a woman,* he thought.

That night, Kelton Turned her. She barely reacted. She passed out for a few minutes, shaking slightly, then she sat up and the blackness was in her eyes. Quickest he'd ever seen anyone Turn.

"All right," Feller said when the two of them crawled out from behind the curtains where the small bed was. "I think I've worked out how we can break into a supermax. And even better, how to get us back out."

"That's great," Kelton said. "You're a mastermind. But Laura and I have some business to attend to first."

He explained that he'd once held three girls captive in his house, but they had escaped.

"Laura here doesn't look like a captive," Feller said.

"Laura is a natural," Kelton said. "But the other two—they need to be taught a lesson. And Laura here knows where they're hiding, don't you, sweetie?"

"I'm coming along," Feller said.

CHAPTER 14

Once the three boys stopped actively hunting vampires, they seemed to lose all caution. They never even bothered to look back. Patty was able to follow them fairly closely, so closely that when the clouds broke a couple of times, letting the sunlight through, she was able to scramble to cover and wait, and still catch up to them when the clouds returned. The teens were laughing and jabbing at each other with the baseball bats, and otherwise roughhousing and carrying on.

They were walking toward the hills, heading inland from the downtown area, and had soon crossed into housing developments that Patty hadn't even known existed. This had all been farmland when she'd been a kid.

There were a few fancier houses high in the hills, and the three boys wandered up the wide, well-maintained roads that wound among them. These mansions had always been there, lording it over the humble town below. Patty started getting a funny feeling, as if she'd been here before. As they continued to climb, the terrain became more and more familiar. Sure enough, they went to the very top of the hill, where a huge house dominated the skyline. It was perched at the edge of a cliff, like a castle.

Before Patty was old enough to be in school, whenever her mother couldn't find a babysitter, she'd bring Patty to work with her. There was a small area behind the house where the servants parked, and her mother would lower the backseat of the car, cover the back with blankets, toys and books, and leave

Patty there for her entire shift. "Don't tell anyone," she'd say. "No one should know."

After a few hours, Patty would sneak out of the car, bored and restless. She would avoid the dirt trail her mother took up to the house and instead explore the landscape, getting higher and higher until she found herself on the little hill opposite the mansion's long deck. From there, she could see inside. She'd catch glimpses of her mother vacuuming, doing the dishes, coming outside and washing the windows. She couldn't see much of the mansion's interior, just the outlines of things, so she'd try to imagine what it looked like inside. When she'd sense her mother was getting ready to come back, she'd slip back to the car. Patty would pretend to be napping when her mother got into the driver's seat and looked back at her with a tired smile.

"Did you have a good time?" she'd ask, and Patty could always genuinely say that she had.

She'd spent years in the Monster's basement pretending that she lived in that giant house. She wandered the many imaginary rooms in her mind, making up the furnishings and décor—all gold and silver, everything lush and soft. The view from the hill would come back to her, as if she was a princess surveying her realm.

Now she remembered that just before she'd gone there for the last time, there had been a new baby, who had his own room, and a huge playground built for him outside, though it would be years before he would be old enough to use it.

Then Patty's mother had lost her job, accused of stealing—which was ridiculous, because her mother never did anything wrong. Her mother had returned a bank bag once with more money in it than Patty had ever seen, not even taking a single twenty-dollar bill, though it would have bought them dinner.

The store owner had snatched the money bag out of her hands, glaring at her as if it was her fault the bag had gone missing in the first place. They had stood there for a few moments, mother and child, hoping the woman would give them a reward. Then they had turned away, empty-handed.

That had been the beginning of the really hard times, when the car hadn't just been a temporary playground for Patty, but had been their home.

It gave Patty a queasy feeling to be here again. She was almost afraid the reality of the mansion would tarnish her memory of it...but it was every bit as grand as she remembered. The three boys walked up the dirt trail her mother had always taken and entered through the same side door Patty used to see her mother disappear through.

But these weren't servants. One of these boys was the little prince she'd once seen, all grown up.

She followed them. They couldn't keep her out now. She didn't feel inferior, or subordinate, or any of the things her mother must have felt. She was vampire, and vampires lived by a different set of rules.

The first room was huge, a basement that extended deep into the hillside. It was like a stadium, with high walls. There was even a basketball hoop at the far end. The floor was concrete, and the space was being used for storage. The everyday castoffs of a rich family, broken furniture, old microwaves and coffeemakers and other defunct electronics, were scattered about. There was a pool table and a ping-pong table, and both were piled high with boxes. One whole wall was filled with books, haphazardly stacked. There was enough stuff down here that Patty and her mother could easily have lived off it for years.

Patty had avoided thinking of her mother. The only good thing about her death was that it had happened before Patty's kidnapping. She tried to imagine what that would have done to her mother. The rest of the family hadn't mattered—all the aunts and uncles and cousins who hadn't lifted a hand to help them when they were struggling, and who probably had posed for the camera, cried crocodile tears and then forgotten her.

Laura, of course, had no family—only foster parents who in some ways had been worse than no parents at all. Of the three of them, only Simone had a family to go back to. Patty had asked her why she didn't call her parents, but Simone had flushed and shaken her head. While Patty and Laura had no one who cared, Simone had a family who maybe cared too much, who put pressures on her that she would barely acknowledge. Now, Simone was probably too embarrassed, too humiliated to contact them, certain her family would reject her as damaged, forever soiled. Perhaps, if they hadn't been turned vampire, it might have been different.

Patty could hear the three teens climbing stairs, the light from which she could barely see behind all the detritus. She easily picked her way through the darkened room. Its shadows were as clear as day to her. The light on the stairs went out, but she didn't hesitate to follow the boys. At the top of the steep steps was a door. She stopped and listened. The boys' voices were still receding.

Patty opened the door and stepped into her dream house. It wasn't anything like she expected. The first room was a kitchen. It was all modern and spare, with metal appliances, open cabinets and marbled granite countertops. The room beyond was a huge living room that was also decorated in muted tones. She had imagined something old-fashioned and lush, but the colors were subdued, and there was lots of black and white. There were tile floors instead of soft carpets, and Scandinavian-style hardwood furniture instead of plush chairs.

Still, the overall effect was one of wealth, more spectacular than her wildest imaginings.

Beyond the living room, which looked new—or at least rarely used—was a room the family probably actually used, a den-like area with furniture that was a little more comfortable and scuffed, and a small amount of clutter. There was an enormous TV on the wall, almost the size of a movie screen. The boys were sprawled on the couches, playing video games and drinking beer. There was an odd odor coming from the hallway beyond the den.

Patty stood at the entrance and tried to blend in with the shadows. One of the teens seemed to sense her and looked over his shoulder. She kept completely still, and he stared at her but didn't seem to see her, then shrugged and took a sip of his beer. She moved further into the big room, sticking to the shadows. The boys started yelling at the game on the screen, jumping up and raucously waving their arms. Patty slipped into the darkened hallway beyond the den.

Following the strange odor, Patty was pretty sure what she'd find. She was getting accustomed to the smell of death. Even so, when she opened the door, the stench almost knocked her down. She went inside and quickly closed the door behind her. It was the master bedroom, and the little prince's parents were sprawled on the bed, half-eaten. Insects were swarming over them and their skulls were beginning to show. They were still in their nightclothes. They probably hadn't been alive long enough to know what had hit them.

Patty stared at the bodies. Parts of them had been eaten, but only after they were dead. It was obvious that blunt objects—perhaps something like baseball bats—had crushed their skulls.

She left the room and started back toward the den. As she passed a second door, she heard a faint scuffling coming from the room behind it. If she hadn't been vampire, she probably wouldn't have heard it. She opened the door. It was completely dark, but she could see clearly. A teenage girl was on the bed, naked. She was spread-eagled, her hands and feet tied to the four bedposts, and she was gagged. Her eyes met Patty's, and each could tell the other girl was a vampire. A feeling of familiarity passed between them.

Overwhelming rage washed over Patty. These boys were doing to this girl what the Monster had done to her.

The girl looked to be about seventeen years old. The look in her eyes wasn't fear—it was a cold, calculating anger.

Patty raised her finger to her lips and the girl nodded. Then Patty closed the door and tiptoed back toward the den.

"Damn, man, your parents are really starting to stink, Kerry," one of the boys said. He was small, with long, floppy black hair and a narrow face. His chest seemed to hunch in on itself, as if he didn't have any shoulders.

The boy in the middle scrunched up his face. He was opposite in appearance to the first speaker—tall and broad and blond. "We got to wait, Sam. Make sure it looks like vampires."

"It's not like there is going to be any doubt. How are you going to explain not reporting it sooner?" the third boy said. He was a good-looking kid with a well-manicured appearance. Even his T-shirt seemed to be free from wrinkles; his tennis shoes were bright white.

"We were out of town, you know? Camping? That work for you, Dennis?"

"That might work. I haven't been home for days."

"I called Dad," Sam said. "But I didn't tell him where I was."

"Besides, all you have to do is show the cops your sister," Dennis said. "After we kill her, of course. I kind of hate to do it, you know. I never thought I'd say it, Kerry, but your little sister turned out to be pretty hot."

"Yeah, I'd like one more go at Kate," Sam said, "before we turn her in for the bounty."

Kerry kept playing his video game, barely paying attention to his friends. "Sure. Whatever. Have at it."

Dennis and Sam got up, and Kerry turned his head slightly. "But I warn you, I'm turning her in today, 'cause I want to get some brew."

His faces of his two friends lit up with anticipation.

"You go first," Dennis told Sam. "I'm going to see if I can find any more liquor bottles hidden away in the kitchen. Kerry's mom was pretty good at concealing them, but I know how drunks think."

"You just like sloppy seconds!" Sam taunted, and started walking toward the hallway.

Patty retreated into the shadows and stood still. The boy walked right by her. She waited until he was past, then took his head and twisted it as hard as she could There was a grinding snap, and Sam went limp. Patty lowered the kid to the floor, then had second thoughts and picked him up and carried him to the parents' bedroom, where she deposited him on the carpet.

Dennis came along about five minutes later, probably figuring his friend was done by then. This time, Patty hid behind the master bedroom door and waited until the boy actually entered Kate's bedroom. She followed silently and came up behind him as Kate's eyes grew wide. She bit into the boy's throat, making sure she tore out the vocal cords. Then she dropped him onto the floor and put her foot on his neck until he stopped struggling.

Patty went over the girl's bed, took out her gag and started untying the ropes. She fumbled with the knots and finally leaned down and severed them with her fangs.

"What do you want me to do to your brother?" she asked, without preamble.

"Kerry's my half brother. If you don't mind, I'd like to take care of him myself."

"I thought you might," Patty said.

As soon as Kate left the room, she turned to the boy on the floor. He was still alive, barely, as Patty started eating him. In the background, she heard the full-throated screams of a young man, which were abruptly cut off.

I think my dream house is now mine, she thought. *That is, if Kate doesn't mind sharing.*

CHAPTER 15

They were alone together. That fact was pretty hard to ignore. But Rod was still waiting for Simone to make the first move—if she ever did. She was beginning to seek him out as soon as they woke up, staying at his side until they went to bed in separate rooms. He was pretty sure she liked him. Rod had upended his hours for her, staying awake during what he thought of as "vampire time," sleeping during "human time." He didn't mind. He just wanted to be with her.

Patty had left more than a day ago, and there was still no word from her. Dusk was approaching and they had just gotten up when they heard an insistent knock on the door. They looked at each other. "What do we do?" Simone asked.

"Nothing. We answer the door."

"But what if it's the cops?

Rod didn't have an answer to that. He knew he'd try to talk his way out of whatever situation they found themselves in, but he wasn't sure what her reaction would be. He'd already seen that a vampire's response to danger was more antagonistic, less predictable than a human's. He was probably lucky to have survived the initial encounter with the girls. He was certain that Simone was trying hard to control her aggression, but he wasn't so sure about Laura and Patty.

The man at the door was either a well-preserved ninety-year-old or a badly preserved seventy-year-old; Rod couldn't quite tell. Smelling the alcohol on the man's breath, he suspected the latter. He was overweight and looked sloppy in dungarees and a dirty linen shirt, and had a full white beard and long hair.

"Who are you?" the man demanded, without so much as a greeting.

"What?"

"I said who the *hell* are you?" the man shouted as if he thought Rod might be deaf.

Rod smiled uncertainly and put out his hand. "My name's Rod Parker."

"You know what? I changed my mind. I don't give a damn *who* you are, what I want to know is *what* the hell are you doing here?"

"Yeah? Who are *you?*" Rod demanded in an equally strident voice.

"Name's Lee Awbrey. Mean anything to you?"

"Should it?" Rod answered. He'd decided to answer belligerence with belligerence. In response, the man was already lowering his voice.

"Seeing as how my nephew Stephen Awbrey owns this house, it ought to. He asked me to look after this place, and he hasn't told me any different."

Actually, now that he thought about it, Rod had heard the name Awbrey. The street they were on was Awbrey Lane. When he'd gone around to the neighbors to introduce himself and try to buy livestock, more than one of them had said not to bother the guy at the end of the street, that he'd just slam the door in his face. "Lee Awbrey thinks he owns this street because it all used to belong to his family," one of them had said. "It's nobody's fault but his own that he sold it all to buy more booze.'

Rod had taken their advice and had never gone to the house in the overgrown lot at the dead end of Awbrey Lane.

"Oh, Stephen!" Rod said, as if he'd just remembered the name. "He's the guy renting this place to us."

Lee Awbrey had calmed down a little, and now just looked slightly puzzled.

"Who is it, dear?" Rod heard a voice call from the other room. Simone came around the corner, and Rod saw her as Awbrey must have seen her—tall and sleek, with shining black hair and dark eyes, looking like an exotic flower in the dirt and grime of the countryside. She walked up beside him and took his arm, as if they were a long-established couple. Rod really liked the sensation. It was easy for him to imagine it was all true—that they were a comfortable couple who could read each other, who could finish each other's sentences.

"This is our neighbor, Lee Awbrey—he's the uncle of the fellow who rented this place to us," Rod explained.

"Like hell!" Awbrey was flaring up again. "He'd have told me."

Simone's voice hardened. "I don't see what business it is of yours, mister."

At the tone in her voice, Awbrey seemed to go a little crazy. "It is my business, you little bitch!" he shouted. "As soon as I can get ahold of Stephen, I'm coming back. And next time I'm bringing my shotgun!"

"Hey, hey, no need to call her names," Rod was saying when Awbrey surged toward him, all two hundred fifty pounds of him, and pushed Rod against the door. Rod heard a hiss, and saw out of the corner of his eye that Simone had extended her fangs and claws—then just as quickly retracted them.

The big man let go of him abruptly. "I...ah, I'm sorry," he said to Rod. His eyes flicked toward Simone in fear. "I'll get ahold of Stephen and see if we can't clear all this up." Then he turned and hurried away.

"Do you think he saw?" Simone asked.

"I'm sure he did."

"I'm sorry, I think I made things worse. I saw how, when

you confronted him, he seemed to back down, so I tried the same thing."

"Yeah, difference is, you're a woman. I don't think this guy likes women."

They went back to the kitchen and sat down at the table. They sat in silence for a few moments, then Simone reached out and took Rod's hand. "I'm sorry," she said again. "For everything. I never should have dragged you into this. You should get out of here while you can."

He squeezed her hand. The look on her face made him wonder. She didn't look like she really wanted him to go, he realized. She looked like she wanted him to…

He leaned forward and kissed her lightly on the lips.

She grabbed his neck and kept him there, and pressed her mouth more tightly to his. Rod didn't know how long they spend awkwardly bent toward each other, kissing, but it seemed like hours, and then when it was over, it seemed like only a moment.

Simone smiled. "I'm glad we finally did that."

"Me to," he said. "I mean, I've been wanting to."

"I know, Rod. Thanks for waiting until I was ready."

There was nothing to do after that but to stand and hug, and the hug turned into another kiss. Rod was holding Simone so tightly that he was lifting her an inch off the ground. Realizing this, he started shuffling toward the bedroom, his lips still locked on hers. She started to guffaw into his mouth, and he started laughing too, their lips still locked together as they trembled with laughter.

He stumbled to the bedroom and fell backward on the bed with Simone on top of him. They stopped laughing then and looked deep into each other's eyes. To Rod, it was if they were one set of eyes, their souls mirroring each other.

We really should get out of here, he thought. But when she pulled at his shirt, he let her draw it over his head. Then it was his turn to take off her shirt. They fondled each other for awhile, bare skin to bare skin, then eagerly broke apart at the same moment and scrambled out of the rest of their clothing.

The bed was old and creaked, and they started laughing at the absurd rhythm of the squeaks—but they didn't stop.

"What do we do now?" Simone asked again, after a long silence in the afterglow of their love.

"I think we'll have to leave," he said.

There was, of course, another solution. They were both thinking it. Rod was proud of her for not mentioning the option of tracking down Lee Awbrey and silencing him. Rod could never have followed through with that, but he wasn't completely sure about Simone. He loved her—with all his heart—but she was vampire, and though he felt safe with her, he couldn't be completely sure how she might react to anyone else.

"What about Patty and Laura?" she asked. "What if they come back?"

"We can try to leave a note. Somewhere only they could find."

Again they fell silent, both of them racking their brains trying to figure out a solution.

"All right," Simone said finally. "I think you're right. We have to leave. But where do we go?"

"We'll go to my house," Rod said. "We'll be left alone there. I hardly know my neighbors."

Simone got up and started putting on her clothes. Rod watched her, still not believing his luck in finding such a beautiful girl. She glanced back at him shyly. "I'll get ready; we can leave tonight."

He nodded reluctantly, then followed her example and started dressing.

The knock at the door came before they were ready to leave. Simone wanted at least a couple of hours of darkness to escape in, but they were still scrambling around for a place in the shadows where they could leave a note. They had just decided on the closet, which they knew Laura would check if the two girls returned together. At the sound of insistent knocking, they exchanged glances and, without a word, moved quickly and quietly toward the back door. Rod opened it and started heading for the patch of trees. A voice out of nowhere spoke directly into his ear. "Hey, don't leave yet."

Simone snarled. That made the stranger jump backward, and Rod saw him materialize out of the darkness. It was a young man—or rather, a young vampire. Kind of a nerdy vampire, with floppy black hair and heavy rimmed glasses. "Hey, no need for violence!" he said. "We're on your side!"

From the direction of the house, a second vampire emerged. Even in the darkness, Rod could make out her features. She was tall, with long, wavy blonde hair, and pale skin and eyes. She looked grim, and when she tried to put on a reassuring smile, it was anything but. "Terrill sent us," the blonde vampire said.

"Terrill?" Simone looked puzzled, but Rod quickly broke in. "Thank God you came!" he said with relief.

"Don't thank God," the male vampire said. "Thank Terrill."

The tall female vampire rolled her eyes. "Yeah, thank Terrill, who had to be convinced by me. Could you give it a rest, Marc? Terrill isn't some revered being, he's just like us."

The vampire she'd called Marc didn't seem convinced. He shook his head. "Someday you'll see, Clarkson. He is nothing like us."

"I still don't understand," Simone said.

Rod put his arm around her waist. "Remember when I told you of *The Testament of Michael?* How there was a powerful

137

vampire who preached coexistence with mankind? I left him a message on the Internet. I hoped if Terrill was as powerful as he was rumored to be, he'd find us."

Clarkson nodded. "I found your blog."

"On the Internet," Simone repeated doubtfully. Even though she had spent hours exploring Rod's cellphone apps, it was clear she still didn't get how wide-reaching the technology was that had developed while she was a captive. But even the relatively tech-savvy Rod couldn't help but be impressed by how quickly the vampires had found them.

"If we found you, others can too," Clarkson said, all business. "The message mentioned there were three women. Where are the other two?"

"They're gone," Rod said. "But I'm not sure they would have wanted to join us anyway."

Clarkson nodded. "Then come with us." She started walking toward the front of the house, followed by Marc. There was a big black SUV parked in front, with tinted windows—which was a good thing, since dawn was only an hour away.

Just as Clarkson's hand reached for the door handle, a loud voice boomed at them from near the doorway of the house. "Where do you think you're going?"

Rod turned and instinctively tried to shield Simone when he saw the big neighbor, Awbrey, standing there with a shotgun pointed at them. Simone gently pushed him to one side and stood in front of him instead—which made more sense, he admitted to himself.

Awbrey edged around them so he could get a clear shot at all of them. Clarkson tensed, and for a moment, Rod wondered if she would attack. From what he understood, these Golden Vampires wouldn't kill a human. *But what about in self-defense?* he wondered.

"My nephew has never heard of you guys," Awbrey said. "So I'm thinking you owe us some rent money for your squatting."

"We'd gladly pay you," Rod said. "But if we had any money, we wouldn't have been squatting."

"Just as I thought," Awbrey said. "Why don't we let the sheriff sort it all out, then? You can work for the county for awhile in an orange jumpsuit, and we'll garnish your wages." Still holding the shotgun with one hand, he fumbled for a cellphone with the other.

"Hello, dispatch? I got a situation here. I…" His voice cut off abruptly and a strange look came over his face. Then a kind of gargling sound came out of his throat, and a gusher of blood flowed out of his mouth. He dropped to the ground, unmoving, his head semi-detached from his neck.

Out of the darkness behind him came a vampire who was nearly as massive as Awbrey was, but taller, wider in the chest and narrower in the waist.

Rod heard Simone gasp. "The Monster…"

CHAPTER 16

Hoss was cloistered in his hotel, which was on the opposite side of London from the Council of Vampires offices and Council chambers. It was obvious to him now that the distance was deliberate. While Peterson paid for the lodgings and was constantly telling Hoss how important his "New World" viewpoint was, the old vampire seemingly had no intention of letting him get mixed up in politics—whether or not he was a Council member.

New World? Hoss thought. *How is America new to anyone who isn't centuries old? It's ridiculous.*

He asked to check out the IT services at the hotel, and Peterson looked at him as if he didn't know what Hoss was asking for. "Oh, computers!" he finally said. "I think we have a room for that somewhere around here."

Hoss found the little room on his own.

He stood in the back and watched the young vampires there. It felt familiar to him, as if he'd finally come home. They were so engrossed in their work that they didn't notice him at first. Finally, the big, rawboned vampire who was walking from station to station as if supervising the efforts turned around. He was lanky, but wore loose fitting shorts and a baggy t-shirt. He was growing a black beard, out of simple neglect it appeared.

He jumped in surprise. "Who the hell are you?" he shouted.

"My name is Hoss."

"As in *Councilor* Hoss?" The big vampire stared at him suspiciously. "The newly elected councilor from America?"

"That's me," Hoss said. Then he asked a question about some coding one of the vampires was doing, and the conversation quickly evolved into technicalities. The time flew by, and before Hoss knew it, it was quitting time for the IT gang. The big vampire stuck out his hand. "I'm Jared," he said. "Come by any time, Councilor Hoss. I think you're the first lord high mucky-muck to bother to come down here."

So it was that Hoss embedded himself with the younger vampires there, who were frustrated and angry at how they were being ignored by the old guard.

"So ignore them back," Hoss said after a few days of listening to the IT gang complain. "Let's do what needs to be done, and to hell with asking permission. I'm a Council member—I'll take the heat."

It was as if he'd freed them from chains. They had a thousand ideas, some good, some bad: some of them were fully fleshed out and just awaiting permission to be implemented. Hoss was happy to provide that permission. "Information is always good," he said. "Go ahead."

Of course, he took great pains to make sure none of this activity could be traced back to its source. But little by little, the Rules of Vampire were reaching a wider and wider audience, promulgated throughout the social networks and going viral in exponential leaps.

Public surveys were showing that a wider and wider segment of the population was beginning to believe that vampires existed. Hoss had decided they couldn't stop that—there was too much evidence out there. There were dozens of very convincing YouTube videos from the Crescent City incident alone.

But he could try to shape how vampires were perceived.

He didn't promise that vampires were harmless to humans; it would be many centuries, if ever, before most vampires could peacefully coexist with humans. It was the rare vampire who could turn Golden. Even Hoss had little inclination to follow Terrill's lead. He liked feeding on humans too much.

So the message Hoss tried to shape was that vampires weren't numerous enough or dangerous enough for most humans to be worried about. He argued, through a thousand sock puppets and trolls, that if people took precautions to avoid vampires, vampires would probably avoid them. A vampire attack was like being attacked by a cougar while out jogging: the chances were so slim that you might as well not worry about it.

Of course, even as he argued this, Hoss was out every night on the town, looking for victims. He felt a twinge of guilt, but not enough to stop doing it. No—he was being practical. Vampires had been discovered, vampires were going to feed; there was no getting around that. The Rules of Vampire were the best way to keep the situation from getting out of control.

His two young friends, Jimmy and Pete, were out with some of the younger vampires every night, painting the town red— literally. Jodie was even more voracious. She still crawled into Hoss's bed at night, but he was certain that he was just one among many to whom she granted her favors.

That was all right. He was losing interest in her. She was a simple soul—vicious and insatiable. If it weren't for him, she probably would have gone Wildering. When Jimmy began paying more and more attention to her, Hoss signaled that it was fine with him.

Sometimes Combs asked him over, and at a sumptuous banquet table, he was fed a nice young victim, one who was usually completely intoxicated or drugged so he could get a nice buzz on too.

"Why do we have to kill them?" he asked one night. "Why can't we just take their blood?"

"Have you ever tried?"

"Well, yeah."

"And how did that go?"

"I couldn't stop feeding once I started," Hoss admitted.

"We are vampire," Combs said.

They went back to eating the prostitute whom Combs or one of his surrogates had picked up off a local street corner. She was diseased, but such things didn't seem to affect vampires and indeed, added a little flavor to the meal. Hoss wondered if vampires had evolved to feed off less-fortunate humans, to cull the herd, which was beneficial to both vampire and human.

"I've been watching your activity online," Combs said, looking up and wiping his mouth. "I approve. However, I think you need to be careful. Most of the old vampires don't completely understand this new way of exchanging information They might think that you're breaking the Rules of Vampire."

"I doubt they'll even notice," Hoss said. "I think Peterson wakes up at dusk and asks his servants to bring around the horse and buggy."

Combs laughed. "He probably does. But then he fully wakes up and gets into his Ferrari. Don't underestimate us old vampires. Over the centuries, we've had to learn to adjust to change. Fitzsimmons especially has become very adept with the new technologies."

"Then Fitzsimmons had better damn well return from wherever he is," Hoss said. "He should be taking care of business. Peterson has done nothing. He seems to only care about consolidating his personal power."

"It's possible Fitzsimmons can't return," Combs said.

"What do you mean? You've hinted at this before. If you know something, just tell me."

"As you said, young Hoss, Peterson is consolidating his

power. How do you suppose he is doing that? And why is Fitzsimmons letting him?"

Combs, wily old vampire that he is, is still not answering the question, Hoss thought. *Probably never gets his own fangs bloody.*

"Well, something better happen soon," Hoss muttered. "The world is changing fast. Vampires have been exposed. Yet the Council of Vampires does nothing."

"What would you have us do?" Comb asked.

Hoss looked up from gnawing on a piece of gristle. The old vampire seemed genuinely curious.

"The way I see it, we have three choices," Hoss said. "First, we can try to stay hidden, use every trick we know to hunker down and obfuscate our existence. As I've said, I don't think, in a world of cellphones and social networks, this is possible. Second, we can slowly emerge from the shadows, but try to peacefully coexist with humans. Delay, delay, delay. This will be tricky and might require a rewriting of the Rules of Vampire. We would have to control our feeding, if not completely eliminate it."

"So you expect us all to follow Terrill's example?" Combs asked.

"Not possible. But we can pretend to—do everything we can to reassure humans that we aren't really dangerous. Maybe in the future, the situation will change. I admit, this isn't a very good solution, but it's the only solution I can think of."

"And the third option?"

"We go to war. We kill humans when and where we please. We try to gain the upper hand."

"But you don't like that last option."

"We would rouse the entire human military-industrial complex. We are outnumbered a hundred thousand to one. We wouldn't stand a chance. We would come closer to extinction than any time before the Rules of Vampire were promulgated."

"But this new strain of vampirism?" Combs mused. "Couldn't we increase our numbers dramatically? In a very short time?"

Hoss shook his head emphatically. "The Battle of Crescent City showed how that would turn out—and the humans didn't even have to bring the full force of their resources to bear."

"But if you hadn't intervened," Combs said, suddenly sounding very passionate. Hoss was startled. Usually Combs seemed above it all; he almost never got emotional. But here he was, arguing. "If your followers and Terrill's hadn't joined the humans, it seems to me the Wilderings would have won."

"Yes, but then what? The human response would have been even bigger and more severe."

"The Wilderings would have also increased exponentially!" Combs shouted.

Hoss fell silent, astonished at Combs's response. But even as he watched, Combs's expression went blank, as if a curtain had been drawn over his thoughts.

"Well, that was invigorating!" the old vampire said. "I guess we'll never know what would have happened, eh?"

"Thankfully, no."

"Still…" Combs mused. "Have you ever done a computer simulation?"

Hoss shook his head, somewhat surprised that he'd never thought of it. As soon as he left here, he decided, he was heading for the computer room to present the problem to the IT vampires.

They finished the meal with small talk. Hoss had visited most of the tourist sites in London, and Combs told him about less-known but fascinating locations. Hoss left the dinner slightly buzzed from the intoxicated victim and almost forgot the argument he'd had with Combs.

But as he walked down the stairs of the high rise, he remembered what Combs had said about Fitzsimmons. He needed to look into that. If the president of the Council of Vampires was in America, there should be a record of that somewhere. Sure, Peterson released a steady stream of messages from Fitzsimmons—but that was the problem; it was all coming through Peterson.

Combs had surprised him tonight, and for the first time, Hoss began to question his new mentor's motives. Hoss didn't know exactly what was going on, but it was clear that he was caught up in some Machiavellian dealings. It was invigorating—just the kind of thing that Hoss liked, and which the small town of Crescent City never provided.

Almost without thinking about where he was going, he found himself outside the IT room. There were three or four vampires in there, as there almost always were. They greeted Hoss as one of them. He presented them with the problem he'd been mulling over.

"A simulation?" Jared asked. The vampire in charge of communications appeared to be a middle-aged man and had only been Turned a couple of decades before—young by vampire standards. He'd been a geek before being Turned, and he was still a geek. "Why didn't I think of that?"

They immediately set about creating the program, and it drew in other IT vampires, who called their friends, and soon they had a dozen techies working on the problem. By the next morning, they had come up with a rough simulation.

"It could use some fine-tuning," Jared said. "But it should give us an approximate answer."

They ran the program.

First they ran what had actually happened. The Wildering

plague took off, growing at an alarming rate, a red stain that began to cover the Northern California coastline. Then the Golden Vampires appeared as a small yellow patch, but one that had an immediate effect on the growth of the red stain. Then Hoss's vampires—the followers of the Rules of Vampire—appeared, and the red stain was beaten back and eventually extinguished.

But not completely, Hoss noticed. There were still red splotches scattered throughout the area. *Do you suppose the humans know that?* he thought.

"OK," he said. "Let's see what happens if only Terrill and his band arrive."

They ran the simulation again. This time, the red stain was beaten back only temporarily, but before it could regrow significantly, the projected outside human forces came to the rescue. Again, the red was reduced to a few scattered spots.

"All right. What happens if Terrill never shows up?"

The simulation looked exactly the same, right up to the point where Terrill and the Golden Vampires had originally entered the picture. This time the red stain grew. Not only did it overwhelm the defenses at the Armory in Crescent City, it also completely drowned the entire area.

Jared reached over and pressed a key, and the area shown by the map expanded. Soon the entire area north of San Francisco and south of Bend, Oregon, was submerged in red.

The room fell silent. Jared expanded the map to all the states west of the Mississippi. "That's as big as we programmed it," he murmured.

It seemed to take only seconds before the crimson stain exploded. Not only was it growing bigger, it was doing so at a faster and faster pace. In the end, the entire map was blood red.

"Well," Jared said. "That was unexpected."

Hoss sat before the screen, stunned.

This changed everything. Combs had known this would be the result. That's why he'd argued so vehemently. So what were the old vampire's true intentions? Whose side was he really on? Was he trying to manipulate Hoss?

He turned to Jared. "Where do the communiqués from Fitzsimmons come from?"

The entire room went still. Jared shook his head. "What do you mean?"

"I mean, where's Fitzsimmons?" Hoss asked bluntly.

"In America," Jared answered. "Where else?" There was a look on his face that Hoss couldn't quite read. The IT chief had deliberately turned away from the rest of the room, and he was raising and lowering his eyebrows as if trying to semaphore a message to Hoss.

"OK…" Hoss said. "Just wondered."

The room slowly relaxed. As the IT vampires started excitedly talking about the simulation, they seemed to forget Hoss's question. Eventually, Jared surreptitiously signaled for Hoss to follow him out of the room.

"What's going on?" Hoss demanded.

"Not yet," Jared answered, leading him farther away from the others. He didn't stop until they turned around a corner and moved into the stairwell.

"The messages aren't coming from America," Jared said. "They're coming from London. The first one to notice that—and the only one to ever mention it aloud—was a guy named Harold."

"So let me talk to Harold."

"You can't. He's gone. A day after he brought it up, he disappeared. No one has dared mention it since."

"So you think there is a spy." Hoss didn't phrase it as

a question.

"Maybe more than one. Peterson is pretty free with his money, and most of the techies are young vampires who haven't accumulated much wealth. So yeah, I'm pretty sure that Fitzsimmons is either dead or a captive."

"So what happened?"

"Why does it matter? Why should I endanger my life over an asshole like Fitzsimmons? I mean, give me a choice between Robespierre, who wants to guillotine everyone in sight, or Danton, who only wants to guillotine, well, *almost* everyone, and I'll pick the latter."

Hoss didn't say anything, but it offended his sense of order. Fitzsimmons was the elected president of the Council. If he was removed by any method other than a vote, then it was a coup. Pure and simple.

Once the rules broke down, they became meaningless. Either all the rules must be followed, or none of them.

The following morning, before he went to sleep, Hoss vowed to find out what had happened to Fitzsimmons. He called Jared and asked him to track down the source of the messages.

"I'll do that," Jared said. "But don't ever call here again. If you have something to say, say it to my face."

"Right," Hoss said.

Jared hung up. A moment later, Hoss heard a second click.

CHAPTER 17

Hoss wandered the broken Twilight lands outside the giant walls of the eternal city. Mankind was extinct, all of them either Turned or consumed. The Wilderings preyed on each other. Some banded together under strong leaders; others wandered as ronin vampires, alone and in hiding.

Very rarely, a Wildering became so powerful that the immortal gods behind the walls noticed. The gods would then either reward or destroy the Wildering, or even more rarely, raise him or her up to join them.

Hoss was ronin for a long time—and he was left alone, for the price of challenging him was too high—until one day, almost by accident, he became the leader of the largest clan of Wilderings. Their old leader tracked him down and confronted him, leaving Hoss no choice but to kill him, and Hoss became his successor. From that base of strength, he conquered the rest of the Wilderings. Now his army was camped outside the eternal city, ready to besiege the mile-high walls.

The god came to him in broad daylight, materializing inside his tent. He appeared as a huge shadow against the hanging tapestries.

"You have done well," the god said. "The immortal gods have decided to let you join us."

"Not interested," Hoss said.

"You will never have to fight again. We offer you eternal life, safe from danger. We still have humans living behind our walls to serve us, and we breed them for the most succulent flesh.

Come, join us, and let this Wildering riffraff go back to their wandering ways."

"There is no such thing as eternal life, nor safety from danger," Hoss said. "As you will soon find out."

"Do you not realize what will happen?" the god said, sounding puzzled. "Can you not see our power?"

"You made a mistake. I see before me not a god, but a vampire. No vampire has ever defeated me."

"Ah, I see," said the god. "Then you must be taught a lesson. For I am no simple vampire—I am indeed a god."

The creature began to grow, filling the tent like a black cloud, but the darkness was deeper than black; it was nothingness, a hole in existence that sucked up all light, a Shadow from which nothing escaped.

Hoss lifted his spear and threw it with all his might into the center of the black void. But the emptiness came roiling toward him and washed over him, and he felt its unending cold, heard its everlasting echo and saw its infinite nothingness, and he was consumed.

Hoss awoke at dusk, his vampire senses alive to the coming night. His heart was pounding. The blue blood that usually flowed sluggishly through it felt liquid and hot.

It is a vision of the future, that's clear, he thought. *But what does it mean?*

Who were the gods? They were vampires, but also something more. There was something that his subconscious was noticing that only his dreams revealed, but like all such visions, it was murky and unclear.

He made his way to the IT room, where he found Jared waiting. Before he could speak, the IT chief grabbed Hoss by the arm. Though he wasn't a big man, Jared was still stronger than Hoss, with his thirteen-year-old frame. He pulled Hoss into the stairwell.

"Don't *ever* call me like that again," he hissed. "The Council owns both the landlines and the Wi-Fi. They can hear everything we say."

"Sorry," Hoss said. "That was stupid of me."

Jared glared at him for a few moments more. "Well…I think I found where they're hiding Fitzsimmons. Not from the messages, but from a strange little rental bill we've been getting every month from a small apartment building in a rundown part of town. I figure that's got to be it."

He handed Hoss a torn piece of notebook paper with an address scribbled on it. "There's a camera in the apartment. I can't access it, but I can turn it off. And I will—at exactly eight o'clock.

"Thanks, Jared. I won't forget this," Hoss promised.

"Oh?" Jared said as he walked away. "Actually, I'd rather you did forget."

The apartment was in Camberwell Green, a part of London that Hoss probably would have avoided if he weren't vampire. Though he was small of stature and he saw some burly lads eyeballing him, none of them approached him. The aura of a vampire wasn't always obvious, but it was there—other predators picked up on it and made way for him.

He trudged up the stairwell, which smelled of piss, and idly browsed the graffiti as he passed. He couldn't make any sense of it. Each successive floor he climbed seemed less populated, until on the final floor, it appeared that only one apartment was occupied.

There was a large vampire standing in front of the door. Hoss wandered idly up to him. As he'd hoped, the guard didn't take a very good look at him, and clearly judged him to be human. It wasn't until Hoss was almost upon him that the guard began to realize who—or rather, what—was approaching.

Hoss covered the last few feet in a bound and landed on the guard's shoulders, sliding down his back and grabbing his neck and chin along the way. He twisted the guard's head as hard as he could as he continued down to the floor, letting his weight do the damage, and heard the crack of the other vampire's spine. The guard dropped backward onto the floor. He twitched and groaned, his eyes bugging out in disbelief. Hoss stomped down on his neck, completing the severing of his spine

Hoss opened the unlocked door and carefully poked his head around it, but there was no one inside the room. He dragged the guard's body in behind him. There was another door at the other end of the room, and he quickly crossed to it and opened it.

Behind it was a tiny room, little more than a closet, with a single lightbulb hanging down over a table with a child-sized coffin on it. Dried blood covered the floor, with hanks of fur and bone sticking out of it. It smelled awful. Hoss approached the coffin, uncertain what he'd find.

The armless, legless vampire lay in a puddle of his own waste, the gastric juices burning away the flesh of his lower torso. His hair and beard were long and gray, and his eyes were blurry. But through all the destruction, Hoss recognized Fitzsimmons.

The vampire tried to focus on him, and there was a small spark of recognition in his rheumy eyes. "You…" he managed to gasp.

"I'm Hoss. Do you remember?"

The pitiful creature managed to nod his head. "You…are one of them?"

"No," Hoss said. "I am no part of this. I'm going to get you out of here."

He took a deep breath, leaned down and lifted the vampire from the muck. There was a sucking sound, as if his torso was stuck, then a sudden release of pressure, and Hoss stumbled backward. Fitzsimmons was slimy and hard to hold onto. Hoss managed to maneuver his way out of the room before the vampire's torso slipped out of his grasp and dropped to the floor with a thud.

Fitzsimmons glared at him, but at least it seemed to wake the old vampire up. *Anger is better hopelessness*, Hoss thought. He saw a bathroom off to one side, found a soiled towel and grabbed a roll of toilet paper. The water was a little brown-looking, but preferable to the slime that covered Fitzsimmons. It took the entire roll of toilet paper and constant rinsing of the dirty towel, but eventually, Hoss managed to get down to skin.

Once his body was dried, Fitzsimmons was easier to carry. Hoss lifted him again, wondering how they were going to get out of there without being observed by the human population. Even in this part of London, someone carrying a limbless torso around would be remarkable.

He felt something nip at his throat and pulled Fitzsimmons's face away from his neck. Sure enough, the other vampire's fangs were fully extended, and there was a crazy look in his eyes.

"Not me, damn it," Hoss said. "Wait just a second."

He went over to the guard's body and dropped Fitzsimmons on top of him. He didn't have to do any more than that. The voracious vampire had no trouble tearing his way through the body using his fangs alone, consuming everything but bones within a few minutes.

When Fitzsimmons finally looked up, Hoss could see that the spark of intelligence had returned to his eyes.

"How much time do we have?" Hoss asked.

"Sometimes they come twice a day. Sometimes once.

Sometimes not at all. If they're coming twice today, they'll be here within the hour."

Hoss sighed. No time to call for help. Not to mention, Jared had insisted that Hoss not use his phone for that purpose again.

He took the guard's bloody coat and covered Fitzsimmons's head and torso. "Don't move," he said. "Until we get to the car, you're just a parcel, understand?"

"Of course."

Even with Hoss's vampire strength, by the time he reached the ground floor, his arms were so tired he thought they'd fall off and he'd join Fitzsimmons in being limbless. He stumbled the last few yards to the car, getting a few curious glances but nothing more. He opened the back door, dropped Fitzsimmons onto the seat and slammed the door. He got in the driver's seat. "Just a little longer," he said.

Hoss's hotel had an underground garage, and he pulled into a parking space without incident. He carried the other vampire to the elevator, and a few minutes later, he had deposited Fitzsimmons in his suite's huge bathtub and was running water into the tub. "Can you sit up?" he asked.

Amazing, Fitzsimmons had already sprouted a couple of inches of vestigial limbs. He pushed against the side of the tub with his flippers and pulled himself up an inch or two. "I'd rather not drown."

Hoss stared down at him. Fitzsimmons's flesh was already healing. "A couple more feedings and I think you'll be as good as new," he mused.

"Could you bring me a live one?" Fitzsimmons asked. "I haven't had a live one in ages."

Hoss grunted. Bringing back live victims was always more difficult. It required persuasion, usually, rather than brute force.

"I'll see what I can do," he said. Actually, eating a live meal sounded appealing to him, too. He turned off the faucet when the water reached Fitzsimmons's neck. He left the bathroom and got dressed in his night-on-the-town clothes.

"I'll be right back," he shouted as he headed out the door.

Perhaps because he actually needed them to be, the prey weren't very cooperative tonight. The girls seemed to sense Hoss's desperation. He finally flashed a big wad of bills and coaxed one of the less-attractive streetwalkers from the corner of her alley. She was a big girl—lots of flesh. As he'd hoped, he saw a large man start to trail them. Perfect. Let the pimp spring his little trap, and there would be plenty of meat for both Hoss and Fitzsimmons.

Conveniently, the pimp didn't try to jump Hoss until they were safely in the darkness of the parking garage. Hoss tripped him and slammed his head into one of the concrete pillars. The man dropped like a misshapen bag of manure. The girl started screaming, so Hoss reached into her throat and removed her larynx. He'd become practiced at this move, so now the meals usually didn't expire right away.

He dragged both of the humans into the elevator by their ankles.

Back in his suite, he let Fitzsimmons have most of the meat. When they were done, the other vampire's vestigial limbs had grown by another six inches.

"Thank you," Fitzsimmons said, looking sleepy.

"Let me help you to the other bedroom," Hoss said. He half-dragged, half-carried the other vampire into the room and dropped him onto the bed. "Sleep it off. The sooner you can start moving around on your own, the better."

He closed the door behind him, then sat at the dining table and wondered what to do next. He'd defied Peterson, who was the most powerful vampire alive. It probably wouldn't take long for the old vampire to figure out who the most likely culprit was.

Will Combs help me? he wondered, then shook his head. Combs would do whatever was in his own best interest, and Hoss simply didn't know enough about what that was. He didn't fool himself into thinking the wily vampire would endanger himself to help Hoss. Sure, Combs had pointed him in this direction, but was it because he wanted Hoss to succeed, or to fail?

No, his only hope was for Fitzsimmons to fully recover and present himself to the Council. It was going to be a race between recovery and discovery.

As if in response to this thought, there was a pounding at the door that seemed to make the whole suite shudder. Hoss realized immediately that the Council had come for him.

He looked around. There was no escape—no other exit. The windows were sealed. *Something to chalk up to experience*, he thought. *I'll never get caught like this again.*

He walked to the door as it shook again from the pounding. "Yes?" he said, opening the door.

Three vampires had come for Hoss, more than enough to control him: big, beefy vampires who dwarfed him.

"You're under arrest by order of the Council of Vampires." The one speaking was the biggest and meanest-looking. Hoss had seen him in the proximity of Peterson more than once. It was one of his creatures, James, or Janes, or something like that. James, that was it.

"On what charge?" Hoss asked.

"Charge?" James repeated. "Let's just say all of them. Every damn rule; is that good enough for you?"

"We'll see," Hoss said. He spoke in a neutral voice, which only seemed to enrage his captors.

"You coming willingly or do we have to drag your carcass out of here?"

Hoss said, "I'll come gladly—to clear all this up."

"Yeah, sure. That's a good idea. Do that."

Hoss forced himself not to look back at the closed bedroom door. But the three vampires seemed only interested in him. Whatever he was being arrested for, it apparently wasn't for breaking Fitzsimmons free. Chances were, they didn't even know about that yet. The quicker Hoss led them away from Fitzsimmons, the better.

"What are we waiting for?" he asked. "Let's go!"

James stepped back and eyed him suspiciously. He cast a glance over Hoss's shoulder. Then he shook his head and motioned for the other two vampires to grab their captive. Hoss heard the door click shut behind them.

He could only hope Fitzsimmons recovered enough to be ambulatory soon...because it was possible that only Fitzsimmons could save him now.

CHAPTER 18

All her newfound strength and confidence deserted Simone when she heard the Monster's voice. She was little girl again, chained in a basement, a mere sex toy. She cried out and started to run back toward the house, but Rod was there. He grabbed her and gently swung her into his arms.

"He won't get you," he murmured.

Simone could feel his brittle human bones as he held her. Even before the Monster had been Turned vampire, Rod wouldn't have stood a chance against him, but here he was, putting himself between her and her worst fears. Her resolve began to return, pushing against her fear, overcoming it, and when she stepped in front of Rod and spoke, her dread was a hollow feeling in her stomach, but her anger was a fire that burned through it.

"You won't take me again," she said to the Monster. "You'll have to kill me first."

"But you liked it, honey," he sneered. "I know you did. Isn't that so, Laura, dear?"

Laura stepped out from behind the Monster's bulk. "She liked it. We all liked it. She was just begging for it."

"Oh, Laura!" Simone cried. The cry was wrenched from her amid a feeling of despair that broke the ties that bound them. Laura had betrayed them.

Laura stared back defiantly. There was not the slightest doubt that she had gone with the Monster voluntarily.

Clarkson took her hand off the SUV's door handle and

turned around. "Go away," she said in a voice so cold and steely that even the Monster seemed to pale a little. "You aren't welcome here."

"Vampire lady, I'm not welcome anywhere. Never stopped me before. Just step away and I won't have to kill you. This girl is my property."

"No vampire is property," Marc spoke up. "*The Testament of Michael* says tha-"

"Shut up, you little pipsqueak," the Monster growled.

Marc paled and backed up a step.

Another vampire emerged out of the darkness. Simone blinked—with her vampire night vision, she should have been able to see him before, but until he stepped into the artificial glow of the porch light, he'd been invisible, as if wrapped within the shadow of a shadow.

"I recognize you," Clarkson said. "You're the FBI vampire hunter, Feller."

"*Was*," Feller corrected her. "Was a vampire hunter; now I'm a vampire who hunts."

"How ironic," Clarkson said. "How appropriate…"

"And I recognize you, too," Feller said. "Clarkson, Council of Vampires, and one of the new so-called Golden Vampires."

"I have the blood of gold," she acknowledged. "But I doubt the Council of Vampires will claim me now. If you know about my powers, then you should know not to challenge me."

Feller looked amused. "I've heard about you. Very impressive—blood of gold, daywalker, all that."

"Then go! We don't have to fight."

"Ah, but here's something you should see," Feller said. He pulled his sleeve back from his arm and bit into it. Blood welled up in a blackened, sluggish flow. "There is more than one new kind of vampire in the land. We who have evolved alongside you were bred in the shadows, as you were bred in the light, but we are even stronger than you gold bloods. We are the Shadow Vampires, and our blood is black. Kelton here is more powerful than any vampire who has ever existed."

"Oh, my God," Marc exclaimed. "As it was foretold in *The Testament of Michael*: 'Just as the Blood of Gold has been created to redeem vampires, from the darkness shall come the Shadows, who, in their evil, shall bring about the reckoning, the…the final…'"

Everyone was staring at him, and he stuttered to a stop.

Clarkson didn't take her eyes off of the Monster, but she directed her voice toward Simone and Laura. "There is an abandoned motel by the beach. There are other vampires there. Run. I'll hold this creature back. The dawn is not far away. If I survive, I'll find you."

Rod looked at Simone doubtfully, but she didn't hesitate. She took his hand. "Come on," she said, pulling him along as she ran toward the back of the house.

Rod started lagging. "What?" she exclaimed in exasperation.

"We should take the car," he said.

"But we would be abandoning them here," Simone said.

"They have blood of gold. They will survive the dawn, but you won't."

They headed back. As they turned the corner of the house, they saw that Clarkson had moved to confront the two Shadow Vampires, with Marc behind her, obviously more reluctant. The blonde vampire saw them, and as they headed toward the SUV, she nodded her head in approval.

Rod took the wheel and Simone got in the passenger side. Only seconds later, the first rays of the sun broke through the morning clouds and washed over the clearing. Behind the tinted windows of the SUV, Rod gave a big sigh of relief.

Simone barely noticed her narrow escape. She was focused on the tableau outside the windows. In this light, Clarkson appeared as a shimmering, golden presence, and Marc just a little less so. In front of them were two shadows—a deep blackness, which the light seemed to avoid.

As Rod peeled out onto the driveway, sending dust into the air, the light and the shadow converged, and it seemed to Simone that they obliterated each other. The clearing in front of the house appeared empty. She closed her eyes and shook her head, and when she looked again, she could see frenzied movement—and then Rod turned the corner and they were gone.

Marc didn't think he was a coward. He'd taken a lot of moral and ethical positions in his life that had required real fortitude. He'd endured the mockery of those less enlightened, but he'd never actually been in a physical fight. He'd seen a couple of fights after school, and they had been alarming violent. So he'd always cultivated a knack for talking himself out of any confrontation.

This is the real thing, he thought. *A life-and-death struggle.*

He wanted to move up beside Clarkson and play his part, but he couldn't quite get there. He probably looked more like he was hiding behind her than backing her up.

He could barely think, he was so frightened. Clarkson and the big vampire were facing off. The other Shadow Vampire, Feller, was—was looking at *him*, with an evil grin. There was no other word for it: evil.

When Clarkson began her attack, both Marc and Feller stepped back, as if mutually agreeing to let the two Alpha vampires fight it out first. But Feller also gave him a look that seemed to say, *You're next.*

The two fighters moved so fast that Marc didn't so actually

see the blows land, but instead saw the reactions to those blows. Clarkson fell backward with an alarmed expression. Then a look of determination came over her face and she entered the fray again, and this time, after a flurry of dizzying motion, it was Kelton who stumbled, nearly falling to his knees before recovering and growling at Clarkson.

Marc saw light flowing around her, and then saw shadow enclosing it. Then the shadow blinked out and a flare of light took its place. Back and forth the light and shadow flowed, creating a blurry whirlwind of color and void.

On the leaves and dirt of the clearing, a black and gold Pollack painting was being created as the blood of both fighters flew. A black globule hit Marc on the cheek, and it burned. He wiped it aside. Then a gold drop hit him on the forehead, and it emboldened him for a moment.

Then there was stillness and quiet. The fighters broke apart and faced each other, breathing deeply. Their clothing was shredded and they were covered in wounds, which weren't healing. Clarkson looked small in comparison to her opponent, and Marc realized that her spirit—which had appeared to make her his equal—had somehow been diminished.

He heard her speak, gasping. "I can't win this. He's too strong. You must go tell Terrill. Tell him what happened here. He has to know."

"But what about him?" Marc said, pointing at Feller, who looked like he was getting ready to fight.

Clarkson turned and gave the ex-FBI agent a mirthless grin. "I can hold them both back, Marc. But only for a short time. Run, damn you! If you stay, we'll both be destroyed and the others will never know what happened here. Run!"

Marc backed away and Feller started after him. In a blur, Clarkson was on him, tearing into him. Feller cried out in alarm, and pieces of his body started landing on the ground, splattered with black.

As Marc turned, he saw an amused expression come over the giant vampire's face, as if he wanted to see what happened and was willing to let Clarkson destroy his confederate to find out.

Feller was on his back, and Clarkson raised her claws to land a killing blow. Only then did the other Shadow Vampire react. She cried out in frustration as his huge hands closed over her neck. Her claws ripped at his hands, but still he held on. Her cries became more and more strangled as he squeezed, and the light—the golden light that had pervaded the clearing—began to dim.

Then Marc was running, mindlessly, toward the line of trees in the distance.

He stumbled, rolled and, amazingly, landed on his feet again, and kept running. Halfway to his goal, he glanced over his shoulder. He didn't so much see two figures as two black shadows pursuing him. Feller went in and out of the darkness. He was limping and struggling to move. But the other shadow kept coming, deep and relentless. Marc realized he wouldn't reach the shelter of the trees, and even if he did, he doubted it would matter.

He gave up. All thoughts of escape abandoned him. A strange sort of peace came over him as he slowed and turned around.

He stood still, waiting. He wasn't a brave man, as it turned out, but he could try to be brave in this last moment of existence. *The Testament of Michael* was written—he was pretty sure that was what he'd been put on this Earth to accomplish. His job was done.

As the shadow approached, he grew ever more still. He closed his eyes and waited for the end.

A shadow washed over him, and then past him. He stood

there for several moments more, but nothing happened. Confused, he opened his eyes. The other vampires had gone by him as if he wasn't there.

He turned his head and saw the two shadows, with Feller dropping in and out of view, reach the trees. Then, as if they'd seen the movement of his head, they turned and rushed back toward him.

Again he held perfectly still, but this time with his eyes open. They thundered toward him like death itself, but faltered, slowed and then—just a few feet away—both the large vampire and Feller stopped, looking perplexed.

"Where'd he go?" Feller asked.

"It must be their gold blood," Kelton said. "It makes them invisible during the daytime, just as our blood makes us invisible at night."

"Then he could be right here," Feller said.

"Yeah," Kelton agreed, but then he waved his hand around at the hundreds of yards of meadow and the miles of forest beyond it. "Anywhere around here. Why don't you stick your arms out and start waving them around?"

Marc held his breath. That might actually work—but they didn't know that. He had never been so still in his life, but his muscles were starting to stiffen. He tried to relax, sensing that if he started quivering, they'd notice the movement.

He thought back to the feelings of rightness that had washed over him as he wrote *The Testament of Michael*. He closed his eyes and tried to be invisible—a spirit, nothing more. A ray of light.

"Screw it," Kelton said. "Let them come. If she was the best they got, we don't have anything to worry about."

"Don't forget Terrill," Feller warned.

"I ain't forgetting him. I'm looking forward to meeting him."

Then they were moving away.

Long after they were out of view, Marc kept standing there, feeling at peace, knowing that he had time. *It is going to be all right,* he thought. *Light is stronger than shadow. I'm sure of it.*

Then he remembered that last look on Clarkson's face, and a shadow crept into his heart.

Sometimes the light is blocked, he thought. *And the shadow hides beyond the light's reach.*

Simone and Rod kept driving until they were halfway to Brookings.

"Where are we going?" she asked finally.

"Hell if I know," he said, slowing down. "I feel like a coward."

"There wasn't anything you could do," she said. "You're only human. Maybe I could have helped, if anyone could've."

"No," Rod said. "You saw her. That blonde vampire was faster than any vampire I've ever heard of. She seemed to know how to fight, too. You wouldn't have lasted a second. Besides, it was dawn."

"Still…maybe I could have helped her." Simone started crying.

"You couldn't have helped," Rod said, feeling helpless himself in the face of her tears.

"I know," Simone sniffled. "I'm crying about Laura. I knew she was screwed up—who wouldn't be, after all that happened to her? But I never thought she'd join *him.*"

Rod reached out and took her hand, and the gesture of sympathy sent Simone into another crying jag.

They drove north, over the border to Oregon and up the coast. Hours passed, and Simone finally stopped crying.

"I'm heading back," Rod said. "I think I know what place the blonde vampire was talking about."

They drove all the way back to Crescent City. There, beside the beach, was an abandoned, boarded-up motel with a restaurant attached. Rod pulled into the parking lot. The sun was sinking into the ocean. They waited until the last rays blinked out and then got out of the car.

He knocked on the door to the office. As the last light of day faded, the door opened. A little girl stood there, blinking up at them.

"You're human," she said. "You better not come in here."

Simone stepped forward. "He's mine," she said.

"OK," said the little girl, and opened the door wider. "Don't say I didn't warn you!"

CHAPTER 19

"You little weasel!" Peterson yelled. "I brought you all the way to London and this is how you repay me?"

"I'm sorry, but do you mind telling me what my crime is supposed to be?" Hoss asked.

Peterson fell silent and sat back down in his office chair. Hoss was standing, handcuffed, in front of a long desk, which was so polished that he half expected to see himself reflected in the surface. He shook his head. Sometimes he almost forgot he was vampire.

The guards had left the room, leaving just the two of them. They were in the president's chambers, which were attached to the Council offices. A row of CCTV screens lined one wall, showing everything that was happening throughout the offices of the vampire complex.

One of the screens was blank, Hoss noticed. *Does Peterson know I released Fitzsimmons?*

"You know damn well what you've done, Hoss," Peterson continued in a more moderate voice. "You've been telling the world about us, exposing the Rules of Vampire to humans."

"It's not like they don't already know," Hoss said. He knew he shouldn't be relieved that the charges were less serious than he'd expected, because they were still more than enough to get him in deep trouble—not to mention true to boot. "I'm just trying to explain what the rules are and how they can help."

"*Never trust a human,*" Peterson said, quoting Rule One. "That rule, above all others, must be obeyed. Disobeying is punishable by death."

The door of the office opened. Councilor Combs entered, followed by two bodyguards. He stopped just inside the doorway, acting surprised. "What have we here?" the dapper vampire asked. "What are you doing to poor young Hoss?"

Peterson looked disgusted. "I see your spy network is efficient, as usual. I heard you and Hoss were getting friendly."

"Spy network? I was just dropping by!" Combs protested. "I must admit, however, I did hear a rumor. What has Hoss done?"

Peterson snorted. "Hoss has been telling the humans all about us—without approval of the Council. He must be punished."

"So he will be," Combs said. "Friend or no friend, he will get what he deserves just as soon as the full Council has heard the charges. But we shouldn't be too hasty. Perhaps we should wait for Fitzsimmons to return before we start condemning any more members to death."

Peterson flushed and flashed a glance toward the empty screen. As if in response, one of his lackeys hurried into the room and whispered in his ear. Peterson's eyes flicked toward Hoss and grew cold. "Check his apartment," he said. "Find him."

Hoss tried to look unconcerned. If Fitzsimmons hadn't recovered enough to make good his escape, then they were both doomed. Hoss wasn't sure it mattered. Peterson had apparently decided he was an unreliable ally and would be seeking the ultimate punishment in any case.

"Business doesn't stop just because Fitzsimmons isn't here," Peterson said. "The rules must be enforced."

Combs sighed. "I was afraid you were going to say that. I hope you don't mind, but I have already called for a Council meeting," he checked his wristwatch, "in about three hours."

"You had no right!"

"Oh, and you do? I never did see that letter of authorization for you to assume leadership."

"I was elected vice president of the Council."

"Strange that Fitzsimmons is only contacting you, isn't it? He was always so good at keeping in touch, cozying up to the membership. Always willing to press the flesh, give a speech, make a phone call—the consummate politician. Very odd that he should fall silent."

"He's been busy."

"Yes, no doubt he's been very preoccupied."

Both vampires turned to Hoss as if they expected him to say something. "I'm sure he's up to his elbows in work," Hoss said. *That is, if he has any elbows*, he thought.

Peterson frowned. "Very well, let's see what the Council decides."

A few hours later, the Council of Vampires was called to order. It was nearly a full session, since a regularly scheduled session was only days away. The members from South America and Australia wouldn't arrive for another day, but since their votes usually cancelled each other out, it probably didn't matter.

Peterson had the majority of votes on most subjects, but he couldn't always get his way if the issue was contentious. Public exposure through new technology and media was something most of the Council, being composed of the oldest living vampires, didn't fully understand. Because they didn't understand it, they were more likely to trust the opinions of the younger vampires on such things.

They didn't get much younger than Hoss.

He stood and made his case. Peterson had relented and taken off the handcuffs. For the first time, Hoss felt his youth. His adolescent voice faltered and broke embarrassingly. He thought he had some convincing arguments, but he could see that he wasn't swaying anyone. Combs and maybe a couple of others were on his side—that was it.

The vampires had remained concealed for so long that they

simply couldn't see that hiding wasn't possible anymore.

"If we can't remain secret, then it is up to us to shape the message," he insisted. "We must attempt to make the humans understand that vampires don't wish to destroy them all."

"We don't?" This came from the large Dutch woman, Belinda. She hadn't liked Hoss from the start—that he was young and American seemed to be strikes against him.

"We certainly don't want them to *think* that," Hoss said, "whatever the truth. And isn't it true that we don't wish to kill them all, but to keep them alive until we need them?"

"So you suggest that we just lie to them, and if we lie well enough, they'll believe us."

"Some will, some won't. Humans can be gullible. But isn't it better to keep them docile?"

"The best way to keep them docile is to keep them ignorant," Peterson insisted. "President Fitzsimmons has been very clear about this."

At the mention of Fitzsimmons, there was an uneasy ripple around the conference table. More than one councilor had lost his or her life by defying Fitzsimmons, whereas Hoss had no power or influence. Hoss began to feel as though he was being submerged under a cloud of suspicion. It was clear which way this was going.

"Even if he is guilty," Combs said, "does Hoss deserve the death penalty? Look how young he is! I would think a warning should be sufficient. Or perhaps banishment."

Hoss looked around the table, and his heart sank. Combs's words had had the opposite effect of what he'd wanted—unless finding Hoss guilty *was* what Combs actually wanted. It was as if the plea for leniency had merely confirmed Hoss's guilt. There probably wasn't a worse tactic one could use in front of a group of vampires than to plead for mercy, especially since most of these vampires didn't have a compassionate bone in their bodies.

In the end, when the vote was taken, it wasn't even close. Hoss lost by three votes.

The guards entered the room. Hoss looked over at Combs, who shrugged regretfully. *Yeah, thanks a lot,* Hoss thought. *I don't know why, but you probably set this whole thing up.*

Hoss held out his hands for the handcuffs.

The lights went out. The room disappeared into darkness. Ordinarily, this wouldn't have mattered—vampires could see just as well, if not better, in the dark. Still, it was unusual. Vampires normally used indoor lights so as to not stand out. Most of them had gotten used to always flipping the light switches when entering a room—unless, of course, they were using the darkness to stalk their prey.

There were shouts in the outer chamber, then the sounds of a scuffle and bodies slamming against the floor. The door burst open and a dozen vampires entered the room, led by Jared. Jimmy and Pete were in the group, and they grinned at Hoss. Jodie followed them in, her eyes shining with excitement. There were more vampires beyond the door, and Hoss sensed that there was a small army of them outside. It was the entire crew from the IT room, along with a few other young vampires whom Hoss didn't recognize.

"Let him go," Jared said, pointing at Hoss. The guards looked confused and glanced toward Peterson, who had his hands under the table.

"You can press the alarm button all you want, Vice President Peterson," Jared said. "All the electronics in the building have been turned off. It's just the Council of Vampires and us."

"This is outrageous!" Peterson shouted. "Treason! I'll make sure you all die for this!"

"You aren't in a position to make threats, sir," Jared said. "I have more than a hundred followers outside this room, all of them sick and tired of the way you folks are running things. I don't think you want to fight all of us."

"On the contrary," Combs said. "I believe we will indeed have to fight all of you." The words weren't overly loud, but they seemed to fill the room. Combs stood up, and though he was shorter than anyone else present, including Hoss, he dominated the gathering. "As much as I regret it, I have to agree with Councilor Peterson. This coup cannot be allowed to stand, or all will be chaos. You and your fledgling followers have underestimated us, young sir. Any one of us on the Council can take on a dozen of you. You will lose, do you understand? Back away now and we'll let you live."

Jared squared off with Combs, with Jimmy and Pete at either shoulder. Jodie stood just behind them, looking delighted that there was about to be violence, but none of the other three looked confident. Hoss could see the older vampire tensing, as if ready to leap.

"Stop!" Hoss cried. He believed Combs—that the older vampires would make quick work of the younger ones. He had heard the certainty in Combs's voice. "I submit to my punishment!"

"That won't be necessary," another voice said. Fitzsimmons squeezed his way through the intruders, dressed in his finest suit and looking none the worse for wear—though perhaps a little more slender, a little more gaunt. "I'm back..." he hesitated, then said, "...from America. What I learned there has made all of this unnecessary. Back down, everyone. No one will be punished because of the events here today. It will be as if it never happened."

Combs relaxed first. "President Fitzsimmons, welcome

back." He shrugged and sat down, then looked over at Hoss and smiled. He raised his eyebrows as if to say, *Well played.*

Everyone seemed to realize it was over—except Peterson. "You!" he shouted. "How did you..."

"Yes, I have returned," Fitzsimmons said, cutting him off. He walked over to the white-haired vampire at the head of the table and put his hand on Peterson's shoulder. Peterson seemed to shrink under the weight of the gesture. "If you don't mind, I'll be taking my chair back," Fitzsimmons said. "I've been told you've done a splendid job while I was gone, Peterson. You can be sure I will be rewarding you soon for your efforts on my behalf. Very soon."

Peterson got up and moved aside, but didn't take the seat to Fitzsimmons's left. He hesitated, looking indecisive, as if wondering whether he should stay and fight. Instead, he turned to leave. As he did, Fitzsimmons grabbed the cane out of his hands. "You won't be needing this anymore," he said. "I think I can find a use for it."

Peterson looked from the sword cane to Fitzsimmons's face and then back to the cane. Then he hurried from the room, not looking back. There was the sound of a scuffle in the next room, and a muffled cry. Fitzsimmons ignored it. He brought down the head of the cane on the table as if it was a gavel and said, "The world has changed, and we must change with it. A new kind of vampire exists, and we will soon have to make a choice as to whether to try to ignore them or join them."

"There is a third choice," Combs said from the other end of the table. "We can resist them."

"You haven't seen these Golden Vampires, but Hoss here has, haven't you, young man?" Fitzsimmons asked.

Hoss had sat down in relief. Jimmy and Pete had made their way over to him and were standing behind him. Jared was standing near the door, shifting from one foot to the other as if unsure what to do next.

"I think we should invite Jared into our consultations," Hoss said, "as well as a few of his followers. This Council needs the advice of some younger, more tech-savvy members."

"Agreed," Fitzsimmons proclaimed, slamming the sword cane down on the table again. "Come, stand behind me and be my advisor, Jared. I'll be glad to listen to your advice. Meanwhile, Hoss, please tell us about Terrill and his followers."

Hoss rose to his feet. He sensed that Fitzsimmons wanted nothing but the truth, so that's what he told—how the vampires with blood of gold could walk in the daylight and were stronger and swifter than any other vampire.

"How wonderful!" Belinda exclaimed.

"But at a cost," Hoss said. "They must vow not to harm humans, no matter the provocation. I don't believe that most of us can do that. And if you are given the blood of gold and you aren't sincere, it will destroy you."

Most of them had already heard this, but there was still a moment of silence in the room. Very few of them had the inclination to stop feeding on humans.

"I have read this *Testament of Michael*," Combs said. "I believe it is a dangerous path that will lead to our extinction. We mustn't give in to the humans or pretend to be like them."

"But what can we do?" Belinda said. "Terrill is beyond our reach. We cannot control him."

"Perhaps we cannot," Combs agreed. "But I have learned that Terrill is not the only new kind of vampire. Just as the Wilderings appeared suddenly, I have learned that they have also produced another kind of vampire. Evolution has worked in the opposite direction as well. These vampires, whom I call Shadow Vampires, are equal in strength and power to the

Golden Vampires, but are more savage yet—creatures of the darkness who will protect all of us, who will look after our interests."

Even Fitzsimmons seemed surprised. "I have not heard of these Shadow Vampires. How do you know they exist?"

"Because I am one of them," Combs said.

He had been standing, his head barely reaching the top of the chair behind him. Now, it was as if he grew—though it was not his body that grew, but his shadow. His body faded into the blackness. Even in the darkness, the other vampires could see his shadow lengthening and growing, and the councilors on either side of him scrambled out of the way. Combs's voice began to change, as if it was coming from deep inside a well, cold and distant, yet loud and clear.

"Vampires will have to choose—there will be no middle ground. You must choose the darkness, the everlasting eclipse, the void that dispels the light, or become useless, creatures at the mercy of the humans—so-called Golden Vampires. All vampires will have to take a side and take the test, and those who fail or chose wrongly will be destroyed.

"But those who join the Shadow will own this world, and between us we will bring down the eternal darkness. Those who oppose us will die, and those beneath us will be our food. The day is coming when you must choose."

Hoss looked around the table. Most of those present were caught up in the words of the Shadow Vampire. Only a few seemed troubled and were trying to hide their reactions. But Fitzsimmons—he was nearly levitating in his excitement.

"I don't need to wait," he cried. "I will join you now!"

The shadow lifted off the floor and floated over the table. Most of the councilors scrambled back, as if afraid to be touched by the void. But Fitzsimmons stood waiting with shining eyes.

The black mantle settled over him, and there was the familiar sound of blood being sucked, and Fitzsimmons cried out. The muscles in his body contracted, and he fell forward onto the table and started shaking. He flopped over on his back, then tensed one last time and grew still.

When he arose again, it was if he was part of the same shadow as Combs, and his voice had the same coldness. "The Council of Vampires is now dismissed. You are no longer of any use to us. Soon you will be given a choice: you will join us or be destroyed. You may try to hide, but we will find you eventually."

Hoss saw Combs behind Fitzsimmons. It was as if the president of the Council was his puppet and Combs was speaking through him.

"We are going to America," he said, and the sound echoed as if they were in a vast cavern. "Terrill and his abominations must be destroyed."

Fitzsimmons turned to Hoss. "You are going with us, Hoss. You will be our guide. Soon you will be allowed to join us—or you will be discarded, like the rest of this soon-to-be-extinct species.

"Everyone is going to have to make a choice."

CHAPTER 20

Terrill first noticed the young man at the back of the audience. He was chubby and quiet, with a scraggly goatee and mustache, and long hair tied back in a ponytail. He seemed to be both listening and not listening, as though he wanted to be present and yet run away.

Every night, Terrill had one of his "discussions"— he refused to call them sermons. He didn't think much about the young vampire at first, but when he began to move closer and closer to the front as the days passed, the look on his face became more and more intent, until Terrill found himself speaking directly to this one listener, as if he represented everyone Terrill was trying to reach.

"All vampires will soon have to make a choice," Terrill said. "To stop preying on humans, or to forever become creatures of the night, hunted and scorned. They must choose the light or remain in the dark."

"But why is it wrong?" the young man asked. Everyone grew quiet, and by that reaction, Terrill realized that others had watched the ponytailed vampire's progression the same way he had. It was the first time he'd spoken since he'd joined them.

"It is a simple concept: to kill is evil. All vampires kill. Therefore all vampires are evil."

"Are there no exceptions? What about killing in self-defense?"

"To kill is evil," Terrill repeated.

The young vampire shook his head. "We aren't human. So why is it evil to kill them? Why is it any more evil than it is for humans to hunt and kill deer, for instance?"

"As *The Testament of Michael* says, we were born of humans, and therefore we are part of them." Terrill almost hated himself for quoting the Testament, but it often said things better than he could, and it seemed to add authority to his words. "We must learn to live amongst humans or we will be destroyed."

"Why?" It was a blunt question, and one that none of the others had asked—at least, not so directly.

"Humans become ever more numerous, their weaponry ever more effective," Terrill explained. "Their information and communication systems are nearly instantaneous. We have fewer and fewer places to hide."

"But hasn't it always been so? Surely we can adapt, just as we have always adapted. You yourself formulated the Rules of Vampire, which have helped keep us hidden."

"We are hidden no more."

"Oh? Most humans *still* think we are a myth. My own parents—I tried to show them how I had changed, and they wanted to take me to the doctor to see if I had a blood disease! I bet if we laid low, they'd forget all about us again."

"The Wilderings have eliminated that options," Terrill said. "There are constant outbreaks, all over the country."

"So we eliminate the Wilderings. We impose the Rules of Vampire so that no more are created. Each vampire becomes responsible for those they Turn, and suffers the same fate."

"Come here," Terrill commanded.

The young vampire approached with his head down, as if embarrassed to be the center of attention. The crowd parted silently. There were usually about fifty or so followers at any one time, nowadays. About one in five would ask to partake of the golden blood. The others drifted away, still in doubt or outright rejecting his message. Many came to him and pleaded that they were too weak, that they could not stop hunting humans.

About one in five of those who asked to take the Blood of Gold passed the preliminary tests and were actually accepted. So far, all had survived. There were now about thirty Golden Vampires in existence. At this rate, Terrill thought, it would only take a few more thousand years to convert them all.

"You're not in trouble," Terrill reassured the ponytailed vampire. "Sit in front of me. You're the first vampire to really challenge what I've been saying. For that, I thank you. What's your name?"

"Matt Conroy."

"Continue your questions, Matt."

"I'm sorry, Terrill, but I don't understand why we have to change. You're asking too much. We are vampire; it is our nature to kill, to drink the blood and eat the flesh of humans."

"We are also thinking, reasoning beings. We choose our own fate, control our own actions."

"Do we?"

Again with the blunt question—so much more effective than the roundabout philosophy that most of his followers spouted. *This young man got over his shyness quickly*, Terrill thought. "We are given the ability to choose. Our actions are our own."

"Are they?" Matt asked. "If so, why were we given this nature to begin with? Why don't vampires get our sustenance from tomatoes, if we weren't meant to kill? Why is it evil?"

"Because it's wrong!" Terrill shouted, unable to control his exasperation.

"It's evil because it's wrong? It's wrong because it's evil?" the young vampire asked, rolling his eyes. "But why? Who says?"

One of the other disciples spoke up. "*The Testament of Michael* says that God has forgiven us. He had given us the choice to turn away from evil."

"Ah, yes...God. But why should we believe God exists?" Matt asked.

"You're not asking for much, are you?" Terrill said. This question touched on his own doubts. Most of the time, he, too, had a hard time believing that there was a God in heaven. If so, why had He created them this way? And yet, Terrill could not deny how much he had changed. When he had turned away from killing, everything around him had changed as well.

In the end, Terrill had decided it didn't matter what he believed. He didn't need to know whether this choice came from God or from some other source. With or without God, the blood of gold *did* exist, and vampires had been given the choice to turn away from killing.

"Have you touched a cross, Matt?" he asked. "Have you tried to enter a church? Have you been sprinkled with holy water? If God doesn't exist, then why would these things hurt us?"

"But wouldn't that mean that we belong to the Devil?" Matt asked. "Shouldn't we be worshipping him instead? Asking for *his* help?"

There was an angry murmuring in the crowd. Terrill raised his hand. He began to unbutton his shirt, and the crowd fell silent. He exposed the scars left by the cross that had been fused to his body. "I renounced killing, and by some miracle was made human again. When Michael turned me back to vampire, he gave me the blood of gold. I don't know why, Matt. I can't tell you why I was chosen except to say this: I believe it is evil to kill another sentient being. To do so is wrong. That's all."

Matt looked frustrated, but he didn't question Terrill any further that day.

After that, Matt rarely left Terrill's side. They discussed the hard things, the things no one else wanted to talk about. Terrill let Matt see his doubts, and in some ways the student became the teacher. Then, one day, Matt announced that he wanted to take the Sacrament of the Blood of Gold.

"Are you sure?" Terrill asked. "You still seem so full of questions."

"As do you, Terrill. And yet…"

"But you must look in your heart, Matt. You must be certain."

"I am. I am convinced you are right. The killing must stop."

Terrill examined his disciple's resolute face. He sighed. "Very well, but you must undergo the tests that Jamie and Sylvie have created. If you pass those tests, we will proceed."

A week later, Jamie came to him. "Matt passed all the tests," she said.

Terrill saw the look of doubt on her face. "But…?"

"He's so scary-smart that he might just have supplied us the answers we were looking for. I don't think he's ready."

"I don't see how we can refuse him."

Terrill still insisted on bestowing the Sacrament of the Blood of Gold on the converts, even though any of the Golden Vampires could have done it. The time was coming when he would send his disciples out into the world to teach his words and to find converts. But until then, he was responsible for every success and every failure.

There were three converts that day. The first two took the sacrament reverently, with no difficulty. "The blood of gold shall transform you, absolve you, make you one with God. Partake of my blood and thou shalt be redeemed, reborn in God's grace," Terrill assured them.

Matt waited on his knees. He looked up at Terrill, and there was no doubt in his eyes.

"This is my blood," Terrill intoned. "Accept it and be one with me."

The blood dripped down into Matt's mouth. He sat back on his haunches and swallowed. Everyone was watching, as if all of them understood that a true test was being administered.

"Oh, no," Matt muttered. "I thought I was ready." He convulsed, falling on his back, and his body began shaking.

"Damn it!" Terrill cried. He knelt at Matt's side, holding back tears. *Please, God, help this vampire become one of us,* Terrill thought. He couldn't remember ever praying before. *This young man truly wants to be part of your grace. Please, God, accept him into your arms.*

Matt arched his back, then slammed into the ground again.

"Forgive me!" Terrill exclaimed. "I should have known."

Matt shook one last time and was still. He turned his head toward Terrill. "I wanted to believe."

Then he was gone.

Terrill wouldn't leave the trailer. The crowds grew larger, if anything, in his absence, but he wouldn't show his face. Others began preaching from *The Testament of Michael* in his stead, and they preached with greater fervor, drawing in even more supplicants. The list for the Sacrament of the Blood of Gold grew ever longer.

"You must do it," Sylvie pleaded. "Everyone is waiting."

"No," Terrill answered in a dead voice. "Matt was right. Vampires aren't ready. I have no right to ask it of them. Who am I to preach anything? Every day, I feel the desire to kill."

"You aren't the one asking," Jamie said. "You are but a conduit. It isn't your job to question."

"No," Terrill said. "I won't do it anymore." He rolled over in his cot and pulled the blankets over his head.

"If you won't do it, I will," Jamie said.

"Go ahead," Terrill answered. "I won't stop you."

From that day forward, the number of Golden Vampires increased by leaps and bounds. Once it was accepted that Jamie could give of the blood, others started to take it upon themselves to perform the sacrament. The failures began to multiply, but everyone understood it was part of the risk. It was starting to be whispered that even the failures were accepted into heaven.

"This is Terrill's blood," the new ministers would say. "Accept it and be one with him."

When some of the converts began to leave, Jamie and Sylvie didn't stop them. It felt as though everything was out of their hands, as if God was taking a hand in things. God had spoken, even if Terrill no longer wanted to listen.

"Terrill, I have returned."

Terrill dimly recognized the voice through his fog. He turned over and lifted the blanket. It was Marc, the damn vampire responsible for *The Testament of Michael*. It was his fault all this was happening. It was all because of that stupid book.

"What do you want?"

"Clarkson is dead," Marc said.

Terrill sat up inadvertently. His mind struggled to create meaning out of Marc's words. "Clarkson? What do you mean?"

Marc began to tell the story, and by the end, Terrill was completely awake.

"What do these Shadow Vampires look like?" he asked.

"They are the opposite of light, Terrill. They reek of the pit."

"How did you escape?"

"I hid in the light. They couldn't see me." Marc explained how he had stayed still and quiet until the sun was directly overhead. Only then had he moved. The Shadow Vampires had disappeared, along with Clarkson's body. He wasn't sure, but he thought that Simone and Rod had escaped.

Terrill closed his eyes. He remembered the hordes of Wilderings, killing indiscriminately, overwhelming the little town of Crescent City. Now he had a vision of Shadow, with vampires who could walk in the daytime and were as powerful as Golden Vampires, but evil.

Matt had asked if vampires belonged to the Devil. It had been a good question, one for which Terrill hadn't had a good answer. Now it appeared that at least some of the vampires did indeed belong to the legions of the damned. It was suddenly clear to Terrill what he must do. The Golden Vampires had been created to fight those of the Darkness.

All other vampires were going to have to choose sides.

He walked out of the trailer and stopped, astounded at the sight of the crowds filling the meadows around the camp. Cars lined the narrow dirt road as far as he could see. He heard cries of "Terrill!" and "It's him!" Sylvie and Jamie rushed up to him, along with some of the other early followers.

Apparently, by disappearing, Terrill had only added to his mystique. *Good*, he thought. *It will add weight to my commands.* "Give everyone who asks for it the Sacrament of the Golden Blood," he said.

Jamie spoke up immediately, opposing him. "That isn't a good idea." Robert was standing with his arms around Jamie, and he nodded in agreement.

But Terrill was convinced he was right. "Everyone will have to make a choice," he said.

"Are you sure, Terrill?" Sylvie asked. She reached out her hand and rested it on his arm. "Is this really what you want?"

"We're going to Crescent City," Terrill said. "If God wants us to confront evil, then that's what we're going to do. It's time for the vampires to choose, once and for all. They must become part of the Golden Light or join the Dark of Shadow."

Behind him, he saw Marc scribbling, and Terrill knew that *The Testament of Michael* was about to get another codicil. For the first time, Terrill felt like the prophet that everyone else thought he was. Before it was over, he suspected, Marc was going to be adding a whole bunch of new codicils.

CHAPTER 21

Patty and Kate holed up in the hilltop house for another few days, feeding off the three young men until they were nothing but bones. Finally, hunger overcame them and they ventured into town. Patty was dressed in clothing that she'd found in Kate's mother's closet. It was conservative, but Patty was feeling conservative these days. She never wanted to feel sexy again.

Kate was only a senior in high school, but in many ways, she was considerably more worldly than Patty. Her clothing was skimpy, revealing—it wasn't the kind of clothing that Patty would have ever been allowed to wear, or would have wanted to wear, for that matter.

Kate was the bait when they went hunting.

It was easy enough to lure men into the darkness behind the bars and taverns—but once there, Kate couldn't bring herself to let Patty kill them.

"They're just horny," Kate said. "It isn't their fault."

"Who cares whose fault it is?" Patty objected. "We need to eat, and eat soon, or we'll be too weak to do anything about it."

They robbed the men of their money but not their lives, and used that money to buy raw meat at the supermarket. That would have been sufficient, if not very satisfying, except that it soon became clear that in Crescent City these days, anyone buying raw meat was under suspicion. Going to the same supermarkets night after night was even more suspicious. Store-bought meat wasn't going to do the trick for long.

They more or less stumbled upon a solution to their problem

on the fourth night. Kate was getting weaker and weaker from lack of flesh, and Patty had already determined to kill soon, whether or not the younger girl objected. After letting young men buy both of them drinks all night—which, strangely, had no effect on them—Kate started feeling faint.

Patty led her outside. There was a picnic table in the alley and a dim light over the door. Kate lay down on top of the table.

"I'll be all right in a moment," she said, slurring her words.

"Stay here," Patty said. "I left my purse inside. I still have enough money to buy some meat. We'll try that little market near your house."

She went inside and searched the area of the bar where they'd been sitting. None of the men bothered her. Without Kate, she was invisible. Kate was always the one who attracted them, and they treated Patty like she was the unwanted third wheel. For some reason, Patty didn't mind. She didn't have the slightest attraction to these callow boys.

The bartender watched her searching for a while, then reached under the counter and proffered the purse with a questioning look. She smiled at him gratefully, took the purse and checked inside. The money was still there.

Maybe Kate is right, she thought. *Maybe all men aren't bastards*

It was probably the last time she would ever have such a generous thought. She walked out into the alley and stopped cold. There was a young man on top of Kate, his pants around his ankles, while two others cheered him on.

She dispatched the onlookers without a thought. A sharp claw penetrated the first one's back, puncturing his heart. She tore out the second one's throat, and he gurgled, spouted blood and fell over on top of his friend.

The guy on top of Kate was so engrossed in his act that he didn't even notice what had happened to his two friends. Now that it was quiet, Patty could hear his grunts.

She walked up to him, stopping where he would see her when he opened his eyes. "Having fun?" she said.

The man froze. He looked up at her, his face white. "She wanted it," he said. "She asked for it. She was des-" He coughed, and blood came out of his mouth instead of words.

Kate had her fangs fastened onto his throat. There was a loud snap as she bit into his neck. She sat up and pushed the body away. The young man's corpse flopped off the table, bounced off the bench and landed on top of his two friends.

"In a way, he was right," Kate said. "I *was* asking for it. I wanted to see what he'd do if I acted helpless."

"I thought they were 'just horny,'" Patty said scathingly.

"Horny is one thing," Kate said. "But you at least have to ask a girl nicely first. Buy her a drink or something."

Patty snorted. "If you say that makes it all OK, I'll believe you. Personally, I find these guys disgusting." She reached into the first corpse's jeans pockets, then the second one's, where she found some car keys. She pressed the button and heard a pickup beep on the edge of the parking lot.

"Stay here," she said. "I'll drive the truck as close as I can."

They loaded the bodies into the back of the pickup and made it back to the house just as dawn was breaking.

After feeding, they decided to take turns having a shower. Patty went first, washing away the blood that seemed to cover every inch of her body. She came out and grabbed a towel. Kate was sitting on the edge of the tub.

Patty was startled. She didn't think anyone could sneak up on her unnoticed anymore. But then, she'd never had a vampire do so before.

"I didn't hear you come in," she said. For some reason, she was conscious of her nudity. She knew she had a nice body, when she wasn't covering it up in frumpy clothing. Her face was pretty plain, especially without makeup, but when she was relaxed, she had a soft beauty.

Kate was still covered with blood. She stood up and took off her clothes. They landed on the tile floor with a wet splat. She was petite, with tiny breasts and a narrow waist. Patty tried not to stare.

"I can never get the blood off my lower back," Kate said as she stepped into the shower. "You mind helping me?"

Patty hesitated. It was getting harder and harder to conceal her interest in the younger girl. Standing next to her in a hot shower, rubbing her hands all over her body, it would be impossible to hide her desire.

As it turned out, Kate didn't want her to hide it. As soon as Patty touched her, she moaned, turned around and put her arms around Patty's neck. Patty made love that night for the first time in her life.

"I still like boys," Kate said as they lay in bed afterward. "Horny boys."

"You can have them," Patty said sleepily.

For the next two nights, the same thing happened. Kate would act helpless and appear to pass out someplace where men could find her. She'd suddenly recover if they acted helpful, which happened a few times.

But just as often, the man—or one of the men, if it was a group—would look furtively about, then start to unbutton her blouse. Sometimes they stopped there, and then Patty let them live, because she knew that they fell—just barely—under the strange, seemingly arbitrary "only horny" standard Kate professed to follow.

But if they dared try to go farther, Patty would kill them, usually by breaking their necks so as not to lose any blood.

Then the girls would load them into the back of the pickup and drive them back to the house. They'd feed, then hurry into the shower and then to bed.

Patty felt alive for the first time in her life. *Now that I'm technically dead,* she thought, *I feel alive.* She laughed at the irony.

After several days, the house was really beginning to stink.

"We either have to bury the remains or leave," Kate said, wrinkling her little button nose.

"Easier to leave," Patty said. "Unless you want to stay. I mean, it's your home, right?"

"I don't have any fond memories here," Kate said. "I loved my parents; they didn't deserve to die, but they were cold and pushy and pretty self-absorbed. I spent my childhood at private schools, because they didn't want me around. My brother… well, you met my brother."

Patty was sitting on the couch with Kate lying against her. She felt so content. At that moment, she had an image of Simone's no-nonsense expression and Laura's typical perplexed look. She stiffened.

"What's wrong?" Kate asked, sitting up.

"I forgot," Patty muttered. "How could I have forgotten?"

"What did you forget?"

"I haven't told you anything about myself," Patty said. "I wasn't just an ordinary girl when I got Turned."

"I noticed that," Kate said, laughing.

"I don't mean *that*," Patty said. Then she began to tell Kate about how she had spent the last ten years of her life.

Kate stared at her when she was finished, her face white. Then she draped herself in Patty's arms, seeming to want to get as close as possible, to touch every inch of her. "I'm so sorry that happened to you, Patty. Why didn't you tell me?"

Patty shook her head. "I really did forget, almost. It was as if once I was Turned, nothing that happened before really mattered—and what little mattered, I wanted to forget. Then I met you, and all I wanted to think about was you. But now…I think maybe I should have kept looking for Laura. She was so helpless. And Simone didn't deserve to be left in the lurch like this."

"We'll drive over there tonight," Kate said. "I know exactly what house you're talking about."

"Thank you, Kate," Patty said, feeling relieved that her friend was going to take care of things.

"I'd like to meet Simone," Kate said. "She sounds like a pretty cool person."

Patty felt a moment of wild jealously, which she immediately shook off. She'd seen how Simone and Rod were circling each other. In fact, that was one of the reasons she'd volunteered to go search for Laura, because she figured they needed time alone. Unless she missed her guess, those two had been all over each other the minute she'd left the house.

"Meanwhile, come to bed, dear girl," Kate said softly, as if she could read Patty's mind and see the jealousy there. "I think I understand now why you don't care much for horny boys."

Sergeant Butler got the call late in the afternoon. It was still bright out, or he wouldn't have responded. He'd taken to ignoring any emergencies after dark. Too dangerous. He'd seen how fast the vampires were when they were in their element—and how invisible they became. But he figured he could handle one more call for the day. He was feeling good. He was starting to get rich. He had plenty of "fuck you" money, as long as he was careful. If the department asked too much of him or it got too risky, he could quit.

The call was to a house he'd been called to many times before. Lee Awbrey was always complaining about his neighbors, though more often than not, he was the one at fault. *Routine call, another hour of overtime,* Butler thought.

He almost missed the body lying by the side of the road. It was in a slight ditch and had fallen into shadow. From the size of the body, he guessed it was Awbrey, who was a big, sloppy man.

Butler kept driving until he reached Awbrey's house at the end of the lane. He stopped the car and thought about it.

Turn around and go back? he wondered. *Pretend I didn't see the body by the side of the road?*

There were houses all along the road, and the neighbors had probably seen him pass by. Might be hard to explain that away. He looked up at the faltering light of day. Unfortunately, he'd have to see this through.

Butler pulled his gun as soon as he got out of the cruiser. He started walking toward the body, then changed his mind and went back to the car. He opened the truck and pulled out his crossbow. *This is most likely a vampire incident*, he thought, *way out here in the boonies.*

He loaded the crossbow. He'd bought it on recommendation of the FBI agents who'd been in town until a few days ago. They'd pretty much ignored him, but he'd swallowed his pride and followed them around like a puppy, trying to pick up vampire hunter tips. The knowledge had served him well once he'd started on his own bounty hunting expeditions.

He approached the body carefully. It looked uneaten, which was unusual. Either the victims of vampires were Turned with a bite or they were killed. When they were killed, they were usually consumed.

He was about ten feet away when the body twitched. That's all the warning he had; then the giant vampire was on his feet and charging.

Butler fired when the vampire was only inches away, and the bolt went straight into Awbrey's heart and kept going until it protruded most of the way out of his back, catching only on the last fletching of the arrow.

The vampire was still moving. An arrow to the heart would eventually kill him, but beheading him would be safer. It was getting dark. Butler sighed and trudged back to the cruiser to fetch his axe. By the time he got back to the body, there was another vehicle parked in the driveway.

Two girls were getting out. He nearly called out to them, but at the last moment, something in the way they were moving stopped him. It was getting so that he could recognize vampires from the smallest of indications. *Probably why I'm still alive*, he thought. *Because once night falls, anyone you meet could be a vampire.*

He'd left the crossbow behind when he retrieved the axe. He hesitated. All he had was his sidearm. Would it be enough? Against two vampires?

The girls were talking loudly, as if they didn't have a care in the world. They weren't even looking around. He decided to try to sneak up on them.

"Doesn't look like anyone's home," the smaller, younger-looking of the two said. There was just enough light to see her face, and Butler thought she looked familiar. A cheerleader at the local high school, he decided. He never missed a high school football game.

The other girl was unfamiliar, but she jogged a memory. What was it that vampire who paid rewards had said? "The oldest one, about twenty-six, is tall and skinny, kind of plain, with mousy brown hair."

This girl wasn't quite skinny; in fact, now that he was examining her closely, he could see that she had a nice body, but she fit the description in every other way.

"Can't tell if anyone's home just because the lights aren't on," the taller girl was saying. "Simone was being pretty careful."

They knocked, and after a few moments, they opened the door and went inside.

Butler ran to the side of house and poked his head up until he could see through one of the windows. He could hear them talking.

"Where do you suppose they went?"

"They could be anywhere," the taller girl said. She sounded depressed, which surprised Butler. He'd never really talked to a vampire, or even overheard them much. He'd just assumed they were heartless, soulless killers. It never occurred to him that they would have everyday conversations.

These two girls seemed almost normal. They were also exceedingly nonchalant, considering their situation. Weren't they aware that the region was swarming with vampire hunters, all looking for a bounty?

He remembered what the FBI agents had said about newly turned vampires. "Baby vampires," they were called, and without the guidance of a Maker, these vampires were often naïve and trusting.

The two girls met in the living room after searching the house, and Butler saw them hold hands.

"What do we do now?"

The younger girl hugged her friend. "Don't worry, Patty. We'll find them. I have an idea, actually. When I was first Turned, before my brother and his friends caught me and tied me to the bed, the rumor went around that there was a safe haven for new vampires at an old abandoned motel near the beach. We could go there. We'd at least be safe for the time being."

"Yeah, I don't feel safe here," Patty said. "Something

happened. Something bad."

Butler could barely restrain his excitement. He'd hit the mother lode. For days he'd heard rumors about a local hideaway where all the surviving vampires were supposed to be congregating. He hadn't really believed it, because it was too good to be true.

He knew exactly what motel they were talking about. It surprised him that he hadn't thought of it earlier.

Now the only question was, did he call the authorities and collect on the bounties, or did he call the strange vampire who was willing to pay him for information about three girls?

Why not both? he thought.

As the two vampire girls got in their pickup and drove away, Butler pulled out his phone and started dialing.

Patty and Kate made it to the motel in about five minutes. It looked deserted. They could see a glimmer of light over the coastal mountains. Whether there were any vampires here or not, they needed shelter.

Patty knocked on the door. "If there's anyone there, we'd rather not be standing here when the sun comes out," she called.

The door opened and a grimy hand reached out and pulled her roughly into the room.

CHAPTER 22

"I heard you were dead," the supervisor said. "Or shitcanned, or some such bullshit."

"You can't believe any old shit you hear," Feller said, flashing his badge. This guy had never liked him, he recalled. Salvatore was his name, or something Italian, or maybe Spanish. He had dark good looks, and had been shunted off to the prison system because Feller had graded him low on his tests. Didn't matter. They just needed to get inside long enough to bite someone—maybe this asshole, if he accompanied them.

Salvatore examined the FBI badge, casting one last suspicious look at Kelton's huge bulk. Feller had insisted the big vampire shave his beard, cut his hair and at least try to fit into a suit. Which is what he did—approximate wearing a suit. It looked more like a sack draped over his shoulders. Laura had wanted to go with them too, but Feller couldn't think of a plausible excuse to bring her along. They had left her pouting on the steps of Halliday's trailer.

"I'll send Perkins with you," Salvatore said. "He's worthless enough to be your nursemaid."

"Fine."

"Perkins!" the supervisor shouted.

"I'm right here, sir," said a low voice from behind them.

"Shit, Perkins! I swear, you're always sneaking up on me. That's why I said you're worthless. Didn't mean anything by it."

"Yes, sir," Perkins said, but there was loathing in his face. He was an average-sized man with lots of baby fat. He looked soft.

"Yeah, well. Take Agents Feller and…"

"Kelton."

"Take Agents Feller and Kelton to SHU."

Perkins looked surprised and a little troubled. The Secure Housing Unit was where they held the worst of the worst, the meanest of the mean. Those inmates didn't care how many guards or inmates they injured or killed; they knew it didn't matter, because they weren't getting out anyway, not ever. It drove most of them crazy.

"Sir, they aren't allowed visitors," Perkins said.

"These aren't visitors. These here are the high and mighty FBI."

"Yes, sir."

"Oh, and Perkins. Be careful. The prisoners on the Island haven't killed a guard in days and days, so they're probably feeling deprived."

The SHU was called the Island because it was in the middle of the facility, surrounded by barren ground and its own fences.

Perkins led them away without a word.

"Healthy work environment," Kelton said.

"Real esprit de corps," Feller agreed.

Perkins finally spoke up. "Yeah, well try working here. It fucks with everyone's head, but Salvatore is a special kind of asshole."

There was only one corridor to the entrance of the Island, and it had secure guardhouses on either end. The SHU control room itself was encased in concrete, with such thick windows that a missile couldn't have gotten in. From here, the guards would open one cell at a time, every few days, the hallway led to the showers and then to a small courtyard open to the sky— open, that is, if you considered twenty-foot-high walls covered in razor wire "open."

There were only two guards inside the blockhouse. There wasn't any need for more. Since it was night, everything was in lockdown.

Perkins knocked on the door.

"What do you want, Perkins?" a voice said, crackling over the speaker beside the door.

"We have a couple of FBI agents here," Perkins said into the speaker. "They're here to question a prisoner."

"That isn't allowed."

"That's what I said. Go tell it to Salvatore."

"Salvatore. Shit."

There was a brief buzzing sound and the door opened. The room was small, lined with tiny screens keeping an eye, day and night, on the prisoners' cells, which were bare concrete with no windows. Most of the prisoners appeared to be asleep, except one guy who seemed to be literally bouncing off the walls.

"Isn't he going to hurt himself, doing that?" Feller asked, nodding at the screen.

"God, I really hope so," the guard sitting before the screens said. He was chubby and probably not too tall, though it was hard to tell with him slumped in his chair like he was. The nameplate on his uniform said Carl Winters. "But somehow, he always just seems to bruise himself enough to get a little hospital bedrest. Kind of smart really," Carl concluded in a tone of begrudging admiration.

The other guard, who was apparently in charge, got up and shook hands with Feller and Kelton. He had a rifle in his hand. From this room, he could fire into any of the cells. He was older-looking, with almost completely gray hair. His nameplate said Bill Thomanson. He was probably just a year or two away from retirement. *Sorry about this, old fella,* Feller thought. *You almost made it.*

"Which guard are you wanting to—inappropriately, and as far as I know, against the rules—talk to?" Thomanson asked.

"How many prisoners you got in this block?" Feller countered.

"Two hundred," Thomanson said, looking puzzled by the question. "We're full up. So which one do you want to talk to?"

"All of them," Kelton growled.

"Come again?" Thomanson requested, looking even more confused.

"I want to see all of them in the exercise yard."

"What kind of joke is this?" Thomanson said. He was raising his rifle ever so slowly. Kelton grabbed him by the throat and squeezed, and the shout Thomanson was trying to give was choked off. The rifle clattered to the floor, and there was a loud snap in the small room as Thomanson's spine was broken.

Perkins was trying ineffectively to pull his sidearm, but Feller merely had to turn slightly to sink his fangs into the young guard's neck. He fell to the ground, twitching but still alive.

Then Carl Winters got up. He was taller than Feller had expected. He was also unarmed, and he held his hands out toward the vampires as if to ward them off.

"What are you doing?" he asked incredulously. "Do you know you can't get out of here? I couldn't open these doors even if I wanted to."

"We don't want to get out," Feller said. "We want you to release the prisoners."

"That's impossible," Winters said, his voice quivering. "We can only open one cell at a time."

"What if there is a fire?" Feller asked.

A flicker of doubt crossed the chubby guard's face, and Feller knew his hunch was right. "Show me how to open them right now," he said, trying to sound reasonable, "and I won't kill you."

The guard pointed to a red button at the end of the console. It was surrounded by a cage of wire, which Feller twisted loose.

"You press that button and every alarm in the most secure supermax in the country will go off," Winters warned. "I really don't understand what you think you're accomplishing here, buddy. You're just going to end up in one of those cells, especially if any of these monsters get outside."

Feller nodded and pressed the button. Sure enough, alarms started sounding throughout the complex. Echoes from the far walls competed with the higher notes of the nearby alarms.

The doors to all the cells flew open, and within seconds, the prisoners were pouring out. Kelton had the older guard's keys, and he went to the far end of the room and opened the door. Feller dragged the still-twitching body of Perkins over and tossed him into the corridor. He turned and addressed Winters, who was so frightened he couldn't stand and had flopped back into his chair. "You too."

"What? You said you wouldn't kill me!"

"And I'm not killing you. Now get out there!"

Kelton walked over, picked Winters up as if he was a child and threw him out into the corridor. Then he closed the door again.

Out in the hallway, Perkins was waking up. He stood up, twitching; his arms and legs seemed to have their own controls. Then his red eyes fixed on Winters, and in seconds, he had his fangs in his coworker's neck. He sucked the man dry in what seemed mere moments and dropped his body, then whirled around at the sound of more prey coming toward him.

The first of the inmates turned the corner about then, a huge man, his face and bald head covered in prison tats. A wide grin lit up his beefy face when he saw an unarmed guard running toward him. Only at the last second did he seem to sense the danger, and he turned to run. Perkins leapt on top of him, riding his back, looking like a little kid getting a piggyback ride from his father—except he had his teeth sunk into the prisoner's throat, and blood was painting the walls.

"Now what?" Kelton said.

"Now we wait. We find out who really *is* the worst of the worst."

In the end, of the two hundred prisoners, only about half actually made it to the open yard. The others were shredded and gnawed on, and their remains littered the corridor. About fifty of these casualties hadn't been able to handle the black blood of the Shadow Vampires. Like Perkins, who had burst apart only minutes after passing on the infection, these fifty prisoners must have still had a few redeeming characteristics. It had doomed them.

The one hundred survivors had apparently agreed not to turn on each other. Now they were milling about the open space, uncertain what to do. After a few squawks, Feller figured out the loudspeaker system.

"Jump out of there!" he said, and his voice echoed back at him. "You are Shadow Vampires; you can reach the top of the wall."

The prisoners looked at each other, saw the blood on each other's faces and realized that the voice coming over the loudspeaker was telling the truth. First one of them, then several more, then all of them were trying to leap the twenty-foot walls. They couldn't achieve that height at first, but with a few more tries, some of them started to almost make it...

...only to get hung up on the razor wire and sliced to pieces, screaming. But the others soon figured out that they could crawl over the bodies of the trapped prisoners, and soon the courtyard was empty.

"What are you going to do now?" Salvatore's voice came into the room. "You're trapped there. The prisoners will just be shot even if they manage to get off the Island. You haven't accomplished a thing."

"Go ahead, shoot them," Feller said, assuming Salvatore could hear him. "The prisoners are vampire now; a special kind of vampire. You can't stop them."

"But what about you?"

"You can't stop us either," Feller said. He nodded to Kelton, who took out his cellphone and punched some numbers. There was the sound of a far-off explosion. The lights flickered off and then came back on again, though with less intensity.

"We have backup generators," Salvatore said, sounding triumphant.

"Yes, but not for the floodlights," Feller answered. He motioned to Kelton, and they moved into the cellblock and down to the exercise yard. Where the bodies were piled deepest on the razor wire, the vampires stuck there still alive, they leaped up and then dropped into the darkness on the other side of the wall and disappeared.

The next morning, Feller and Kelton rounded up the survivors. It turned out that black blood called to black blood, and Shadow sought Shadow. In the end, they found only twenty-one of the Pelican Bay Shadow Vampires alive. The prison guards had had night scopes, and since these new vampires hadn't been taught how to hide in the darkness, most of them had been picked off with headshots.

"We just saved the great state of California a whole lot of money," Feller said.

Kelton only grunted, worried that the Master—who was due to arrive any day now—wouldn't be happy with the results.

Still, they did better than the teacher, Miller, who returned with only four Shadow Vampires, and a whole lot better than the banker, Smith, who was a huge disappointment, having been hunted down by a full squad of FBI vampire hunters and gotten himself killed in the first few days.

They went back to Halliday's trailer. Feller and Kelton slept inside and let the new vampires fend for themselves outside. The neighborhood was wiped clean of humans pretty quickly. The Pelican Bay vampires concocted a game among themselves: they delighted on knocking on the door of a house and seeing if they could talk themselves inside. Since most of them had prison pallor, lousy haircuts and neck tattoos, this wasn't easy. Sometimes they used Laura as bait, but that was considered cheating. Most of the time, they failed. The humans lost the game even when they won, for the vampires would force their way in in any case.

"If the Master doesn't arrive soon, we're going to have to move again," Feller said.

Kelton was silent, as usual.

Feller went to sleep on the dining room cushions, while Laura and Kelton took the little bed. In the middle of the day, Feller sat upright and grunted.

"What's wrong?" Kelton asked.

"You don't hear it?" Feller groaned.

"I feel a tickling, I think. What is it?"

"He's coming."

CHAPTER 23

It wasn't until they were on the road to Crescent City that Terrill realized that he and Sylvie were alone—maybe for the first time since they had left Bend. One of the followers had offered the couple his small motor home, and when Terrill had been about to turn him down, Sylvie had gently interrupted and thanked the man. From the gratified look on the follower's face, Terrill knew that Sylvie had, as usual, discerned the ways of the heart better than he.

He and Sylvie made the most of their privacy, hoping that the rocking back and forth of the little motor home wasn't too noticeable. They vampires were parked, caravan style, in a state park outside of La Pine in Central Oregon, preparing the make the final push to Crescent City that night.

Sylvie lay in Terrill's arms late into the day, but he couldn't sleep. They were headed into extreme danger, Terrill and the followers of *The Testament of Michael*, all of whom were vampires.

All but Sylvie.

Vampires weren't easy to kill. You had to behead them, more or less, though a stake left in the heart would kill most of them eventually. Fire and the sun would do it, of course. But these were Golden Vampires, and even those methods weren't enough anymore.

That Clarkson, the most capable vampire outside of himself and Michael that Terrill had ever known, had been defeated by one of these so-called Shadow Vampires meant they were in a real struggle for survival.

In spite of everything, Terrill still had less than thirty Golden Vampires as followers. Twenty-nine of them, to be exact. When he'd laid down his ultimatum, "Accept the blood of gold or else," most of his wannabe disciples had fled into the hills.

One of the recipients of the blood of gold had failed and disintegrated before their eyes. At that point, Robert and Jamie had taken Terrill aside and pleaded with him to stop.

"This isn't right," Robert had said. "You must let them choose when they are ready. To insist is to risk their lives. They want to believe you, Terrill. Some of them want to become one of us so badly, they convince themselves they are ready before they are. "

"We don't have time," Terrill had said. "The Shadow Vampires are coming."

"But if we force vampires to risk their deaths, we are no better than them," Jamie had said imploringly.

Terrill had looked over at Sylvie, who'd looked away. For a moment, he'd had doubts. If Robert Jurgenson and Jamie, the two people he admired more than any others, were against his plan, maybe he was wrong.

But again, he'd seen a vision of a land of Wilderings and darkness, and he'd shaken his head. "It has to be done. Let them run away, if they must."

In the end, only five more Golden Vampires had been added to the rolls. If, as Terrill suspected, the Shadow Vampires were their antithesis, he had to wonder how many converts they had managed to turn. Knowing the human/vampire heart, Terrill wasn't hopeful.

He didn't know how he knew, but he knew that the Shadow Vampires were also the result of long-planned evolution, probably by someone nearly as old as Michael, but without his compassion.

11

Terrill fingered the metal cross fused to his chest. He'd been vampire, then human, and now he was a combination of both. It couldn't be a coincidence that the Shadow Vampires had suddenly appeared when he'd been transformed.

He remembered what he'd said to Matt. "All killing is evil. All vampires kill. Vampires are evil."

Only Golden Vampires didn't kill to eat. Until now, Terrill had hoped to persuade his former brethren, the blue-blooded vampires, to join him. He'd been under no illusions about how long it would take.

But he kept coming back to that basic syllogism: "All killing is evil. All vampires kill. Vampires are evil." *Can vampires be only partly evil?* he wondered. *Can I look the other way any longer?*

With the rise of the Shadow Vampires, he didn't think he could. The Shadow Vampires—and whoever it was that controlled them—weren't going to wait. They were going to seek out other vampires and Turn them to Shadow, or destroy them.

Terrill couldn't see that he had any choice but to follow their example. But he'd give vampires a different choice: renounce evil once and for all, or be damned.

"Can't sleep?" Sylvie spoke against his chest, and he felt the huff of her breath on his skin.

"Here and there," he said.

"What's wrong?" She sat up, pulling her long black hair away from her face. Her breasts emerged from the sheets and he had an impulse to dive into them and continue the day the way they had begun it.

"You can't go with us, Sylvie," he said. He hadn't even realized he'd made the decision until the words were out of his mouth. "It's too dangerous."

She laughed, but uncertainly. "I'm surrounded by Golden

Vampires. How much safer can I be?"

"You don't understand, Sylvie. How can I fight effectively if I'm worried about you all the time?"

"I'll be fine," Sylvie said. "Jamie will take care of me."

"Clarkson died, Sylvie. I would have bet she'd outlast us all. She never took chances; she always knew how to fight. If a Shadow Vampire defeated her, he can defeat anyone."

"But not you," Sylvie said. It was a statement, not a question.

"Perhaps…"

She sat up next to him and patted his leg. "Don't worry. God is on our side, right?"

"Yeah, how many times have I heard that over the centuries, just as some army was about to massacre some other army? Funny thing is, until the battle started, both sides were convinced God was on their side."

"You were chosen by Michael," Sylvie said.

"Oh, what a load of crap!" Terrill cried. "I knew Michael better than anyone, and he was just like the rest of us—except maybe a lot older. Don't be believing all this nonsense Marc is putting out. I don't know where he's getting it. Michael was just a guy. Just another vampire."

"But *you* aren't," Sylvie said. "I saw you turn from vampire to human, and that would not have happened if the good, the light, God, whatever you want to call it, wasn't on your side."

Terrill didn't answer at first. There was a time when he would have accepted this mantle of power. He would have thought it his due. He would have reveled in it. He wouldn't have had any doubts.

Funny thing about that, he thought. *It wasn't until I had doubts that I was given the power.*

"That still doesn't keep you safe," he said finally. "You're too vulnerable. I think we should leave you here in La Pine, book a room in one of motels. I'll come get you when it's over."

"Do you believe I'll be safer here if you lose?" she asked.

Terrill groaned and threw his head back into his pillow. "Shit, shit! Probably not."

Sylvie reached over and ran a soft hand across his cheek. "Poor Golden Vampire," she muttered. She leaned over and kissed him, then ran her hand down his body and grabbed hold of him.

He kissed her back as if was the last time, for he realized that that might indeed be the case. He sensed that she wouldn't stay here, not matter how much he tried to convince her.

This time, they didn't worry about the motor home rocking back and forth, and when the springs began to squeak, they couldn't help but laugh even as they continued to make love.

Darkness was falling when Terrill woke up. Sylvie was leaning over him, staring at his face with a gentle expression. "OK," she said. "I'll do it."

"Do what? You'll stay here?" His heart leapt. If she were safe here in La Pine, it would be so much easier to fight the coming battle.

"I will let you Turn me."

The words didn't penetrate at first. And then the world shifted and clicked into place, and everything was all right. It was the final piece of the puzzle, somehow. *Damn*, he thought. *I'm getting as mystical as Marc.*

"Are you sure?" he asked.

"I'm very sure," she said. A flicker of doubt crossed her face, but her voice didn't reflect it.

"What…what made you change your mind?"

She put her head back on her pillow and stared at the ceiling. "You were right. It was unfair of me to make you worry. I don't want you to make the wrong decision in the heat of battle because of something I've done…"

Her voice trailed off, and Terrill sensed there was more. "And…?"

She sat up and took his hands. "I was being a hypocrite, Terrill. How could I love you and think you're good, and be so certain that you were on the side of right, and yet at the same time think that vampires are unnatural? It was fear. That's all it was. I'm afraid of what I will become."

"Oh, I don't think you have to worry about that!" Terrill said. "You'll become one of us—like me and Jamie. Trust me, you won't have to do anything against your scruples."

She smiled sadly. "I know."

They heard a knock on the door, and then Jamie's voice. "You guys ready to head out?"

"Give us one hour," Terrill shouted.

"Geez," he heard Jamie mutter. "How many times can you do it in one day, already?"

Terrill felt completely energized. *It is all going to work out,* he thought.

"This will be a little different," he said, getting out of bed and throwing his clothes on. "I have to turn you into a vampire first. With this new strain, you'll be…out…for about half an hour."

Sylvie lay in bed, a serene expression on her face. Terrill's fangs came out and he leaned over her, then pulled back. "Uh, this might hurt a little," he warned her.

"You think?"

He leaned down over her neck and watched the veins in her skin. *Have I ever wondered if it hurt?* he thought. *I don't think it ever occurred to me.*

He hesitated, smelling her clean porcelain skin. He was going to lose the human Sylvie forever. But there would be no difference, right? She would still be Sylvie, only stronger, nearly invulnerable. Isn't that what he believed?

It wasn't turning out to be so easy to overcome the centuries when he had believed differently, when he had known he was evil, that all vampires were evil. Beautiful Sylvie—could he bear to turn her into one of them?

The blood of gold gives us the power to choose right over wrong, Terrill thought. It sounded like one of Marc's sayings, but he was certain he had just made it up.

"You're starting to make me nervous," Sylvie said.

"Sorry."

He sank his fangs into the deep red blood and drank, and it was ambrosia. *The taste for red blood is still in me,* he thought. *And this is the blood of the one I love.*

Sylvie jerked once or twice as her human body resisted dying, but she never made a sound, and soon she was lying pale and ghostly in the moonlight that slanted through the windows of the motor home. She had never looked so beautiful. There was a sharp contrast between her black hair and white skin Her brown eyes were growing dim.

Terrill waited by her side as the minutes passed.

He was so absorbed in watching her that he was startled when someone pounded on the metal door. "What's holding you up, Terrill?" Jamie shouted. "We've got to get moving if we're going to get there tonight!"

Had it been an hour already? He looked down at Sylvie, but she hadn't moved. *Strange,* he thought. *She should've revived a long time ago.*

He heard the other cars and motor homes in the caravan starting up, so he crawled up into the driver's seat, and with one last troubled look back, he led the way out of the park and onto the highway.

Terrill's panic grew with every minute, with every mile.

Finally, a few hours later, as they pulled into the outskirts of Grants Pass in Southern Oregon, he couldn't stand it any longer and pulled over to the side of the road.

Jamie parked behind him as he was scrambling out of the driver's seat, and moments later, she swung open the motor home's door and came inside. "The cops aren't going to like this many cars on the side of the road, Terrill," she said. "Do we really want to call attention to ourselves?"

"It's Sylvie!" he cried. She still hadn't moved. Her eyes had the milky look of death.

"What do you mean?" Jamie said, rushing to his side.

"She wanted to be Turned."

Jamie looked down at her little sister with wide eyes. "Oh, Sylvie. Why?" She whirled on Terrill. "Why'd you do this?"

"She asked me to!"

"And you just went ahead, you selfish bastard?" Jamie snapped. "Did you really believe that's what she wanted? I've never seen a human as happily alive as Sylvie. And look what you've done to her!"

"I don't understand why she hasn't Turned," he said, feeling calmer now that another person was screaming the same blame at him that he was feeling himself. *I deserve it,* he thought. *But I've got to fix it.*

"If this was an old-style Turning," Jamie said, also calming down a bit, "we wouldn't be worried. That took days."

"True," he said.

"For all your vaunted powers, Terrill, you weren't the vampire who started creating Wilderings," Jamie said. "I was. Maybe, somehow, you don't have the same strain of vampirism."

"Shit," Terrill said. "Why didn't I think of that?" Still, he started to feel relieved. Then he remembered that only one in a hundred attempted Turnings by old-style vampires had been successful, and he started to panic again.

Jamie grabbed him by the arm. "Have a little faith, Terrill. We can't have come all this way, have gone through so much, just to lose her now."

He nodded, but found he otherwise couldn't move.

"I'll get someone to drive the rig and you sit here with her, OK?" Jamie said kindly.

Again he nodded. He sat down at Sylvie's side and brushed back her hair with his fingers. "I'll wait," he said.

A couple of hours later, Terrill looked up to see that Robert Jurgenson was driving and they were passing into California.

Later, on one of the winding roads of the coastal mountains, he became aware of his surroundings again as red and blue lights flashed through the windows and a loud siren whooped. Jamie was driving now. Somewhere along the way, they must have stopped, and she had taken her lover's place.

Terrill felt stiff, as if he hadn't moved in hours. He had no idea where the time had gone—he just remembered staring at Sylvie's face as if willing her to move.

He heard Jamie swearing as she pulled over for the cop car.

He heard her talking to the officer, and then their voices started to rise in anger.

"I didn't give you permission to search this vehicle!" he heard Jamie shout as the door of the motor home swung open.

The cop was huge, fat as well as tall, and Terrill immediately sized him up as having muscles beneath the fat. This man was used to literally throwing his weight around.

He stood there at the door, staring at Terrill and Sylvie for a moment, then said, "What the ... ?" and started to pull his weapon.

Jamie or Terrill probably would have gotten to the cop before he could draw his gun, but before either of them could act,

Sylvie came flying off the bed with a banshee screech and landed on top of the policeman, who fell backward onto the road. Terrill heard a loud crack as the man's head hit the pavement.

Jamie got to Sylvie first and trapped the wild girl in her arms. Terrill grabbed Sylvie's kicking feet and they hauled her back into the motor home. "We need rope!" Jamie shouted.

Terrill ran to the bench seats, threw off the cushions and started rummaging through the storage space beneath. His hands landed on some plastic rope almost immediately, and they soon had the screaming, spitting new vampire tied to the bed.

"Wow," Jamie said. "Was I like that?"

"Probably," Terrill said. "A little. Vampires have a saying: The deeper the spirit, the stronger the hunger."

"Big surprise," Jamie said, "little sister has a big hunger."

They were both relieved, if a little alarmed. "I'll get the raw meat," Terrill said. "You take care of the cop. If he's all right, try to glamour him. If not, we'll try to find a hospital."

He almost couldn't believe those last words. The old Terrill would have left the policeman by the side of the road and thought nothing of it. Or he would have eaten him.

As they fed Sylvie big chunks of red meat, Robert managed to get the policeman up and seated in his squad car, placating him with some cop talk. The officer was dazed and confused, and appeared to be convinced he'd been in a fender bender of some kind.

They got the caravan moving again.

CHAPTER 24

The small, dapper man Hoss had known as Combs was gone, replaced by a...by a demon. Hoss couldn't think of any other word for it. He was a demon from the pit, made of cold and darkness and pain. The humans had it wrong: hell wasn't filled with fire, it was empty, a void, a black nothingness.

Once transformed in the Master of Shadow, Combs never appeared again in bodily form. He was a void that blotted out anything it touched. Fitzsimmons was his mouthpiece, and Hoss could sense the former president's horror and humiliation at what he was being turned into, but also his savage joy in his new powers.

In a hollow voice, Fitzsimmons had ordered the entire Council to board the private jet that the president usually reserved for himself. No one disobeyed.

Hoss and Jared and some of his allies, the young, tech-savvy vampires who had thought to overthrow the Council, had pressed up against the wall, hoping they wouldn't be noticed. Fitzsimmons had left the room, and Hoss had let out a big sigh of relief. He'd turned to Jared, about to say that they needed to get out of there fast. Blend into the countryside. Be old-style vampires.

"You, too," came an echoing voice from the doorway. All Hoss could see was a dark hallway, but he could sense the malevolent presence behind the darkness. "All of you."

At the airport, other vampires had appeared, as if summoned. The other two jets owned by the Council were also filled:

every seat, every inch of the aisles and every storage unit and compartment, whether pressurized or not. There were dozens of vampires that Hoss had never seen before. All of these new vampires had a mantle of darkness—an outline of shadow, a sucking emptiness.

They sat on the tarmac for an hour, even though by all appearances, they were ready to depart. Hoss looked out the window and saw Peterson approaching the plane, escorted by four large vampires who blended with the darkness outside.

Peterson stumbled into the plane, pushed from behind. He looked old, not just in appearance, but in demeanor. He didn't look at anyone, just straightened his clothing and marched down the aisle to the front of the plane, where he took the last available seat.

The plane taxied for takeoff, and Hoss looked longingly at the bright lights of London. He suspected he might never see them again.

Fitzsimmons and He-Who-Had-Once-Been-Combs were together at the back of the plane, and it was as if the metal frame of the aircraft had disappeared back there and been replaced by a starless night, empty of oxygen, warmth and substance.

Hoss, Jared and the younger vampires huddled together near the center of the plane, silent, trying to be unobtrusive. Jodie sat next to Hoss, and in the seats in front of him were Jimmy and Pete. At the front of the compartment, the other councilors were conferring. At first they seemed frightened, but as they continued to talk among themselves, they seemed to gain courage from each other. These five vampires had been among the most powerful in the world. They'd always been more ruthless, more cunning, more savage than all their brethren.

There was the big Dutch vampire, Belinda Hanson. She may have had a baby-girl voice, but that didn't fool anyone. She was no pushover.

There was Jerome Bacher, the German representative, who came from a district that had long been infested with vampires—yet he had risen to the top.

There was Isaac Hargraves, who looked like a small boy, but was perhaps the most devious of them all, a survivor who used his appearance to seem harmless while he manipulated those bigger and stronger than himself.

And there was Bogdan Kovalev, from Russia, who had survived decades of police state and a kleptocracy, and was richer and more powerful in his homeland than any of them.

Overnight, their power had been stripped away.

Only Peterson stayed out of the debate, merely glancing over at them with dull eyes whenever they asked him something. They spoke in tones so low that even vampires a few seats away couldn't hear them, but no one had to hear anything to realize a conspiracy was being hatched.

Hoss looked nervously over his shoulder at the darkness that enveloped the back of the plane. He could barely make out the form of Fitzsimmons sitting there, facing forward, unmoving. The rest of the darkness was lifeless, implacable.

The argument among the councilors became heated. It appeared that Belinda was insisting on something, while Hargraves was still in doubt. Finally, they fell silent.

Hoss eyed them uneasily. *This isn't the time to challenge the Shadow*, he thought. He could sense the vast power beneath the emptiness. It was the power to nullify anything thrown against it, to take in the assault and make it disappear. Strength didn't matter, speed didn't matter, willpower didn't matter. The Shadow would swallow anything that opposed it.

Belinda stood up and glared at the other councilors, who stood up a little less eagerly. She led the way to the back of the plane. Peterson remained seated, seemingly unaware of or uncaring about the coming confrontation.

Belinda looked at Hoss challengingly as she passed. They'd never gotten along, but her look seemed to suggest she thought they had a mutual enemy. Hoss turned his head away. Outside the windows, it was dark, but it was a warm darkness, a darkness of the Earth, filled with the currents of life. It was as if it glowed, underneath. Behind him, the Shadow gave off no such warmth.

Fitzsimmons stood as they approached. His face was blank and his eyes had turned completely black.

"We insist on a vote of the Council," Belinda said, her voice rising with every syllable. Faced with the vacuum that was the Master, she seemed less sure of herself.

Fitzsimmons turned his head ever so slightly, as if listening to instructions only he could hear. "Vote?"

"We have a quorum." Jerome spoke up, his voice loud, as if the louder he got, the braver he got. "There are eight councilors on this plane."

"What do you wish to vote about?" Fitzsimmons's voice was toneless, neutral, yet threatening.

"The leadership of the Council," Belinda said. "Us being forced to go along on this trip. Everything!"

"I see," Fitzsimmons said. "Everything." He tilted his head. "*Everything* it shall be. Everything you are, everything you ever were, everything you ever will be."

The darkness behind Fitzsimmons enveloped him and he grew dim, as if black smoke obscured him. He didn't move, but the cloud of blackness rose up and over the four dissenting councilors, roiling about the ceiling of the cabin. They looked upward nervously and backed away.

But it was too late. The Shadow dropped over them, and they were covered in a shroud of nothingness. They disappeared into the darkness. Out of the void, out of the emptiness, everyone on the plane could hear horrific screams. Then it was as if the anguished shrieks were being pulled apart, dissipated, scattered. There was a final small cry, and then there was silence.

The councilors popped back into view, one by one. First Belinda. She looked shrunken, lifeless. She turned and walked back to the front of the plane. Then Jerome appeared, stiff and jerky as he followed her. When Kovalev reappeared, he showed no sign of anything wrong—his face was blank, his movements steady—but he seemed somehow devoid of life. Last to reemerge was Hargraves, who didn't look like a ten-year-old boy anymore, but an ancient, wizened old man the size of a child.

Hoss scrunched down in his seat as if that would make him invisible. He felt Jodie's hand digging into his arm, and next to her, Jimmy and Pete's faces were white in shock.

He had caught the look in the eyes of the former councilors—empty, hopeless, the aspect of the eternally damned.

He saw Jared staring at him from across the aisle, his mouth open, his eyes wide. Hoss shook his head emphatically as if to say, *Don't do anything. Don't do anything at all.* Jared nodded, then followed Hoss's example, trying to squeeze his huge frame back down into his seat.

No one said anything for the rest of the long flight. No one moved when they refueled in New York and continued to California. In the awful silence, time seemed to disappear, and it was as if they had spent all eternity inside this small space, with the maw of complete oblivion only a few feet away.

Hoss closed his eyes. In his mind bloomed the red wave of the Wildering horde in the simulations. That was what this was all about, he was certain of it. The Shadow Vampires were here to make that epidemic happen, to make sure that nothing stopped it from happening. The Shadow had arrived to keep the Golden Vampires occupied while the world of men was overwhelmed by the Wildering infection.

Hoss was vampire. He had little sympathy for mankind.

But he didn't want them wiped out.

He blinked awake, surprised that he had nodded off. But he was exhausted. What harm could it do? He closed his eyes again.

Hoss was back in the Twilight wasteland, confronting the Shadow. The void swallowed his thrown spear and laughter surrounded him.

"You cannot defeat darkness with darkness," said a voice from everywhere and nowhere. "You simply add to the darkness; you become one of us."

Underneath his fear and confusion, Hoss was still defiant. He had spent his entire existence alone, triumphant over others of his kind. He had conquered all the vampires of Twilight. His will had overcome all resistance. "I have no wish to join you," he said. "Kill me, if you wish. But I will not become one of you."

"You have always been one of us, but it amuses us let a few individuals maintain the illusion of free will. The Light was defeated long ago. There is only the void, the Shadow that covers everything. You wander in a Twilight that we allow to exist so that we might know the totality of our victory."

Hoss sensed that falseness of that claim. The Shadow would not tolerate independence; it would not allow the suggestion of free will.

"I exist—and all the lands beyond the walls exist—because you cannot snuff out that last resistance," he said. "If you take me into the Shadow, I will still hold a spark of myself, and from the inside, I will destroy you. That is why you allow the Twilight. Because no matter how hard you try to shroud us, you cannot completely obliterate life."

There was a grudging silence. The voice sounded no less certain when it finally spoke. "Perhaps. But in the end, there will be the void and nothing but the void, and even our consciousness will fade, and all will be nothingness."

"Until that time, I defy you!" Hoss shouted.

He woke up as the wheels of the plane landed on the runway in Crescent City. Inside the compartment, nothing had changed. Everyone was still quiet and frozen in fear. But inside of Hoss, something had come alive. *This is not the end,* he thought. *I don't know how I know it, but I know we must resist.*

He looked over at Jared, who must have seen something in his expression, for a look of hope came over his face. Hoss turned to Jodie, Jimmy and Pete. "Do what I do," he said quietly.

The doors of the plane opened. Fitzsimmons stood up and told everyone to disembark. Hoss checked his watch. Even though it was only three o'clock in the afternoon, it was very dark outside. In fact, it reminded Hoss of the Twilight of his dream.

Everyone started to file out. Hoss made sure he lined up next to Jared. "Pass this along to anyone who wants out of here," he told the other vampire. "At my signal, follow me. Whatever you do, don't look back. Just run."

They walked down the steps onto the tarmac of the small airport.

Hoss almost gave up then. There, lined up in a rough order, stood at least two dozen Shadow Vampires, huge, hulking beasts who radiated malevolence. Positioned in front of them was Feller, accompanied by a massive vampire who wore an ill-fitting suit. A girl in a tight, skimpy outfit stood next to the giant.

Feller, the former FBI vampire hunter, recognized Hoss and gave him a mocking grin.

When the plane had completely disgorged its passengers, everyone stopped cold as they sensed the Shadow emerge; it was as if part of the tarmac had suddenly fallen into blackness. Everyone turned toward it. Fitzsimmons emerged out of the Shadow and walked up to Feller.

"You have done well," Fitzsimmons said. "The final battle approaches."

"You speak for Him?" Feller asked, eyeing him.

Fitzsimmons turned and looked into the Shadow. "You may speak to me as if you are speaking to the Master."

"Good," Feller said. "Where do we go from here?"

"The Master was going to ask you the same thing," Fitzsimmons said. "He seeks the Golden Vampires. They are the only vampires he cannot see."

"I know where to go," Kelton said, stepping forward. "I got a call from an informant, a local cop. He told me there is a motel on the beach where the vampires are hiding. That is where Terrill will go, I'll bet you anything."

Fitzsimmons eyed him doubtfully. "If you are wrong, you will have bet everything."

"You shouldn't speak to him that way," said the chubby girl next to the giant.

"Shut up, Laura," Kelton snarled.

Fitzsimmons turned his head and his eyes went completely black. He started to reach out his hand, and Laura backed up nervously.

Then Fitzsimmons's head flew apart into shards of skull and chunks of brain. Black blood splattered over the faces of Kelton and Feller, who jumped back in alarm. Laura screamed.

The sound of the shot followed, and then another rang out as one of the prison vampires stumbled and fell face-first onto the tarmac, a gaping hole where his heart had been.

"Now!" Hoss cried, and ran toward the vegetation on the other side of the tarmac. Shots kept ringing out, one every few seconds, and there were shouts and cries behind Hoss and Jared and about a dozen others who followed them. Pete was among them, but when Hoss looked back, he saw Jodie watching their flight with a small smile. She shook her head slightly. Hoss's heart sank. He'd always known Jodie had a blacker heart than him. Jimmy was standing next to her, looking around wildly as if torn about which direction to go.

Hoss kept running and dove into the heavy coastal vegetation on the edge of the airstrip, followed by his friends. He crawled back and looked over the hedges. No one was chasing them.

"What's going on?" Jared said. "Did you plan this?"

Hoss laughed involuntarily. "Hell, no. I was hoping for some distraction or other, but I had no idea this was going to happen. Listen, I don't know about the rest of you, but I don't much feel like giving up my free will to those black-blooded monsters."

"We're with you, Hoss," Jared said fervently. The others cried out in agreement. "Fuck that!" one of the IT guys shouted. "Hell, yeah," the lone female techie said. "Get us out of here, man," Pete said.

Hoss nodded, relieved. "We've got to try to warn the vampires at the motel, try to get there first. Maybe some of them can get away. I'm telling you, this is all over our heads. Golden Vampires. Shadow Vampires. What the hell? I want no part of it."

"But what if the Golden Vampires are at the motel?" Jared asked.

"Let's hope they aren't," Hoss said. "But I doubt the Golden Vampires will hurt us."

"Hey, Hoss?" Pete asked. "What about Jimmy?" Hoss noticed he didn't ask about Jodie, who he'd always thought was a little sketchy.

Hoss stared at the small figures on the tarmac. A battle seemed to be taking place. Some of the vampires were rushing toward the air traffic control tower. Shots were still ringing out, and there were at least a dozen bodies lying motionless on the ground. But there were dozens more vampires milling around, and behind them all, there was a still blackness, a void, as if part of the airport had vanished, or had become part of the night sky.

"Jimmy made his choice," Hoss said. "We can't help him—or Jodie—now."

He started running toward the line of houses on the other side of the vegetation, and the others followed.

CHAPTER 25

Special Agents Callendar and Jeffers were picking up their sniper rifles at baggage claim when they saw the first of the medium-sized private jets land, quickly followed by two others. That caught their attention, because those kinds of jets rarely landed at little Crescent City—in fact, they pushed the limits of what the airport could accommodate.

But when they saw the passengers emerge, that *really* caught their attention. Twenty years of vampire hunting had given them certain instincts. They ramrodded the reluctant security guard into letting them take the rifles—which the young man seemed completely uncertain about—and, grabbing the cases and leaving their suitcases behind in the terminal, they ascended into the air traffic control tower.

The lone air traffic controller seemed startled to see them, but deferred to their FBI badges.

"Shut it down," Jeffers ordered briskly. "Shut down the airport."

"But…"

"Do as he says!" Callendar shouted. He was searching for the door to the small platform outside the tower. He shoved it open and the coastal wind, ever-present and always colder than he expected, hit him in the face.

All that sniper training they had just undergone was going to be very useful, he thought.

He swept away the cigarette butts that covered the platform—obviously, its main purpose was so smokers could evade the anti-smoking laws. He opened the sniper case and quickly assembled the brand-new weapon. He'd just had a week of training with it, and he felt confident. It was as scoped in as any weapon he'd ever had.

Beside him, Jeffers was doing the same thing. Neither of them spoke. Both had seen how many vampires there were. Both of them knew what was likely to happen.

But it didn't stop them.

From D.C. they had been sent to Hawaii for a quick refresher course in sniper shooting. The world might be ending from a vampire infestation, but department regulations were department regulations, and they were forced to take the detour to get up to speed. They'd been in Hawaii for only a few days when they got the call from Sergeant Butler.

Butler is an idiot, Callendar thought after the caller identified himself. *But he does seem to have a nose for vampires.*

"Ahhh…" Butler stuttered. He was a little starstruck by the FBI guys. "Um…you told me to call you if I ever got wind of the vampire nest that was rumored to be around here. Well, I think I found it."

The agents were sitting on beach chairs in the hot sand just outside their rented cabin. It was on a part of the island without tourists, and for the first time in years, Callendar wasn't on guard every second. He looked over at Jeffers, saw the old wounds on his chest and shoulders, and knew they should stay, let the sun tan away those white strips of scar tissue, let the sunlight fill their darkened souls.

Callendar almost threw the phone into the ocean. "Whoops, must have lost my phone," he'd say when his bosses asked why he hadn't pursue the lead.

He'd put the phone on speaker, and Jeffers was shaking his head, running his hand across his throat in a gesture of negation.

"Tell me," Callendar sighed.

"Well, there's an old boarded-up motel down by the beach. I overheard two vampires talking about it. Frankly, I'm a little surprised I didn't think of it myself. It's perfect."

Callendar remembered driving by the motel dozens of times. *Why didn't I think of that?* he wondered.

Jeffers sighed and leaned toward the phone. "Have you checked it out?" he asked.

"Not yet," Butler admitted.

"Then don't. We're on our way."

Callendar hung up. "What the hell? I thought you wanted this vacation."

"Hey, we still got our sniper rifles. Let's give them a little workout."

They were waiting to take off from the airport in Hawaii when they heard about the prison breakout at the Pelican Bay supermax. The media was speculating that it had been orchestrated by anyone from white supremacists to al-Qaeda, but the minute they heard, the two FBI vampire hunters knew exactly who was responsible. Jumping twenty-foot walls lined with razor wire? Even for vampires, that was quite a feat.

Strange how vampires keep popping up lately, Callendar thought. In the first twenty years of his career, he'd tracked down exactly five vampires. Three of them had been baby vamps, easy to kill; the other two had taken years to track down and destroy.

Now, all of a sudden, vampires seemed to be everywhere.

Little did we know, Callendar thought as he ratcheted the last piece onto the stock of the rifle.

"How much ammunition you got?" he asked.

"Half a box," Jeffers answered. "We can make a dent."

"Yeah," Callendar said. It wouldn't be enough, but it *would* make a dent.

He saw Jeffers remove one bullet from the box and put it in his pocket. He looked over casually at Callendar, who hesitated and then followed his example.

"You got a target?" Callendar asked. He was giving permission for Jeffers to shoot first. Jeffers was a slightly better shot, not by much, but enough to give him right of way.

"Yeah, I'm thinking that officious-looking bastard walking toward us."

"Go for it," Callendar said, taking a deep breath and setting his own sights on the biggest vampire he could find in the crowd.

Jeffers's shot took the head off the first vampire, and Callendar quickly drilled his own target. Then they were both steadily firing, and reloading and firing again.

Calendar worked his way through the box of ammo. Some of the vampires were running for the far side of the airport, and he almost fired at them, then decided that he'd rather kill the vampires who were running *toward* him.

There were a lot of them.

He was down to his last few bullets when he spotted something that didn't look quite right. But he couldn't figure out exactly what it was he was seeing—or not seeing.

"Do you see what I see?" he said.

"I don't know," Jeffers grunted. "What do you see?"

"I see…Hell, that's just it. I see nothing. That is, I see what looks like nothingness. Shit, I can't explain it."

"Then yeah," Jeffers said. "Now that you explain it, I see what you don't see. Or don't see what you don't see."

Callendar heard a click from Jeffers's rifle. "Sorry," his best friend said, shrugging. "Just hoped I was wrong and there was one left in the chamber." His best friend. That's how they had always presented themselves to the world. Not that it had fooled anyone.

Callendar aimed into the twenty or so vampires who had nearly reached the tower, but the angle was bad and he missed. "Shit," he muttered. "I hate my last shot to be a miss."

He pulled out his sidearm and squeezed off six shots, killing four of the assailants. Beside him, Jeffers was doing the same thing. He hit five. There were still dozens coming their way. They heard the sound of footsteps on the stairwell.

"You bring a throwaway?" Callendar asked.

Jeffers shook his head.

"Me neither. Didn't think I'd need it."

They were quiet for a moment, and then looked into each other's eyes. "I don't know about you, partner, but I don't want to become one of those things," Callendar said softly.

"Me neither." Jeffers dug into his pocket, pulled out his single remaining bullet and loaded his rifle. He angled the barrel toward Callendar, who followed his example.

They heard the scream of the unfortunate air traffic controller, and once again, Jeffers looked into Callendar's eyes.

"You know...I always...I, ahh..."

"Yeah," Callendar said. "Me too..

As the door burst opened, they both lifted their rifles and fired.

CHAPTER 26

"Was I a real bitch?" Sylvie asked.

Terrill was sitting at the small dining table in the middle of the motor home. Robert was driving again, and they were only a few minutes from Crescent City. Sylvie had been growling and hissing for so long, Terrill had tuned her out, so her words caught him by surprise.

He got up and sat next to her on the bed. "No worse than usual," he said.

"So usually I'm bitch," she groaned. "I just knew it! Why do you put up with me?"

"Sylvie, you are the nicest, kindest person I've ever known. I keep waiting for the dark side to emerge, but it never does."

"But I'm not a 'person' anymore, am I? According to your little saying, I must be evil, because I'm vampire."

"You haven't killed anyone," he said. "It is the actions you take that make you what you are."

She stared at him until he met her eyes. "You should remember that, Terrill. I haven't said it, but I agree with Jamie and Robert. You're wrong to force vampires to accept the blood of gold."

Terrill felt himself rejecting her words. *Have I ever rejected anything she said?* he wondered. *Have I ever not believed she was right?* He shook his head. "We have no choice," he said. "The Shadow is coming, and it won't be so patient. We can't let it turn all vampires to the darkness. We have to force them to join us instead."

"'It is the actions you take that make you what you are,'" she said, quoting his own words back to him. "You must give them a choice, Terrill. None of us are all evil, not even vampires. But neither are any of us all good."

Terrill realized he was blocking out her words. He changed the subject. "You hungry?"

"I seem to remember wanting to eat a policeman," she said. "Did that really happen?"

"Fortunately, we caught you before you ripped out his throat."

He went the small refrigerator. It had quit working a few hundred miles back, but they had stopped and filled it with ice. It didn't really matter, though—a baby vampire would eat any meat, rotten or fresh.

It disturbed Terrill a little when he saw how savagely Sylvie tore into the raw flesh. *I did this to her*, he thought. *But I can also fix it.*

From the driver's seat, Robert turned his head and called into the back, "We're almost there, Terrill! You better do whatever you're going to do."

Terrill felt a flash of alarm and turned to business. "Are you ready for the blood of gold?" he asked.

"Well, if you think you're going to leave me like this, you've got another think coming!" Sylvie said. She pulled against her restraints. "I think you can untie me now. I won't eat any unwary humans we come across, I swear."

She had blood smeared about her mouth and chin. Terrill got up, wetted a towel and tenderly washed the red stain away. Then he untied her.

"We'll skip all the mumbo jumbo," he said. "It's the blood that matters, whatever Marc might say. I'll simply feed you some of my blood and you'll transform."

Sylvie nodded. There was no doubt in her face.

Why should there be doubt? Terrill wondered. *There was never any doubt.*

But he hesitated. Was it possible—was there something in Sylvie that would reject the blood of gold? He hadn't doubted Matt either, but something deep inside the young vampire had still rejected the sacrament. Then, as quickly as the niggling doubt had arisen, it was banished. Terrill smiled and bit into his forearm. He leaned over Sylvie and dripped the golden droplets, one by one, into her open mouth. She smiled at him and swallowed.

Just like that, it was done. Sylvie would be his for eternity. *Assuming we survive the day,* he thought with a grimace.

She sighed and settled back into the bed.

At first the tremors were slight. Terrill tried to ignore them. But as they became more and more intense, Sylvie's arms and legs started to thrash, and he lay on top of her, trying to keep her quiet.

All part of the process, he thought. Every transition was different. Some vampires simply shifted; some went through a struggle before finally transforming. Sure, he'd expected her transition to be easy, but young though she was, Sylvie was a complex person, with depths he had only begun to delve into. But he'd known that in the deepest part of her, she was still good and sweet and loving.

She howled at the top of her voice.

He heard Robert mutter, "What the...?" and the motor home slowed down as he took his foot off the gas pedal. "I'm pulling over!" he shouted.

Sylvie continued to scream, her vampire voice louder than any human's, piercing and otherworldly. She was shaking so hard she seemed to be levitating.

"No," Terrill said. It came out flat, because he still didn't believe what he was seeing. But in the pit of his stomach, panic was blooming, working its way up his body, and the second time he spoke, it was with all the denial in his soul. "No! It can't be! I won't accept it!"

He pried open Sylvie's mouth as if he could scoop out the golden blood, and she gnawed into his fingers and more of his golden blood went down her throat. He hastily extracted his hand. She had bitten her tongue, but it was blue blood that flowed out over her chin, not gold.

"No, no, no, no!" he repeated. He wasn't aware the motor home had stopped. The door burst open and Jamie rushed in, and at the same moment, Robert scrambled out of the driver's seat and headed to the back. While Terrill sat frozen, Robert held Sylvie's legs and Jamie lay on top of her upper body.

Slowly, Sylvie's gyrations diminished until she was just twitching. Then she stopped moving altogether.

Terrill stood up and stared down at her, numb. Robert looked up at Terrill, his face pale, as Jamie lavished kisses on her sister's forehead and cheeks. Then Robert stood up as well and gently moved Terrill aside so that he could put two fingers against Sylvie's neck. "She's still got a pulse," he said, and at almost the same moment, Jamie said, "She's still breathing."

"What's wrong with her?" Terrill whispered. He felt like a child, unable to do anything effective. His two friends gently guided him to a seat at the dining room table while he kept his eyes fixed on Sylvie's face. She looked as if she was in pain. *Why is she in pain?* he wondered.

"It's Sylvie," Jamie said, answering his question. "My sister never does anything the easy way."

Terrill heard something in Jamie's voice, and he looked up to see that she was standing next to him, smiling down at him.

"She'll be all right," she said with a certainty that seemed to flow into Terrill and start to unfreeze him. "I have no doubt of it."

Robert straightened up from the bedside. "It's a strange reaction, to be sure, but she didn't reject the blood of gold, or she'd be dead. We just need to wait until she revives. Unfortunately, we don't have any time. We're in Crescent City. The motel is only minutes away."

Terrill heard him talking, but the words didn't really register. He was still staring at Sylvie's face, and as he watched, her features smoothed out and became peaceful. He took a breath and realized he'd barely been breathing.

Someone grabbed him by the arms. He looked up to see Robert's frowning face. "You've got to snap out of it, Terrill. You led us here. This whole expedition is your idea. What do you want us to do?"

Sylvie's eyes popped open. Terrill was at her side in an instant, as if he'd teleported there.

"Sylvie," he said.

There was no reaction. Her eyes showed no understanding. They weren't lifeless—in fact, they seemed to glow with a strange radiance, but they didn't move, and she didn't react to his words.

"Wake up, my love," he pleaded. "Join me." He sensed Robert and Jamie standing beside him. They were all silent as they waited for a reaction from Sylvie.

There was a soft sigh and a smile. Nothing more.

But it was enough. Terrill felt all his resolve return, and his mind cleared of worry. That smile was the smile of saint.

"I don't know what's going on, but she's going to be all right," he said. "I can see that now. Just as well. She can stay here, safe from the fight." He looked up at his two oldest followers. "Are you ready?"

Jamie and Robert were looking at each other, not at him, but they both nodded. Robert went back to the driver's seat. Jamie took her place in the passenger seat beside him. They took each other's hands.

"Let's do it," Robert said.

Feller looked down at the bodies of Callendar and Jeffers, then out over the airfield, which was littered with dead vampires. You had to hand it to these guys—they'd wasted very few bullets. Especially those last two.

Feller had kept the other vampires from ravaging the FBI agents' bodies. He wasn't sure why. He hadn't even liked them—they'd always been in the way of his career trajectory. But…they'd been FBI and he'd been FBI, and to desecrate them was to desecrate the memory of his former life.

All that effort to free the Pelican Bay psychos, and now all that was left was a handful of them. The Master had brought another couple of dozen Shadow Vampires from London, but half of them were gone, too. Their army had been winnowed down.

Feller stayed on the tower's platform for a few moments longer, breathing in the fresh ocean air. Below him, the Shadow was like a black cloud floating over the field, except the wind didn't touch it. If anything, the blackness had spread, as if it had absorbed energy from the deaths of the vampires.

Feller could sense that the creature was absolutely enraged. A pall had settled over all of them, and it felt as if they were going to be pinned to the ground under the weight of it. Personally, Feller wished he could slip away, like that group that had started running when the shots rang out. He didn't want to die for the cause. He was too selfish for that. That's why he'd taken so readily to the black blood in the first place.

But he was a Shadow Vampire. There was nowhere to run—

hell, the Master was probably reading his mind right now, and the only reason he wasn't being forced to throw himself off the tower was because the Master needed all the troops he could find.

Feller felt a tug, a summons. He sighed and slowly descended the steps of the tower.

Kelton was trying to reorganize the surviving Shadow Vampires. Laura was following him around like his personal shadow. Feller walked up to them, and Kelton grunted at him. Feller had never run into anyone who communicated mostly with grunts, but Kelton was surprisingly expressive with his limited sounds.

"Still think we're on the winning side?" Feller said.

"I never thought I was on the winning side," Kelton said. "I was always on the only side I could be on. But yeah, I think the Master is going to be pretty hard to beat. Have you looked into the Shadow? I mean, *really* looked?"

"I've been trying to avoid it, actually."

"How do you defeat nothing?" Kelton said. "It is bottomless, never-ending. Anything that exists becomes nothing when it is thrown into that void."

They finally gathered all the survivors into a rough approximation of a team. Off to one side, Peterson stood alone. The other four councilors huddled together, unmoving. Two other vampires, a young-looking girl and her boyfriend, stood waiting nearby.

"What now?" Feller wondered aloud.

A tentacle of the void shot out, running along the tarmac like a stream of tar, and headed straight for Feller and Kelton. Feller backed up, but Kelton stepped forward to meet the dark ribbon, and it enveloped him. The big vampire straightened up and went rigid, as if a giant had grabbed him by the throat. Then he flopped back down again.

"What's wrong, baby?" Laura exclaimed.

When he turned, Kelton was no more. The Master of Shadow's voice came out of his mouth.

"Turn them," the hollow voice said, and Kelton motioned toward the councilors, including Peterson, as well as the two young vampires.

Feller saw the vacant looks in the former bigwigs' eyes and shuddered. *I'm not letting those zombies bite me,* he thought.

"You do it," he said to Laura.

"Why me?" she whined.

"Because your Big Daddy isn't around to protect you anymore, and I'm ordering you to."

Reluctantly, she went over to the councilors. As if on command, the four fell on her and sank their fangs into her, and she cried out. They sucked deeply of her black blood. She staggered from the draining and fell to her knees.

Right where she belongs, Feller thought. Then he felt the command also, and found himself walking toward Peterson and the two younger vampires. "You are to take my blood," he intoned, but it wasn't him speaking, it was the Master. "You are to become one of us."

Peterson didn't object. He shrugged and bit into Feller's proffered arm. He straightened up, then his eyes turned black. Just like that. Easiest transformation Feller had seen yet.

The girl didn't hesitate either. She muttered "Holy shit" as she started drinking, then fell flat on her butt and rolled over onto her side. She lay there, moaning.

"Jodie!" the boy cried. "Are you all right?"

"It's wonderful!" she gasped.

"What's your name?" Feller asked. The boy was obviously scared.

"Jimmy."

"You have no choice, Jimmy. You have to chose sides."

Jimmy was white-faced, but he nodded. He gingerly leaned over and licked some of the black blood from Feller's open wound.

It was as if someone had cut his legs off. He crumpled where he stood and lay limply on the asphalt. He jerked once or twice, and then his skin started to slough off, his bones broke with loud cracks, and his head rolled away and split in half.

"Sorry, kid," Feller muttered. "You weren't cut out for this."

The four councilors seemed almost animated again, as if they were waking up from a nightmare. Their movements were still jerky, as if controlled from the outside, but intelligence had reentered their eyes.

"Load up the SUV's and let's get going," Kelton ordered.

Feller looked around and realized Kelton was talking to him.

"You heard Kel—uh, the Master. Load up! We're going to war!"

CHAPTER 27

Sergeant Butler took his personal vehicle, a beat-up old pickup he took camping and hunting, because it was less conspicuous than his cruiser. He pulled into the parking lot of the redwood sculpture stand across the street from the motel, and there, nestled among the carved gnomes and dragons and bears, he began his stakeout. He didn't know when Callendar and Jeffers would arrive, but he wanted to make sure he got his fair share of the bounty.

The big vampire he had called might arrive first, but he only seemed interested in three girls—or two, now—so that was OK. Maybe, if Butler could get a free shot at them, he'd take them down when they left.

He opened the glove box, pulled out the small binoculars he kept in there for hunting and examined the boarded-up building. Even now, his eyes wanted to slide off it. It was as if there was a powerful glamour emanating from the structure. *Don't look here,* the aura seemed to say. *There is nothing here.*

But now that he was focused on the motel, Butler found he could ignore the warnings. And he was absolutely certain it was infested with vampires. For one thing, the parking lot was streaked with tire tracks as if cars were arriving and leaving all the time. Butler put down the binoculars and looked around. Sure enough, there were a number of cars parked along the beach highway, even though there didn't appear to be any beachcombers at the moment. It was too dark and windy, and a little chilly. So who did the cars belong to?

It soon became a moot point. As he watched, a caravan of cars, vans and motor homes pulled into the parking lot. A whole crowd of people poured out of the vehicles and milled around as if waiting for instructions. The last motor home pulled in, and the newcomers gathered around it. The door opened and a beautiful redhead emerged. A tall man got out of the driver's side and joined her, putting his arm around her.

Butler was holding his breath. His instinctive vampire radar had already been tingling even before he saw the tall man. It was Robert Jurgenson, the police officer who had first trained Butler and most of the other Crescent City police officer.

And then another tall man emerged, dark-haired, handsome, but not someone Butler normally would've looked at twice on the street. But something about the way he held himself, as if he was aware—but trying *not* be aware—that he was special, made Butler recognize him. Unless he was very much mistaken, this was the legendary Terrill—the oldest vampire in existence, it was said. The bounty on him was in the millions, the last time Butler had checked.

The door to the motel restaurant opened and about fifty vampires emerged. They acted tentative, uncertain, looking up at the sky as if they expected the sun to come out at any moment, and peering nervously up and down the highway as if they expected the vampire hunters to descend on them.

Now that he thought about it, *Where are the damn vampire hunters?* Butler wondered. A little backup would be nice, though even Callendar and Jeffers would have to think twice about taking on this crowd. Butler pulled out his phone, but hesitated. He'd get credit, he supposed, in a bureaucratic sense— some sort of plaque or medal. But if he officially reported this conclave, he'd get none of the monetary reward.

He put the phone back in his pocket and pulled his gun

instead. He ducked down under the dashboard, letting only the top of his head and his eyes show, and raised the binoculars again. The two crowds of vampires weren't mingling—indeed, they seemed to be keeping their distance from each other. The vampire he guessed was Terrill was standing in front of the vampires who had emerged from the motel, and he was saying something important, if his arm gestures meant anything.

Terrill wasn't getting through to them. "You don't understand," he said insistently. "You must join us—you must take the blood of gold!"

"But didn't you just say it kills anyone who isn't pure of heart, or something like that?" This came from a mousy, skinny vampire who had her arm around a beautiful younger girl.

"Are you Patty?" he asked.

She stepped back in surprise, almost stumbling. The smaller girl caught her and helped her stay steady. "How could you know that?"

"We were contacted by someone named Rod. He told us about three vampires who had been held captive: Patty, Laura and Simone."

"I'm Simone." Another vampire girl stepped out of the crowd, followed by a young human Terrill guessed was Rod.

"You are all victims," Terrill said, pointing at each of them. "You didn't wish to become vampire, nor did you choose this life. I'm offering you a chance to turn away from evil, from killing."

"But that's just it, mister," a little girl said, stepping forward. "We're vampire." She was grimy from top to bottom, her blonde hair ratty and snarled, but she had a confidence beyond her years. "Hoss told us to wait for him here, and that's what we're doing. We've been abiding by the Rules of Vampires, which I always heard you created, Terrill. What's wrong with that?"

"It isn't enough," Terrill said.

"Did I hear Rules of Vampire?" a voice said. From the beach side of the motel, a teenage boy emerged, followed by several other vampires.

"Hoss!" the little girl cried, running to him.

"Hey, Charlotte," Hoss said, lifting her up. "Keeping everyone in line and safe, are you?"

"Trying to, Hoss," she pouted. "They don't always follow my instructions."

"Well, no one is used to taking instructions from a six-year-old girl, even if she's the smartest girl in the world," Hoss said. He dropped his smile and turned toward Terrill. "You'd better get ready, Terrill. The Shadow Vampires are on their way. They are powerful; more powerful than you can believe. And the Master—I do believe he is evil incarnate. I'm not sure even you can withstand him, Terrill. How many Golden Vampires do you have here? Twenty? Thirty? The Master has three times as many followers, if not more. You might want to get out of here and fight another day."

"No," Terrill said. "Today is the day when all of you need to decide, once and for all: will you renounce your killing and turn to the light, or will you continue to be vampire, or will you allow yourself to be turned into something even worse?"

Hoss looked stubborn. "I refuse to choose either side," he said. "It is up to each of us to decide our own fate. If you force us to choose, you are no better than the Master."

Butler couldn't believe they were just standing there—nearly a hundred vampires, in plain sight.

He put down his binoculars and looked up and down the highway. Sure enough, vehicles were stopped for what looked liked miles. No one wanted to drive down this stretch of road right now. Butler saw the lights of police cars in both directions down the highway, about a quarter mile away.

And here he was in the middle of it all. He fumbled with his phone and checked the charge. About fifty percent. Well, no help for it—he'd record what he could. He put his binoculars and gun on the seat and started recording.

He heard sirens going off to the north and turned his head to look. It looked like some big SUV's were breaking through the cordon. He turned his camera to catch the action.

Feller drove the lead van because, other than Kelton—who was now the voice of the Master—he was the only one who knew where the motel was. He started running into traffic and soon had his hand on the horn almost continuously. Most vehicles pulled over, getting out of his way, though he had to bump a few to get the message across.

He saw the police cars blocking the highway and had to make a quick decision. It wasn't a serious roadblock, the kind the cops put up when they really wanted to stop someone. It was more like a courtesy stop, the kind they put up when they had to direct traffic around accidents.

He plowed right through a gap in the roadblock, hitting the back end of a couple of cruisers and spinning them off the road. He looked back saw that the other SUV's had had no trouble following.

He saw the crowd in front of the motel and slowed down. *What the...?* he wondered. He'd thought maybe they'd have to wait for the Golden Vampires, even root them out. Maybe send a challenge. Yet here they were, conveniently waiting. He put his foot back on the gas and sped toward them.

Butler kept recording as the second wave of vampires arrived, their vehicles sliding to a stop. All thought of reward had left his mind. He wasn't even worried about being seen, sensing that none of the vampires cared about little old him. There was some kind of vampire Armageddon going on, some final confrontation. And he was watching it all from a few hundred feet away.

The new arrivals piled out of their SUV's.

Butler put down his phone for a second and stared at them. There was something different about them. It was as if they carried the night with them. That was it: they were surrounded by darkness, even though it was still daytime. A huge vampire took the lead, and it was as if he trailed a black cloak, hundreds of feet long, behind him. The other vampires seemed to gravitate toward that darkness.

As Butler picked up his phone to start recording again, he recognized the huge vampire as the one who had been looking for the three girls. But there was something different about him. He didn't lumber or loom or bluster, the way Butler remembered him doing. No, he seemed to almost float on a shadow.

Butler recognized Feller, the FBI agent, who he'd heard was dead. He followed the dark vampire with his camera.

"You must choose now!" Terrill cried as he saw the Shadow Vampires arriving. "Drink of our blood and join us!"

No one stepped forward, and Terrill almost jumped amongst them, ready to make them drink. He felt a strong hand on his shoulder and turned to see Robert shake his head.

And then it was too late.

The giant vampire approached, sheathed in black. He moved slowly, like the increasing darkness of night. From the crowd of vampires from the motel, Terrill heard someone cry, "It's him! The Monster!" He stopped directly in front of Terrill. Behind him was the FBI agent, Feller, and a young woman.

"Laura!" cried the same voice that had yelled "Monster." Terrill saw that it was Simone, one of the girls who had been held captive. "Why are you with him? Come over to us!"

Laura gave a mirthless grin. "Why should I join you? You are all going to die."

The voice that emerged from the Monster was loud, as if it was coming from a loudspeaker, and yet it also seemed to come from far away. It was cold, pitiless, devoid of human sympathy or understanding.

"Terrill is right," the voice said. "You must choose."

Terrill was stunned when he heard the ultimatum, so much like his own. And at that moment, he understood that he'd been wrong. It was not for him to compel faith. He'd been brought here to protect these vampires, to give them chance to decide for themselves what path they wanted to take.

Most of the vampires were running, some back into the motel, others toward the beach. Some even risked running toward the lights of the police cars. Hoss and his followers didn't join Terrill, but stepped to one side as if to say, *We will fight for neither of you.*

Only the Golden Vampires stayed to fight.

They were outnumbered two to one. Terrill fixed his eyes on the huge vampire in front of him, whom he now understood to be the manifestation of the Master of Shadow. Terrill didn't know how he could defeat a Shadow, but he could destroy the huge vampire who represented that Shadow. If he could defeat the leader, perhaps all the others would flee or give up.

But even as he moved forward, he feared he might not be strong enough.

CHAPTER 28

The Shadow Vampire stood waiting for him, not even raising his claws in defense. Terrill ripped out the giant vampire's throat with one swipe and dug into his chest with another blow. Almost instantaneously, the shadow that surrounded the Monster swirled and flowed into his wounds, black blood replacing torn flesh, and soon it was as if the wounds had never been there.

Terrill felt himself flying backward, and only in midflight did he feel the pain from the giant gash in his shoulder. He glanced down at the wound, but it wasn't knitting together instantly like the Shadow Vampire's wounds had. No band of light came out of nowhere to heal Terrill. It was going to take a long time to repair a wound this severe, and meanwhile, his left arm was useless.

The Shadow Vampire was still standing in the same spot, a small smile on his face. Terrill staggered to his feet. Vampires were fully engaged in battle all around him. He saw Robert trading blows with Feller, heavy blows fueled by all the hate and anger they possessed toward each other.

Jamie was fending of the chubby little vampire, Laura, who moved like a swirl of black smoke, there for a second, then gone. A swipe from Jamie gusted the smoke away, and then it was somewhere else, somewhere closer to her. Jamie staggered forward as the smaller vampire materialized behind her.

Terrill approached his opponent cautiously and tried to lift his damaged arm. To his surprise, it moved. He swung his nearly useless claws at the Shadow Vampire, who batted Terrill's arm away. Terrill followed up with a blow from his good arm that, had it landed, would have taken his foe's head off.

The Shadow Vampire blocked the swipe, but only at the last moment, as if he hadn't anticipated Terrill's speed.

Terrill backed away, feeling a surge of hope. So the Shadow Vampire wasn't going to let him simply tear away chunks to be replaced by the black cloud around him. That must mean such repairs weren't as easy as they looked. Instead, the vampire had chosen to block his attack this time. Not only that, the defense had come just in the nick of time.

Terrill's enemy grunted and lumbered forward as if suddenly compelled into action, and just before he reached Terrill, he glided into the air, the black void lifting him. Then he was directly over Terrill and striking downward with all his force. Terrill dodged to one side just in time and felt the swoosh of his opponent's vicious strike whizzing by his ear.

He turned and struck blindly, and to his surprise, he caught the bigger vampire still recovering from his leap. Terrill's claws went deep. He found himself near the other vampire's neck and, without thinking, he sank his fangs into his opponent's throat.

The Monster tasted vile. The black blood boiled in Terrill's mouth, gushing outward, spewing from the sides of his mouth, but he hung on and sucked. He felt dizzy, and it was as if all the events of the last year went rushing through his body at once: he was a blue-blooded vampire again, then a red-blooded human, then a vampire again. He felt strong, then weak, then even weaker. But finally, the blood of gold prevailed, and he felt himself reversing the flow. Golden blood was forced into his enemy's body.

The Shadow Vampire roared. He grew and grew until Terrill's feet were lifted of the ground. Terrill lost his grip, his fangs tearing away at the Monster's flesh, and he fell backward.

The vampire who embodied the Master of Shadow stood glaring at Terrill, his hands pressed against the wound in his neck. The black, inky fluid flowed into his wound, but not quite as fast as before, nor was the healing complete this time. When the Monster took his hand away, there was still a raw wound there.

Terrill looked around. The battle had faltered. The Shadow Vampires had pulled back, as if confused. There were three Golden Vampires on the ground, but only one of the Shadow Vampires had been vanquished.

But something had changed. It might have been Terrill's imagination, but it seemed to him that the darkness had diminished, that the Shadow was being pushed back by the last light of day.

Then the darkness deepened. The sun finally sank into the ocean, and the light faded. The Shadow Vampires seemed invigorated by the darkness.

Terrill felt a moment of fear. He'd been so sure he had right on his side, that God would somehow protect them. But as he had told Sylvie, every army went into battle thinking it had right on its side. Only one side could win, and the side that won was usually the one with the most men, or the most weapons, or the advantageous terrain.

To one side of Terrill, Robert rushed forward and engaged Feller again. Both men were bleeding from multiple wounds, and both were moving more slowly than before. Laura screamed, an inhuman cry of rage, and flowed toward Jamie, who stood waiting with a look of determination on her face. Terrill's first follower showed no fear, only the resolve to win.

Three more Golden Vampires were now on the ground, along with two of the Shadow Vampires. Some of Terrill's followers appeared to be fighting more than one enemy at a time.

Terrill looked over at Hoss, who was standing in the shadows of the motel with his crew. The young vampire looked troubled. "Hoss," Terrill called. "I'm sorry! You were right. I was wrong to insist you join me. But the Shadow Vampires won't give you a choice!"

Hoss looked away.

Terrill felt the onrush of darkness and turned to block a brutal jab to his head. The Shadow Vampire, revived by the night, was faster than ever, as if he had just been getting warmed up before. It was all Terrill could do to defend himself. For a few minutes, he steadily retreated, foot by foot. His back came up against an obstacle, and he realized that he was leaning against the motor home that contained Sylvie's sleeping form.

He looked up at the Shadow Vampire, whose eyes flicked toward the door of the motor home, and Terrill knew without a doubt that the Master of Shadow wanted more than just to kill him. The Shadow wanted Sylvie.

Terrill's vision seemed to expand, and he could see the entire battle and could tell what direction it was going. They were being crushed, one by one. For every Shadow Vampire who fell, there were two more to take his or her place. But it wasn't an equal battle. The Golden Vampires were being defeated—and there was no one to take their place.

Terrill was infused with a sudden strength, the strength of desperation. Sylvie was helpless inside, and he would die before he let this Monster near her.

He lifted his left arm and felt enormous pain, but found he could use it again. Great damage was being done to the tissues, but he didn't care. He surged into the Shadow Vampire, pushed him back into the center of the battle and started swinging, landing blow after blow. The Monster staggered under the onslaught, and Terrill went in for the killing blow.

He missed, and with that miss, all his newfound energy left him. He stumbled, almost unable to stand. The Shadow Vampire stepped back, a glint of triumph in his eyes.

Then the Monster was flying through the air, landing on the asphalt with a loud grunt. Hoss had him by the waist, while around the Shadow Vampire's head and shoulders, there was a flurry of movement from a small, vicious creature. The movement slowed for a moment, and Terrill could make out the furious face of the little girl vampire, Charlotte, as she stabbed into the big vampire's eyes.

Then it was her turn to go flying through the air. She hit the ground with a soft crunch and stopped moving. Hoss, too, was flung off, and landed on his back. They were only ordinary vampires, no match for a Shadow Vampire.

Across the battlefield, the same scenario was being played out. There was a brief surge of energy with the addition of the blue-blooded vampires to the fight, but they were quickly beaten back by the Shadow.

Once again, the two sides backed away from each other. The Shadow Vampires no longer looked so self-confident. The Golden Vampires still seemed resolute.

But it was obvious who was winning.

Terrill couldn't think what to do to change the dynamics. If the battle continued the same way, the Golden Vampires were slowly but surely going to be overwhelmed.

The Monster stood up, breathing deeply. The blackness had gathered around him, leaving the other Shadow Vampires in smaller pools of darkness. It was as if the Master of Shadow was gathering all his strength for one last fight.

Feller and Robert still faced each other, but Feller was standing straight while Robert was hunched over.

Jamie was covered in black blood, but Laura was equally covered in golden blood, which looked dim and dirty on her. Laura looked as though she was enjoying herself.

Terrill straightened up. It went both ways, he realized. If he had hoped to demoralize the Shadow Vampires by defeating their leader, then the same thing was true on his side. If he went down, he knew the others would collapse.

He didn't take his eyes off the Monster, who looked smaller somehow and slightly off-kilter, as if he was favoring one leg. Terrill didn't have to look down at his own body to know that he was even worse off. He couldn't even feel his left side, and it was as if his left arm was missing. He felt great pain in his right leg, which was preferable to the numbness in his left leg. Blood was flowing into his eyes from wounds in his head.

As he watched, the inky blackness that surrounded his enemy continued to swirl into the other vampire's wounds, and when it finally stopped, the giant black cloud that had first confronted him resembled a small tapestry of blackness. That gave Terrill one last surge of hope.

But the instant the Shadow Vampire started moving toward him, his heart quailed, for there was a speed and strength in those movements that he knew he couldn't match.

He stood waiting, no longer hoping to win, but determined not to lose.

Butler's phone camera gave out in the middle of the fight. He cursed for a few seconds, but he knew it probably didn't matter. He had the footage of a lifetime. Put this battle up on YouTube, and he'd be the all-time hit leader.

He was in awe. He'd never known that vampires could be so fast, or that they could sustain such damage. After this display, Butler decided his vampire hunting days were over. Too damn dangerous.

He wasn't sure which side he was rooting for. Probably the Golden Vampires, since they were obviously the underdogs.

But this wasn't going to be some inspirational come-from-behind victory. The Golden Vampires were getting creamed. The great Terrill was being worn down, little by little, by the huge Shadow Vampire, though it was admirable how much resistance he was putting up while being torn to pieces.

Butler turned on the phone again and was surprised to see that it suddenly had a lot more juice.

He raised the camera just as the gold light began to glow within the motor home.

It started off as a flash, as if someone had turned a light on, but it quickly grew brighter. It was as if the white metal sides of the motor home were glowing. The door flew open, and standing on the steps in the center of an almost-blinding glow, Butler could barely make out the figure of a naked female vampire.

She walked calmly down the steps and into the middle of the battle. For a second, the fighting stopped. While Butler had been distracted, Terrill had been sent to the ground, and he wasn't getting up. The giant vampire was leaning over him, his arm raised as though to inflict the killing blow.

The Shadow Vampire hesitated as he saw the glowing golden figure coming toward him.

He stood up and grew darker, as if drawing on all the blackness around him. The other Shadow Vampires staggered, as if they'd been suddenly drained of their essence.

The glowing figure stood over Terrill, but didn't look down. It appeared she was beckoning the darkness toward her.

Butler looked down at the flashing red power indicator on his phone. "Stay with me, damn you!" he cried.

He'd only glanced down briefly, but at that instant, the

Shadow Vampire had covered the distance between him and his foes and was wrapping himself around the glowing figure. He was huge, much bigger than the female. Butler could see his giant fangs as they sank into her shining neck. The glow dimmed for a moment, and even from a distance, Butler could hear the Golden Vampires crying out in pain.

Terrill didn't see or hear her coming. As he looked up at what he knew would be his deathblow, he was blinded. Then she was standing over him.

He knew it was Sylvie, though he couldn't see her features through the brilliant light. He felt at peace. He might die, but he knew that Sylvie would live, an angel of light.

Then the Monster was there, smothering her in a cloak of emptiness, ripping into her neck.

"Sylvie, no!" Terrill cried.

She didn't even try to defend herself. Her golden light began to dim. He could see the shape of her body outlined in black, could see her bones as if in an X-ray. The contours of her face suddenly became clear, and she had a serene expression as the light was drained from her body.

She flickered. He heard her sigh.

Then the Shadow Vampire released her. She looked an ordinary woman again— beautiful, to be sure, her black hair once again visible, her porcelain skin as white as the moon. She stood swaying, and Terrill struggled to rise and catch her.

But she stayed on her feet. Then it was the Master of Shadow who was staggering.

A roar emerged from his throat, and his physical boundaries shredded in the otherworldly anguish and horror. His cries strangled to a stop, and he fell to his knees. The blackness was streaming off him, flowing out into the night. The army of Shadow Vampires cried out as one. Most of them fell to the ground and writhed, while a few managed to stagger away.

The darkness that had fallen over them was growing less defined, lit around the edges by the lights of cars and streetlights and other human things. The soft light of the moon and the stars filtered through the blackness, and the darkness felt comforting again, instead of threatening.

The Master of Shadow was now just a single vampire, struggling to maintain his shape. He staggered to his feet, no longer looking otherworldly, but more like a beat-up and degenerate monster of a man.

He let out a grunt, fell flat on his face and lay there, unmoving.

Butler looked down at his phone and saw that by some miracle, it just kept recording. Almost as if compelled, he got out of his battered pickup and walked toward the surviving vampires, keeping his phone camera up in front of him, recording every moment. He started to be able to hear them talking, and then he was in their midst, a human among vampires, totally at their mercy.

But he wasn't frightened, and the vampires appeared to be paying no attention to him.

As if in response to the presence of the camera, the girl started glowing again, still standing in the middle of them all, looking down at Terrill with an affectionate smile.

She turned toward Butler and spoke. "I have not destroyed the Darkness. The Shadow still exists—it will always exist. Just as the Shadow cannot ever completely defeat the Light, nor can the Light completely defeat the Shadow.

"All creatures must choose which direction they wish to go. It is not for us to compel them. This is the meaning of life, for both humans and vampires. Choose your own path, whether it be in the direction of Light or whether you chose the side of Darkness.

"No one but you can decide."

Then she fell silent and helped Terrill to his feet.

Butler looked down at his phone. The power indicator blinked off.

Got it! he thought triumphantly. *I've got the best recording ever made by anyone, anywhere!*

The phone was snatched from his hands. A nerdish-looking vampire with black glasses glared at Butler. "Give me that, you jerk! Get the hell out of here before one of the less enlightened vampires decides to have a human snack."

Butler suddenly became aware that everyone was looking at him. He backed away, turned and ran for his life.

Epilogue

Marc posted the recording that night.

It became a sensation.

Terrill and Sylvie went back into the wilderness of the Strawberry Mountains outside John Day. Whenever they ventured into the small town to get supplies, they had to be heavily disguised. They became cattle ranchers so they wouldn't have to buy raw meat every week. The neighbors didn't understand why they never sold any of their stock.

Other than the occasional visitor, they were alone. They didn't mind. They were done fighting.

The other Golden Vampires spread the message, and Marc continued to refine *The Testament of Michael.*

Somewhere on the other side of the world, someone wrote *The Jeremiad of Kelton.*

Marc showed it to Sylvie on one of his visits.

She just smiled and ruffled his hair.